A
Ca~~nadian~~
Christmas

ALSO BY TILLY TENNANT

FROM ITALY WITH LOVE SERIES:

Rome is Where the Heart Is
A Wedding in Italy

HONEYBOURNE SERIES:

The Little Village Bakery
Christmas at the Little Village Bakery

MISHAPS IN MILLRISE SERIES:

Little Acts of Love
Just Like Rebecca
The Parent Trap
And Baby Makes Four

ONCE UPON A WINTER SERIES:

The Accidental Guest
I'm Not in Love
Ways to Say Goodbye
One Starry Night

Hopelessly Devoted to Holden Finn
The Man Who Can't Be Moved
Mishaps and Mistletoe
A Very Vintage Christmas

A Cosy Candlelit Christmas

TILLY TENNANT

Bookouture

Published by Bookouture
An imprint of StoryFire Ltd.
23 Sussex Road, Ickenham, UB10 8PN
United Kingdom
www.bookouture.com

ISBN: 978-1-78681-217-9
eBook ISBN: 978-1-78681-216-2

This book is a work of fiction. Names, characters, businesses,
organizations, places and events other than those clearly in the
public domain, are either the product of the author's imagination
or are used fictitiously. Any resemblance to actual persons, living or
dead, events or locales is entirely coincidental.

For Mia, always sweet and funny. I'm so proud
to call you daughter. Burn bright and live well.

Chapter One

The university coffee shop was heaving, students with armfuls of books and hefty rucksacks jostling for space at overcrowded tables, a long queue snaking away from the counter where the growl of a coffee machine drowned out the conversation of the baristas. Isla was sitting at one of the packed tables with a group from her psychology class. She frowned over her coffee.

'I wish I could say yes but my mum's hassling me about something and wants me to go straight home.'

There was a collective sigh of disappointment. It was funny, because at school Isla had never been this popular. But something about her frankness seemed to engage her fellow psychology students. Perhaps they saw her as a potential subject? She was certainly screwed up enough, or so she thought. If only they knew the half of it.

'Can't you just put her off for one evening?' Kayleigh, a petite blonde who looked a lot younger than her twenty years, asked. 'It's not often we get a visiting lecturer, especially one from America who's a pioneer in cognitive behaviour. It's exciting!'

'Only you would find it exciting,' George said. George was a year older than Kayleigh, and everyone knew he was so desperately in love with her that he'd never do anything but worship her from afar for fear of the ultimate, crippling rejection. Everyone except Kayleigh, that was. George and Kayleigh were both younger than Isla. In fact, everyone at the table was at least six years younger than Isla who, at twenty-nine, was the unofficial mummy of the group. Perhaps that was why they all liked her so much.

'You've clearly never met my mum, Kayleigh,' Isla said, laughing lightly. 'If she asks you to come home for something important then you bloody well go home.'

'But I can put you down for the end-of-term pub crawl, can't I?' James, George's best friend, asked.

'Well, you can put me down for it but I can't make any promises,' Isla said. 'Besides, once you've done the first two pubs you'll barely notice if I'm there or not. Bunch of lightweights you are.'

'Oooh…' Kayleigh looked up at the entrance. 'Prof. Choudhry. I need to catch her about my dissertation.' Without another word she grabbed her bag and flew in the direction of the coffee shop doorway. George threw a forlorn look in her direction and then got up too.

'I should catch the prof actually. And I'm supposed to go to the library with Kayleigh later…'

And then he was gone. Leaving only Eve and James.

'I'm going to get another coffee,' Eve announced. 'Anyone want one?'

Both James and Isla shook their heads and as Eve left their table, James lowered his voice and leaned across to Isla.

'So, what are you planning to do over the Christmas break?' he asked.

Isla shrugged. 'No idea. Probably a lot of studying – get ahead for the new term, you know? And I always have my mum's side of my family over at Christmas, so it's often bedlam.'

'A bit overwhelming?' he asked.

Isla smiled. 'Sometimes.'

'I know what you mean. I have a load of family in Cardiff and they always land on our doorstep Christmas Eve. Bloody pain.'

'So you don't keep a welcome in the hillsides?'

'No,' James laughed. 'But I was thinking…' He swallowed hard. 'Well, if you weren't busy for the whole time… maybe you'd like to go for a drink. With me. Just me, I mean… not the others. You see?'

Isla gave him a sad smile. It wasn't the fact that she was almost ten years older that bothered her, but she just didn't do relationships – at least not right now. She was too busy, too focused on her studies, too much responsibility at home – too much of everything. A sporadic social life was one thing, but a boyfriend? James was sweet and he wasn't bad-looking but she'd probably only hurt him in the end. She'd had boyfriends before and they never lasted. He was too nice, too young and too full of hope for that sort of life lesson.

'I don't think so,' she said gently. 'I mean, we have a laugh as we are, don't we? And I think we should keep it that way, not complicate things.'

'Right…' James fiddled with his collar and looked hopelessly over to where Eve was returning with her drink. 'Course… cool.'

As Eve got to the table he stood up. 'Sorry guys, got to run… just remembered something.'

Eve raised her eyebrows in mild surprise as Isla cringed inwardly. She hated these situations. When it came to the opposite sex she did her very best to seem unavailable and uninterested and usually that did the trick. James's request was a timely reminder that she couldn't let her guard slip again. She looked at her watch.

'Sorry, Eve, but it looks like you're on your own.'

'You're kidding me! I wouldn't have got another coffee if I'd known I was going to end up sitting here like Billy No Mates.'

'You'll find someone to talk to,' Isla laughed. 'Everyone loves you. And if I don't get going soon I'm going to be late for my mum.'

'Is she really that scary?'

Isla gulped the last of her coffee and set the cup down with a grin. 'I'll take you home one of these days and let you decide for yourself.'

'I'm not sure I'd be brave enough from what you've told me.'

'That's true. It takes a special sort of constitution to withstand a death stare from Glory McCoy.'

Glory had always been beautiful. As a child she'd enchanted everyone she met, with skin the colour of bitter chocolate and huge dark eyes to match. As a teen she'd found grace in her blooming womanhood where others her age found awkwardness. As a young woman she could walk down a street and turn every head, and as an older woman she wore elegance and dignity like a perfectly tailored suit. Isla, on the other hand, had taken time to grow into her looks, a gangly and uncertain girl until her early twenties. It was only now, as she headed towards thirty, that anyone could look and call her beautiful. Her skin was lighter than her mother's – the product of a Scottish father who had branded her with his name before abandoning them both – and she was taller, less curvy than the women on her mother's side of the family, though the angles of her body suited her.

But right now, as both women stood sizing each other up, nostrils flared, an impasse on the horizon, nobody could call either of them beautiful. Unless, of course, your idea of beauty was the great white shark just before it strikes.

'I suppose you thought I wouldn't find out.' Isla glared at her mother. 'I suppose you thought it would go away if you ignored it.'

Glory tilted her chin into the air, trying to reinforce her superior position, though these days, as Isla grew in maturity and confidence, this was harder to do. 'I was going to tell you.'

'When?'

'When the time was right.'

'The time was right as soon as the letter arrived! And why do you get to decide when it's right?'

'You don't know what you're talking about because you don't know him like I do; that's why I made the decision not to tell you.'

'So you were never going to tell me? What else have you kept to yourself all these years? If you weren't going to tell me this then what else haven't you told me because you didn't think the time was right? For God's sake, Mother, I'm twenty-nine years old! I can make my own decisions about what I do and do not need to know!' She shook the letter clutched in her hand at Glory. 'Have you always known where Dad was? Did you pretend not to?'

'Of course I didn't know where he was! Do you think I did two jobs all those years for fun? I had to pawn our furniture. We had to go without holidays, miss out on trips and days out. I had to shop in bargain bins just to keep us afloat!'

'I know it was tough, Mum – I was there with you through it all. I was the one who got bullied at school for my cheap shoes and free dinners but—'

'So don't you think if I'd known where he was I would have made him pay his way – the selfish bastard! And if you're stupid enough to accept this invitation and go and see him after all that, you can tell him he owes me twenty-four years' worth of child maintenance!'

Isla opened her mouth to retaliate but then let out a long sigh, something in her mother's eyes suddenly draining the fight from her. 'I'm not going to see him, Mum.'

'But you said—'

'I know what I said. But I can see how much this is bothering you and I don't want to go to war with you over someone who couldn't even be bothered to make himself a part of my life. We're a team, right?' She offered a tight smile. 'Always have been, always will be. Just you and me against the world.'

For the first time since the subject of the solicitor's letter had been raised, Glory's mask of proud defiance slipped and she looked as if she was about to cry. The wounds ran deeper than anyone could ever know. Isla knew better than anyone the devastation her father leaving had wreaked. Desperate as she was to find out more about him and his new family, about the reasons a Scottish solicitor had gone to such great pains to track her down, about her own past and the DNA that made her the person she was today, would going be worth the pain it would cause her mother? Isla had been angry about being kept in the dark but she could understand Glory's reasons for hiding the letters that had kept turning up.

Glory stepped forward and wrapped her arms around Isla's neck, resting her head on her shoulder. She said nothing, and Isla didn't expect her to. Isla knew her mother would no more offer an apology for her actions than she would offer her soul to the devil himself. As far as she was concerned, she'd done the right thing and no excuse was necessary. Isla wouldn't push for one, either, because there was enough turmoil in her thoughts right now without adding Glory's fury.

'I don't want to fight, Mum. Not over him.'

'I've always done my best.'

'I know.'

'I only wanted you to be happy – to be safe from the pain I suffered.'

'I know that too. Mum, it's OK. You're right – best to stay out of it.'

'Will you phone the number on the letter?'

'I suppose I ought to. They'll only keep chasing if I don't. But I'll let them know I'm not interested in seeing him, or in whatever it is my grandmother has chosen to leave in her will. I doubt it will be anything special anyway.'

Isla stepped away with a tight smile. The last part wasn't true and they both knew it. No solicitor would spend so much time tracking down someone over a worthless inheritance. But what else could she say? She'd reassured her mum that she wasn't going to the French Alps to meet her estranged father and, no matter how curiosity pricked at her, Glory was going to keep her daughter to her word over that. Easier to back down, because no amount of money was worth losing her mum over.

Chapter Two

Isla lay on her back, staring at the ceiling of her room, the letter that had caused so much trouble lying on the duvet beside her. She'd reassured Glory that she wasn't interested in what it might mean, and she had almost convinced herself of the same. But still, the offer wouldn't leave her alone. It wasn't just about money, though. It was about answers.

For what was perhaps the fifth time that hour, she put it to her face and reread it.

Dear Miss McCoy,

I hope this letter finds you well. I have been instructed by your father, Mr Ian McCoy, to trace you and advise you of the sad loss of your grandmother, Sarah McCoy. He has also instructed me to advise you that your grandmother made provision in her last will and testament for you and he would like to see that her final wishes are respected. A copy of the document is with your father in St Martin-de-Belleville in France, and he respectfully wishes you to travel there and meet him to discuss it. You would be fully reimbursed for any expenses incurred. I would urge you to contact

me at your earliest convenience regarding this so that I may give
you further information.
    Yours sincerely,
    Grover Rousseau
    Solicitor

It didn't give a lot away. But it did remind her, forcefully, that she had a father somewhere out in the world. Ian McCoy. The name tasted strange as she spoke it out loud. It was a name she'd barely even heard uttered as she'd grown up, let alone had cause to speak. What sort of man was he? All she had here were the barest of details, formalities sent through a third party. Did he prefer savoury or sweet, pasta or rice, bright colours or muted tones, town or city, summer or winter, wine or beer? What scared him, angered him, made him happy? Her recollections were empty, apart from the vaguest sense of him – the sound of his voice; a profile backlit by the sun through a window; the scent as she nestled in his arms. He'd been gone since she was five years old, but she should have been able to remember him, shouldn't she? But it was like he'd been expunged from her life entirely, as if someone had taken an eraser to her memory and rubbed him out. Perhaps she'd been so careful for so many years trying not to mention him around her mother that she'd almost forgotten him herself. She tried to remember now what he looked like, but she couldn't. And what about the family she'd never met? Would her life be poorer for not knowing them? Would she always feel the sharp edges of the missing jigsaw pieces in her life?

Crossing to her wardrobe, she felt around in the base for a box, tucked beneath stacks of spare blankets and unworn clothes, and lifted it out. Back on her bed she opened it and removed eight small gifts wrapped in thin, faded Christmas paper. Wrapped messily by tiny fingers when the hope of her father's return was still bright and alive. They were gifts she'd saved her meagre allowance for months to buy, still convinced that one Christmas he'd return and she'd be able to give them to him. The first year after he left, her aunt had taken her to the shops without telling Glory, swearing little Isla to secrecy if only she would stop her tearful pleas. The next year, her older cousin took her, and again the year after that until Isla was old enough to go shopping herself. Then, aged thirteen, she'd decided to stop and packed every gift she'd ever bought him into the box, along with any hopes that he might come home.

She turned the first one she'd bought over in her hands and closed her eyes. She didn't need to unwrap it to remember exactly what was in there, and she could recall vividly how she felt buying it – hopeful, certain that he wouldn't let her down at Christmas, believing that the promise of a gift for him was enough to bring him home. She still knew what she'd chosen for him every year she'd waited, even after all this time.

There were unopened cards too, labelled in an uncertain hand with pictures of flowers and houses scrawled over the envelopes. She'd written one to go with every present, but only for Christmas, because she didn't even know when his birthday was. And there, lining the bottom of the box, was a scrapbook filled with good-behaviour certificates she'd won at school, letters of commendation from teachers and local newspaper cuttings from the time she'd performed in the choir for Princess Anne. As if by proving she could be a good girl she could somehow will him back. And then it stopped. While other children stopped believing in Santa, she'd stopped believing in her dad. Just like Santa, she'd decided that Ian McCoy was nothing but make-believe.

Isla sniffed hard. She hadn't shed a tear for that man in a long time now, and she was damned if she was going to start today. She'd become hard and self-reliant but, really, she'd had no choice; Glory worked ten, sometimes twelve-hour days, at her two different care homes, forcing Isla to become independent at a very early age. While girls in her class had horse-riding lessons or days out to theme parks with their parents, she had dishes to wash, rooms to hoover and meals to cook. She went to the post office to pay bills for the mum who was too exhausted to venture further than the end of the garden by the time she got home from work. She pretended she didn't care that the girls in her class had doting fathers and more money than they knew what to do with, and she pretended she didn't care when she was bullied for her scruffy shoes or the blazer she'd long outgrown. She pretended *so* hard that eventually the pretences became reality and she really *didn't* care. Friends were few and far between, boyfriends even rarer. Glory had made choices, but there was no such luxury for Isla – her childhood was entirely dictated by the decisions made by everyone but her.

Gathering up the scrapbook and the gifts, she shoved them back into the box and slammed on the lid. She'd half thought about taking them with her when – if – she travelled to see her dad in France, but what was the point? What would he do with them? It was a stupid, childish whim, and she hadn't been that child for a long time now.

With the box stowed safely back in her wardrobe, she grabbed her phone from her bedside cabinet and dialled her best friend's number. Dodie always seemed to know the right thing to do and say, and Isla needed some reassurance right now. But the number rang out. It wasn't unusual, Dodie's shop – Forget-Me-Not Vintage – was probably busy as it was getting closer to Christmas and Dodie ran it alone so she often couldn't get to the phone, even after closing time when she had accounts and admin to take care of. Putting her mobile back, Isla glanced across at a teetering pile of books on her desk. There were lecture notes that still needed typing up, but no matter how many times she'd tried to get to them that morning her brain simply wouldn't stay on the task. She'd have to force herself sooner or later – she hadn't given up a job and moved back in with her mum to do a university course that she was going to flunk.

Picking up the letter, she read it again. The more she read it, the more she wanted to go to meet her father after all. But she'd promised now, hadn't she? Did her mum even have the right to ask her to promise such a thing, though? If she wanted to meet her dad again, did her mum have the power to say no? She was an adult now and didn't need protecting. She hadn't asked for it and she didn't want it. What she wanted was the whole picture. Her dad was willing to meet her – did that mean he was sorry for what he'd done? Did it mean he wanted to be her dad again? And did Isla even want that? Did she have forgiveness in her? Glory had spent so many years telling her what a cad he was, she'd successfully transferred all her own mistrust of men onto Isla, who could count on one hand the number of healthy relationships she'd had in her life. Perhaps seeing her dad and finally getting some answers would do a lot more than fill in the gap where her father should have been.

She was going round in circles. She needed to talk and it had to be someone impartial, someone who would give her good, solid advice. She dialled Dodie's number again. If there was one person who could make the world seem brighter when it was dark, that was Dodie. By her own admission Isla could be difficult and temperamental and those traits had lost her plenty of friends over the years – the people who couldn't or wouldn't try to understand her. But not Dodie, never

Dodie. Dodie was patient and kind and optimistic enough for them both. She had the biggest heart in Dorset – sometimes Isla would tell her it was a little too big – but as best friends went she was pretty perfect. People mattered to Dodie, and that's why Isla knew that, even if they had the odd spat, when the chips were down, Dodie would be there for anyone who needed her. Right now, she had no idea just how much Isla needed her.

Chapter Three

It wasn't like those films you saw where family assembled in the dusty solicitor's office and gathered around a vast desk to hear the last will and testament of the fabulously wealthy deceased. All it took these days was a simple phone call to the solicitor.

Isla's heart hammered as she waited for the secretary to put her through. It felt like a tipping point – the point of no return. As soon as this conversation began she would live in a world where her dad existed again, somewhere out there, and she'd have to acknowledge that fact even if she did no more about it.

'Miss McCoy?' Grover Rousseau's voice was rich and full, edged with an Edinburgh accent. For a moment, she was transported back to her father's voice and a time long ago, the memories as sudden and cold as falling into an icy lake. 'Thank you for calling me.'

'I thought I should, though I have to admit that I don't know what I'm letting myself into,' Isla said, fighting the quiver in her voice. 'I understand that my dad wants to meet up with me?'

'He does. It's concerning the matter of your grandmother's death, which I was sorry to hear about.'

'You knew her?'

'She'd been a client for many years.'

'And my dad?'

'Him too.'

'Oh.' What did she say next? She wanted desperately to hear more about her father, but his solicitor was hardly likely to give her any detail that meant anything to her in a personal sense. She didn't even remember her grandmother and certainly didn't give a toss about her final wishes, but it was easier to steer clear of that conversation.

She couldn't deny that she was curious about what she stood to inherit, though she didn't want to sound like a gold-digger. She didn't deserve to inherit anything, really, because it wasn't as if they'd had any kind of relationship at all. Perhaps it was all going to be one enormous practical joke on the part of her grandmother, a last insult from the woman who'd been absent from her life even more than her father had. The joke was on her if it transpired that all she'd left Isla in her will was a flea-bitten old rug or a pile of electricity bills.

'Your father has a copy of the will and he asked specifically that he impart the contents to you himself. As he is executor that's entirely reasonable and he wants to do that face to face.'

'He wants me to go to the Alps?'

'He's prepared to pay your expenses from the estate.'

'He couldn't come to see me here in England?'

'It's not possible without causing significant delay to the administration of the estate.'

'Right.'

'I take it you're amenable to that?'

'I don't know. Yes. Maybe.'

'Which of those responses should I pass on to your father?' he asked, though there was no impatience or scorn in his voice, only a mild sort of humour. Perhaps he'd made these phone calls many times before and nothing surprised him any longer.

'Yes,' Isla replied, though she felt far from happy with her decision. 'What would happen if I changed my mind?'

'Then you would be pressed no further on the matter. It really is entirely up to you, Miss McCoy.'

'So why bother contacting me at all? If he doesn't desperately need me to go and hear this thing?'

'That's not quite the case. I'm not at liberty to discuss the contents of the will as your father would like to do that with you himself, but there are conditions which may not be met should you decide not to travel to France to meet him.'

'And what does that mean? I don't get my inheritance? Whatever that is?'

'Miss McCoy...' He paused as though about to say something against his better judgement. 'The fact of the matter is every party who stands to gain from your grandmother's estate would be affected by your decision not to attend this meeting.'

'What does that mean?'

'That's all I'm willing to say on the matter. I hope you understand that I don't do this to be obstructive but merely to respect the wishes of your father and your late grandmother. It is my belief that he very much wants to see you regardless of the circumstances and perhaps that is enough to persuade you?'

It wasn't, and she didn't know if she believed Mr Rousseau's assertions anyway, but she simply sighed. 'So if I don't go it makes things really difficult for everyone else?'

'Yes.'

'And it would make me an unreasonable cow to refuse?'

'That judgement call is one only you can make. Your refusal would certainly change the nature of things significantly.'

Isla's gaze went to the window of her bedroom, where she was holed up, keeping the conversation away from her mother's ears and disapproval. The sky was like dirty dishwater, drizzle spraying against the glass. Something about it felt flat against the monumental turn her life was about to take. At the very least a decision like this demanded thunder and lightning, or a storm whipping up around the parked cars in the street, not a clammy drizzle in a dull sky.

Because it looked like she was on her way to France.

Isla knew telling her mother wasn't going to be easy. With lectures at university now over until the start of the new term and in need of a breath of air before what she knew would be an awkward conversation, she'd decided to head into town and make a start on her Christmas shopping. Ordinarily there would still be time – Isla wasn't someone who panicked and rushed out the moment the trees had dropped their last russet leaf, but if she was going to fly to the Alps before Christmas, she realised that she might have to be a little more organised this year. Not to mention clever with her money with the unexpected extra expenses she might incur for a trip to the snowy Alps. Even if the cost of getting there was covered, her costs for food and other sundries were not. It was safe to say her student loan was taking a bit of a hammering as she trawled Dorchester's quaint high street.

It wasn't yet five but already dark, the gently sloping street crowded with bright shopfronts and ropes of Christmas lights that criss-crossed the main road from roof to roof, dripping into the space between like strings of stars. They'd been switched on only the week before but already felt as if they'd been there forever. The scene as Isla looked down the high street held a certain magic, despite the hurried impatience of rush-hour traffic. Snatches of Christmas music filtered out of shop doorways as she paused at various ones, peering into the windows for inspiration. She didn't have many gifts to buy and most would be silly, token gifts for the many cousins, aunts and uncles on her mother's side, but there were one or two important ones: Glory's for a start, Dodie's too, and then there was her father. She had a box full of childhood gifts for him in her bedroom, but now that the dream of seeing him again was about to become a reality, she didn't know what to do. She owed him no such consideration, and yet part of her – the part that was still ten years old – wanted more than anything to buy him the perfect gift.

What if she took the gifts from her cupboard to France with her and finally gave them to him? It would mean something to her – the action of passing those years of pain on would be symbolic – but what would it mean to him? Could she take the rejection of seeing his confused face at the sight of a box filled with socks, cheap aftershave and childish hope?

At this point Isla rejected the idea, but it didn't help her wrap her head round the etiquette of her Christmas visit. There would be a whole new family she didn't even know the names of yet, what they looked like and sounded like, loved and loathed, what they thought about the idea of the man they knew as father and husband having a life before them. Was she supposed to turn up with gifts, or would that seem strange and forward? What if they'd bought things for her and she turned up with nothing? Perhaps it was one she'd run by Dodie, but then she knew that her friend would always come down on the side of generosity and forgiveness. It was easy for Dodie to be full of optimism and goodwill, though, because Dodie's family had always been stable and loving. Isla didn't want to see it that way, and she didn't for a minute resent her friend's upbringing, but it was hard not to feel bitter about it on her low days.

With her friend very much on her mind and desperate to push the questions surrounding her dad to the back of it, Isla headed into a shop selling handmade organic toiletries and cosmetics. The window was bright with pastel soaps and bottles, and the fragrance wafting from the front door divine – cinnamon and citrus layered with sweet candy. Dodie loved this shop but it wasn't often she treated herself to anything from it; since she'd taken on her business venture in Bournemouth most of her spare money had gone into that, leaving only enough for the bare, value-brand essentials. It was ordinarily out of Isla's price range too, but this was Christmas and if anyone deserved a treat to thank her for another year of loyalty, love and support, it was Dodie. So, Isla pushed aside her doubts and lost herself amongst the divinely fragranced bottles and bath bombs as she sniffed and tested everything to find the perfect gift.

While she was there perhaps she'd pick something up for her mum, too. No Clinique or Estée Lauder for Glory McCoy who, despite taking fierce pride in her appearance, had to make do with supermarket moisturiser – and that was during the weeks when the money was spare. Often, when Isla had needed new school pumps or she'd outgrown her jeans there'd be nothing left for luxuries at all. Nowadays, not much better off but able to fend for herself, Isla often went home with little treats for her mum. Nothing like the luxury she deserved, but a token to show that Isla appreciated all she'd given up. Perhaps there was a spot of guilt now as she picked up a vanilla-scented hand cream and popped it into her basket, because she knew that, as well as delivering this, she would also be delivering news that Glory would find it hard to forgive.

*

'You said you weren't going!' Glory slapped a slab of fish into the frying pan, the hiss as it hit the fat accentuating the resentment in her tone.

'I know, Mum, but I've had time to think and—'

'All the years I've been father and mother to you… Where was Ian McCoy when you had tonsillitis? On all the nights when you sweated next to me with a fever and I didn't dare leave you in your bed alone? When you were sitting your GCSEs? When your first boyfriend broke your heart? When I had to go to school because those bullies stuck gum in your hair?' She sucked in a breath and looked set to start again but Isla placed a gentle hand on each shoulder and pulled her round to face her.

'Mum… you will always be the most important person in my life but it can't always be just you and me.'

'But you said—'

'I know what I said. I hadn't had time to process what meeting my dad again might mean, but I've realised it might be important. He left us both, Mum, and sometimes I think you forget that. He abandoned me as much as he did you, and if you had a chance for closure now, wouldn't you take it? If you could sit across from him and listen to him explain it all, wouldn't you want to do that too? Don't you think it would help?'

'No.' Glory shook herself free of Isla's grip. 'I don't ever want to see that man's face again.'

Isla paused. Glory didn't mean that and they both knew it. 'Well then, wouldn't you want the chance to tell him how he ruined your life, what his leaving meant for us? Wouldn't that help to bring closure?'

'I'd like to swipe this pan across the back of his head,' Glory said, giving the frying pan a violent swish and sending another hissing cloud of cooking oil into the air. Isla took an involuntary step back and out of range. The mood her mum was in, anything could happen, and she rather liked her fish on the plate and not down the front of her blouse. 'I don't need closure; that's just more of your psychology mumbo-jumbo. I wish you'd stop turning me into one of your subjects.'

Isla's features hardened. 'If I wanted a subject to study I'd choose one a lot less predictable than you.'

Glory swung round to face her again. 'What does that mean?'

'You're like a stuck record where Dad is concerned. He broke your heart and everyone knows it, but that was twenty-four years ago and maybe it's time to move on. I need to move on even if you don't and seeing him will either kill or cure me. Right now, I don't care which because it will be movement, and any movement at all is better than living in limbo with you. I want to see him, to work out for myself how I feel.'

Glory threw her hands into the air. 'Always my fault! I suppose you think it's my fault he left us!'

'It doesn't matter whose fault it is – that doesn't change the facts. I'm angry, of course I am. I'm hurt that he never bothered to get in touch for all those years. But he's getting in touch now.'

'Because there's money involved.'

'We don't know that yet.'

'There's a will, isn't there? His meeting with you is a stipulation of the inheritance. Don't fool yourself, Isla; you're too intelligent to let yourself be taken in by any of this. He doesn't want you; he wants his money.'

'I'm not stupid – I know that. I'll have my guard up at all times and I won't get hurt if that's what you're worried about. I just want to see, Mum. I just want answers. You lost your husband, but I lost my dad and it changed me as a person. I just need to get my head around that and I think seeing him will help. Please… can't you understand what I'm saying?'

Glory flipped the fish over. 'I don't see why you have to go to France. Why can't he come here if he's so desperate to see you?'

Isla folded her arms tight. 'Do you really need to ask that question? Look at your reaction to the mere mention of his name. Imagine how much you'd freak out if he came over to England, was even in the same county as you, let alone the same room. You'd be right back where you started when he first left and I don't want that on my conscience.'

Glory sniffed hard but said nothing.

'I don't mind going over there,' Isla said. 'He's paying so if you look on the bright side it's a free holiday.'

'Holidays are meant to be enjoyable.'

Isla rubbed at her arms. She couldn't argue with that but she wasn't going to say so to her mum. She had to sell this idea to Glory if she was going to leave with them on good terms. She'd made up her mind to go anyway, but she'd rather do it with her mum's blessing, if that were at all possible.

'How do you know all this anyway?' Glory added.

'The solicitor told me. He said he felt I might want to go over there, said I might find it beneficial in terms of my inheritance.'

If Glory was annoyed that Isla had made the call she didn't say so. 'I still don't understand why Sarah would leave you anything. It's a bit late for a sudden attack of guilt when she's hardly bothered with you since the day you were born.'

As a child, Isla had often wondered about her grandmother's absence. In some ways, she'd felt that rejection more keenly than her father's, convinced there was something about her which was so distasteful that both her grandmother and her father couldn't bear to be in her life. She had so many questions to ask her dad, and that was at the top of the list. She could understand why he'd left – at least it wasn't unusual for marriages to break down and for the father to disappear from the child's life. But for a grandmother to forsake the child too? Was she so blind to her son's faults that she'd side with him no matter what? Or was something else happening here? She glanced up at her mother, who was now fetching a pair of warmed plates from the oven. Isla loved her mother but she didn't always trust her. Through all the long years she'd asked herself the same questions about why her father's family had forsaken them, she'd also begun to suspect that her mother wasn't entirely blameless in the affair. What she hadn't dared ask, but what she suspected more strongly than ever before, was whether proud, unforgiving Glory McCoy had driven them away. Had she cut them from her life even though they'd wanted to be a part of it?

'I don't really understand it either,' Isla said. 'But the fact remains that she has, and I want to know more.'

'You'll regret it.'

'I might, but it's my decision whether I take the risk or not, isn't it?'

'You've always been headstrong and stubborn,' Glory huffed as she lifted the frying pan from the heat.

Isla gave a faint smile. 'Where do you think I get it from?'

Glory looked up and met Isla's gaze. Though she was trying to hide it, Isla detected the hint of a smile in return.

'Don't think I've given up trying to talk you out of this fool plan,' she said.

'I wouldn't dare,' Isla replied. 'But that fish looks good so could we put this argument on hold at least until we've eaten?'

Chapter Four

The next night brought an easier get-together in the form of dinner with Dodie. Isla was desperate to talk to someone who would give her supportive, impartial advice after the difficult conversation with Glory, and Dodie had cancelled all her plans the minute Isla had called her to say so. Isla was still reeling from the decision; nervous and hesitant one minute, resolute the next, but ultimately terrified for how it might change everything. Already her relationship with her mum had altered; she'd felt it that morning as Glory had bid her a cold goodbye to go to work. Her mother had accepted it, but she would never be happy about it.

As always, Isla had bought far too much food from the Chinese takeaway. She had a gargantuan appetite and Dodie often complained that if she ate half of what Isla did she'd look like a pygmy hippo. In times of stress this intake could grow exponentially, and despite what she'd told her mum, this was a time of extreme stress. After a brief greeting, Isla dumped the cartons on the table. Even if she had ordered too much food, Dodie would find a home for the leftovers with Dorset's homeless, as she always did. As Dodie set out plates and began to investigate what was on offer, talk turned very quickly to the reappearance of Isla's father.

'So this is your dad's mum? The gran you've never met?'

Isla nodded slowly as she unwrapped her spring rolls.

'Bloody decent of her as she's never laid eyes on you,' Dodie said wryly. 'A sudden attack of conscience, was it?'

'That's what Mum said. I suppose it must have been. I don't know much about it really, but the letter requested that I go. Said there was provision in the estate for my travel expenses if I wanted to.'

'Do you have to?'

'I wouldn't imagine I *have* to do anything.'

'What's your mum say?'

'I'll give you three guesses…'

Dodie smiled. 'OK, silly question. I'm surprised she showed you the solicitor's letter at all. Why on earth did she?'

'Perhaps she had an attack of conscience too. Maybe she thought if she didn't tell me about it things would have been a whole lot worse for her if they'd found me some other way.'

'It would have been, I bet.'

'I wouldn't have been pleased. I'm not a kid any more, but sometimes I think she wishes I still was. It seems like Dad thinks so too; it would have been a lot simpler to send the letters direct to me than rely on Mum telling me about them.'

Dodie opened the lid on a carton of rice. 'So if you know it's going to upset your mum I don't suppose you'll be going.'

'That's the thing… he's my dad. I don't know; I've always felt as if my life has been missing a piece and maybe seeing him and getting to know him again will fix that. But then he didn't want me for all these years, so that makes him a twat, doesn't it?'

'I'd have to agree.'

'He's *my* twat, though. I don't know anything about him or his family, only that our name is Scottish. Mum has this total information blackout where he's concerned, and I get why she feels that way so I've never pushed it. At least, not over the past few years, and we've learned to ignore the fact he ever existed.'

'She kept his name when he left,' Dodie said, raising her eyebrows meaningfully.

'You try telling my mum that's significant and she'll chase you around the house with a frying pan. She says it was just easier not to bother changing it, but I know it's because the silly cow has never really stopped loving him. I think that's why she's so adamant we don't discuss him and we don't acknowledge his existence – it just hurts too much.'

'You can't ignore his existence now.'

'Don't I bloody know it.'

'Do you feel as if you need to know about your dad's family? You've already got an enormous family here in England without adding to it.'

'I have.' Isla gave a slight smile. 'On my mum's side at least. And that's without all the folks in Nigeria. We could fill Wembley Stadium with my cousins.'

'It does seem funny,' Dodie said thoughtfully as she dug her spoon into the tub of chicken and put some on her plate. 'Your gran's never shown any interest in you before but she's suddenly decided to leave you some money. Don't you think that's odd?'

'I did. And I asked my mum about it but she gave me the usual response. Which is no response at all.'

'Do you think that maybe they *did* try to contact you over the years but your mum wouldn't let them and didn't tell you about it? Because she *was* pretty messed up for years after he left, wasn't she? And it might be the sort of thing someone who was pretty messed up might do.'

'I don't know what to think. I believe that if she did, it was for the right reasons – at least she would have thought them right, even if they weren't. It's tough to know what to do.'

'What does your heart want to do?'

Isla shrugged. 'I think I want to go. Just to see. I think I'll always regret it if I don't. And it's not just about the money… that's if there is any money, because I'm not sure about that either. To tell you the truth, I'm not sure about anything right now.'

Dodie blew out a breath. 'It's huge, that's for sure.'

Isla pulled the cork from some wine and poured a glass, which she handed to Dodie. 'What would you do?'

'You're asking the wrong person – I wear my heart on my sleeve and I'm as gullible as they come. When it comes to reason over emotion, I'm absolutely hopeless.'

'That's why you're exactly the right person to answer my question. You see the good in everyone and it always seems to work out OK for you. Your instincts always steer you right. Everyone you meet falls in love with you—'

'Try telling that to Ryan,' Dodie interrupted, but she shook her head at Isla's questioning frown. 'Sorry – ignore me.'

'What I mean to say is, perhaps I should just trust my heart and go; see what he has to say. What harm can it do? Of course, I know that I'm bound to be disappointed because he's done nothing but let me down all my life. When he could be bothered to be a part of it, that is. So I suppose there's nothing he can do to make things worse in that respect, but he might show a glimmer of a good side when I meet him and that might make me understand him a little better. That's got to be a good thing as far as I can tell. But then I don't want my mother to hate me, and she will if I go to see him. Not hate me, but she'll be desperately hurt and she'll see it as a betrayal for all the years she thinks she spent protecting me from his influence. More than that, I don't want to find out things about my mother that I'll wish I hadn't known. There's always two sides to every story, isn't there? I'm stumped.'

'The only person you can really please here is yourself. So perhaps you ought to concentrate on that and forget about the rest.'

'But pleasing me depends so heavily on the outcome of the rest. You see what I mean?'

'Hmm.' Dodie took a sip of her wine. 'I suppose you get a trip to the French Alps, which can't be bad. Which part?'

'Some ski resort I can't even pronounce the name of. I Googled it and it looked posh so he mustn't be doing too badly if he can afford to live there.'

'Want me to go in your place?'

Isla smiled faintly. 'I'm almost tempted to say yes. You could come with me.'

'I wish, but there's too much going on here,' Dodie replied. 'You'll probably find you love it when you get there. It might be worth going just for the holiday, even if it turns out that your dad is the arse you thought he might be.'

'I'm not so sure. It'll be bloody freezing for a start, and how is my thin blood going to cope with that? If he'd gone to Barbados, that might be a different story, but if I do go to the Alps I'm certainly not going for the trip.'

'How about a sexy Frenchman?'

Isla raised her eyebrows. 'I know you're trying to make me feel better but it's not helping.'

Dodie put the takeout cartons to one side and took a seat at the table. 'Sorry... I don't know what to say. In the end, it's a decision only you can make. I'm happy to listen while you sound off, but I can't offer any advice because, honestly, I don't have a clue what you should do. The only advice I can give is to go with your gut instinct, because it's what I would do.'

'I wish I could be more like that. I'm all logic and planning and sometimes I wish I wasn't; life would be much more fun with a free spirit.'

'A free spirit often gets you into trouble too,' Dodie said with a slight smile. 'I envy your logic and reasoning – at least you have a plan.'

'You're doing OK. You've got your own business for a start. And a boyfriend. For all my sensible planning I have neither of those things.'

'It's only a matter of time,' Dodie replied. 'When your course is over you'll get your dream job. And as for boyfriends, they're overrated.'

Isla arched an eyebrow as she unfolded a napkin. 'Had a falling-out with Ryan?'

'Sort of. I don't want to talk about it.'

'He wouldn't let you watch *Harvey* again?'

'No.' Dodie laughed. 'It wasn't quite that bad. We had words; it was nothing and I'll sort it out with him tomorrow.'

'As long as you're OK. If you want to talk I'm here – don't forget that.'

'I thought we were supposed to be talking about you tonight?'

'Yeah, well... I'm sick of hearing myself talk about it so everyone else must be suicidal by now.'

'Not me.' Dodie smiled. 'If you want to go over it a thousand times I'll keep listening.'

Isla looked up from her plate and her heart swelled at the sight of her friend's concerned gaze. If only everyone in her life could be as dependable as Dodie Bright. *Don't cry, don't cry...*

'Oh, God!' Dodie squeaked. 'Please don't cry; it wasn't said to make you cry and if you start I will too!'

'I know. I've just realised how lucky I am to have you.'

'I feel the same, so now we've got that out of the way we're going to eat Chinese and say no more about it or we'll both be weeping into our fried rice!'

Isla forced a smile, sniffing back her tears. 'There's a lot to get through too, so I'd better pull myself together and make a start!'

Chapter Five

Isla reread the email. *Looking forward to meeting with you...* he'd signed off. A little formal, perhaps, but what else was he going to say? *Love from Dad? Missed you, sweetie?* She looked up at a light tap on the bedroom door and, as it opened and her mum appeared, slammed her laptop closed. It wasn't like she had anything to hide, but with the situation as tense as it was the last thing she needed was for her mum to see she was in direct contact with her dad, even if it was as vague and impersonal as an email sent with instructions on how to reach the village where he lived.

She forced a smile and Glory placed a neat pile of clothes on the bed.

'I thought you might need some things washing and ironing for the trip,' she said quietly.

'You didn't have to do that—'

'I know. But I was doing some anyway and I thought...'

She was calling a truce. She'd never say it, but Isla never expected her to.

'Thanks, Mum.'

'I was thinking... how are you getting to the airport?'

'I've just booked a taxi to take me there.'

Glory's eyebrows went up. 'Already?'

'I didn't see any point in messing around.'

'And you paid for that?'

'On my credit card. My not so flexible friend…' Isla gave a small smile. 'But I'll get it back from the estate, so I'm not worried.'

'You make sure you do.'

'I will.'

'You make sure he knows just what hell he's put us through over the years too.'

'I think he already knows that.'

'I wouldn't bet on it. But you tell him. Don't be flattered by him, Isla. Don't be persuaded to trust him, no matter what he says. He left us flat and don't you ever forget that.'

'How could I, Mum? I couldn't even if I wanted to. I'm not five; I can work out myself what to do and say.'

'I know, but I don't want…' Glory shook her head. 'Never mind. I wish you wouldn't go—'

'I *am* going. I have to.'

'You can still change your mind.'

'I can, but I won't. Nothing will change between us, if that's what you're worried about.'

'I'm not worried about that. We've both had our hearts broken by that man once, but you might get yours broken twice.'

'A mistake you'd never make, eh?' Isla said, trying, and failing, to bite her tongue on the matter. Since Ian left them, Glory had locked her heart away and nobody had ever been close to touching it again. Inevitably, there was some of that flinty resolve in Isla, though she hated to admit it. 'I'm sorry,' she added quickly. 'I didn't mean that, I only meant—'

Glory shook her head. 'Let's not fight – not now. I only came to bring those things for you to pack.'

'You could come to the airport with me? I could pay for your taxi home again…'

'No. I don't wish you ill, but you know I can't do that, because it would seem that I approve of you going and I don't. I'll be here in the morning to see you off though.'

'I thought you had a shift at the care home?'

'I did, but I swapped it to be here.'

Isla gave a tight smile. It wasn't Glory's blessing, but it was as close as she was going to get.

Chapter Six

Just to make sure Dodie didn't panic at the lack of an update, Isla tapped out a brief text to let her know she was finally on French soil after an uneventful flight. In fact, it had been interminably dull, with not even a hot cabin steward to take her mind off the boredom. She hated being in one place for long, even her own house where she could come and go as she pleased, so even the shortest flight could be purgatory. The textbooks she'd brought to read hadn't helped, nor had the glossy fashion magazines or iPod full of music. When she'd tried to sleep the couple next to her had done nothing but whisper and giggle inanely.

She was in the arrivals hall of Grenoble Airport now, a building that looked like a space-age cathedral flooded with natural light, feeling tiny and lost beneath vaulted ceilings of tubular steel and vast panes of glass, gleaming marble floors stretching for what seemed like miles. It was impressive, but she could have been anywhere in the world. Beyond the windows the sun blazed in a cornflower sky, giving a deceptive impression of warmth, though a quick check of the weather app on her phone told her that outside it was closer to the temperature of the Arctic than Antigua.

No sooner had she sent the text than Dodie had replied, happy to hear things were going to plan. Isla had a strong suspicion that her uneventful arrival was about the only thing that would go to plan from here on in. She had yet to find her way to St Martin-de-Belleville, the place her father now called home, the place she'd Googled and clicked through endless photos of just to get a sense of it, of what she might expect. There she'd found endless Christmas-perfect images of cabins with gently sloping roofs scattered at the feet of mountains. A tiny church with a stone tower framed by iced trees and winding tracks. Skiers expertly navigating slopes of the starkest white set against skies rendered impossibly blue by a burning sun. Restaurants with warm and welcoming wooden interiors, canopies and coloured umbrellas shielding guests from the glare of the alpine sun as they posed for the camera, happy and relaxed with perfect smiles and perfect lives.

Googling photos of the town was one thing, but there were no photos she could scroll through to get a sense of the man she was about to meet – he didn't even have a social media account.

At home, she'd booked a shuttle transfer online to take her from the airport to the resort and now, exhausted from a lack of sleep the night before and her mind-numbing flight, she was glad she had. With an apprehensive tickle deep in her gut, she grabbed her suitcase and began to drag it towards the exit. Eyes trained on the signage for her shuttle company, she hardly noticed the huge lumbering suitcase roll into her path until she tripped over a wheel and found herself thrown into the arms of a stranger.

'What the...' She blinked, horrified as she looked up at the man. But he looked as shocked as she did.

'I am *so* sorry! My case just sort of... veered off... on its own merry way...'

Extricating herself from his arms she smoothed a hand over her jacket and shot him an indignant glower.

'You're alright?' he asked, seemingly untroubled by what Isla thought was her best death stare.

'This time. But it's only through a huge stroke of luck – it could have been much worse.'

As she walked away she could hear him continuing a stammered, shame-faced apology. She was stressed, alone in a foreign land and uncertain of what lay ahead of her – the last thing she needed right now was some goofball trying to floor her with his suitcase and then a fifty-page dissertation explaining how sorry he was. The fact that he wasn't a bad-looking goofball didn't even begin to excuse it. Isla shook herself. He was wearing a tweed jacket for God's sake. And was that an *actual* bow tie? Who in the hell under the age of sixty even wore bow ties these days? This guy and James Bond apparently, although James Bond never wore one that was blue with white polka dots. Isla's thoughts drifted to Dodie. Her best friend, with her nutty obsession over all things vintage and quirky, would probably love this guy. Maybe she ought to go back and get his number – he'd be a darned sight better suited to Dodie than her current boyfriend, Ryan, was.

Isla batted away the idea. Her stress levels were filling her head with the strangest ideas. There was a shuttle seat with her name on it and all she needed to think about right now was getting to St Martin-de-Belleville. The sooner she could see what was waiting for her, the better she could start figuring out how to deal with it.

She woke with a jolt, peeling her cheek from the bus window. She'd been determined not to fall asleep and miss the scenery and yet she'd done just that almost as soon as the shuttle had left the airport compound. The bus was already pulled up in a parking bay, the cut of the engine waking her, and her fellow passengers were grabbing bags and coats in their haste to get off. A low rumble of barely contained excitement and anticipation rippled through the coach. Isla rubbed her eyes and leaned her head back on the seat; what did it matter if she took five minutes or fifteen to get off? It wasn't like she had anywhere to rush off to. At least, not today.

With a yawn she pulled her phone from her bag and flicked to her emails to check the booking details for her stay over the next week. The confirmation message contained a map and a link, which Isla clicked. Her hotel, Residence Alpenrose, was a ten-minute walk, just off the main street of the town, though the hotel's website photo had mountains in it, and she wasn't sure how on earth it could be just off the main street if there were mountains behind it. No doubt her phone's GPS would get her to the right place.

Holding valiantly onto that thought, she pulled her coat and hat on, ready to brave the sub-zero temperatures outside. Already the roads had a generous coating of ice and snow, though the bus had felt so sure and safe as it had whizzed to her destination that Isla wondered how it was that one flake of the stuff in Britain would have had the entire country's road and rail infrastructure at a standstill.

But as she finally stepped off the bus and made her way to the side where the driver was retrieving suitcases from the boot, she looked around herself properly for the first time and stopped breathing. For a lost moment all she could do was stand and stare at the vista that greeted her. The driver cleared his throat and threw her a wry grin as she pulled in a lungful of frozen air and turned to him.

'Your first time?' he asked, his perfect English laced with the most delicious French accent.

Isla nodded mutely, her gaze drawn involuntarily back to the white frosted hulks of mountains bearing down on a town of adorable wooden chalets. It was like standing in the middle of a movie, or a travel brochure, and even though she'd looked at a thousand photos of this very same place before she'd left England, nothing could prepare her for the sight of it now. It was right in front of her, but still hard to imagine a place this beautiful could even exist outside of a snow globe.

She continued to stare as the driver moved to help the next passenger retrieve their belongings from the cavernous space beneath the seats of the bus. She'd seen mountains before on a visit to Scotland; she'd even climbed Snowdonia in Wales one particularly energetic Sunday, but this was like nothing she'd ever seen before. Those mountains were like Lego models against a skyscraper. She swivelled round and in every direction was more of the same – high, jagged peaks that bit into the sky, caressed by tendrils of lazy cloud drifting in a sky of vibrant blue, like a fortress of rugged rock throwing its arms around a town of toy-like wooden chalets which tumbled down the lower slopes.

'Which hotel are you staying at?'

The driver's voice broke the spell. Isla shook herself, now painfully aware that she probably looked like a simpleton standing and staring ahead.

'Oh… Residence Alpenrose. Do you know it?'

'*Oui.*' He stuck his arm out to indicate a track covered by snow. 'Follow this road round to the left and you will see it.'

It didn't look like much of a road, more of a ski run. She almost wondered whether she ought to be wearing skis, or at the very least snowshoes, though it was too late to worry about that now. She wanted to ask if the hotel was any good, but perhaps it was better if she didn't know before she got there. He was hardly likely to tell her if it was no good, and even if he did there wasn't a lot she could do about it anyway. The reservation was made and she was lucky to have one considering the time of year. So she simply nodded. 'Thanks.'

'Enjoy your visit,' he called as she turned to leave.

Beautiful as St Martin-de-Belleville was, under the circumstances that was hardly likely to happen, Isla thought dryly. But he didn't need to know that.

'I'm sure I will,' she said. 'Thank you.'

As she'd feared, madly in love with them though she was, her wedge-heeled boots had turned out to be entirely unsuited to pavements that were layered with a thick crust of solid ice. How she'd arrived at Residence Alpenrose without a broken ankle was a conundrum for the greatest minds of the age to tussle over. One thing was for certain – once her luggage was unpacked, she'd have to head out and get some more sensible footwear. Hefty hiking boots, preferably with crampons or something ought to do it, though they wouldn't go with a single item of clothing she'd brought with her. Luckily it seemed that every other store she'd passed had been dedicated to the pursuit of the great outdoors, so there were plenty of places to get some. At least the down-filled coat she'd purchased the day before she left England had been a sound investment, although by now, as she stood at the entrance of her hotel, she was sweating beneath it from the exertion of staying upright on her dodgy heels and dragging her massive suitcase behind her.

Residence Alpenrose slotted into its surroundings perfectly, almost as if it was a part of the natural landscape. Built in the style of a typically traditional alpine chalet, unlike some of the more contemporary concrete structures she'd seen, it was nestled in pines and shadowed by the mighty snow-capped peaks. It was a cliché, but as Isla turned her gaze once more to the mountains that stood guard over the town, she could swear that eagles soared high over their snowy heads. It was like a tourism video made real, and for a moment she could hardly believe she was actually here. To her left was the patio area of the hotel – deserted apart from a couple sitting at a table, wrapped in ski gear and removing their boots. They looked up and gave her a vague smile, then continued a conversation they'd been having in French. Isla's French was rudimentary to say the least – odd phrases alluding to how fond she was of swimming and requesting the way to the train station were about as much as she could remember from school, and now she was beginning to wish she'd made an effort to improve it before she'd come. Perhaps most of the tourist establishments would have English speakers helping out, otherwise she'd have to get a translating app for her phone or track down a phrasebook in one of the many shops.

She was caught by a sudden yawn. After all the excitement (or trauma, depending on how you looked at it) of getting here, maybe a little nap was in order.

Making her way up to the steps that marked the entrance, tracks on them showing they'd recently been cleared of a fresh snowfall, she let out an impatient sigh. Of course she'd booked the one hotel that had steps to negotiate with a heavy suitcase, the very last thing she needed right now.

As she opened the front doors, however, she quickly decided that she could forgive a few steps. Setting foot in the lobby, she felt immediately at home amongst the rustic wooden furniture, stone floors and warm terracotta-painted walls. She was greeted at the reception desk by a welcoming smile from the grey-haired attendant. '*Bonjour.*'

'I have a reservation,' Isla said, deciding that any attempt to reply in French might lead to a response she couldn't hope to understand. Besides, the hotel website had made a great point of the fact that their staff spoke English. 'At least I hope I do. In the name of McCoy. Isla McCoy…'

The receptionist nodded with that supremely reassuring smile that only hotel receptionists know how to give. 'One moment please,' she said, and it was now Isla noticed that although she spoke perfect English, her accent sounded American. Isla peered over the desk as the woman checked a ledger with a list of handwritten names snaking down the page, intrigued by the quaintness of it and wondering where the computer was hidden. But there was no sign of one, just lists and paperwork and the vast leather-bound ledger. She couldn't help a wry inward smile.

'Oh yes,' the receptionist continued. 'Here you are.' She made a mark against Isla's name on the list and trotted over to a large board covered in hanging keys. She took one of them down and handed it to Isla. 'Room twenty-two. That's on the first floor – you can take the lift over there. Would you like me to get someone to take your bags up for you?'

Isla shook her head as she unzipped her massive coat. 'I can manage, thanks.'

'If you're sure…'

'Yes, thank you.'

'Breakfast is between seven and ten. If you'd like to make dinner reservations come and see me any time. And welcome to St Martin-de-Belleville.'

Isla forced a smile and made her way to the lifts. The doors were just closing as she heard the hotel receptionist greet another guest who sounded English too. She wondered whether there'd be many of them staying at Residence Alpenrose. She was staying there alone and that was just fine, but it might be nice to have the occasional friendly exchange with a fellow guest in a language she could understand.

On the first floor, she located the room easily. No plastic key cards here, just an old-fashioned lock, and Isla turned the key to open the room. It smelt clean and freshly aired, a hefty wooden-framed bed dominating the centre draped in fleecy blankets and furs, ethnic patterned rugs over neutral walls and a huge patio window looking out over the mountains beyond. The room was enormous, with a leather sofa and coffee table, a desk in the corner and bathroom adjoining. Isla wheeled in her suitcase and sat on the edge of the bed. She'd thought Residence Alpenrose a budget option, and it probably was compared to other hotels, but this looked far more expensive than the room she'd booked from the website. Had they upgraded her and forgot to mention? She hoped she wasn't going to get landed with a bigger bill than she'd anticipated because she wouldn't dare present it to her dad. But this was the room the receptionist had told her and it tallied with the number on the keys, so it had to be right.

She shrugged off her coat, her boots quickly following as she kicked them across the room and flopped onto the bed. The temperature outside was bitter, but in here it was cosy – too hot for all the layers she'd arrived in, and now she felt sticky and sweaty. She was sleepy too, but not ready to give in until she'd seen a bit of the place. Perhaps a shower was a way to stave off the tiredness for a little longer.

Without a second thought, Isla pulled the curtains shut, opened her suitcase and took out a change of clothes which she laid out on the bed. Then she stripped down to her underwear. A gorgeous, hot shower was calling and she couldn't wait to get in.

As she reached for the clasp to undo her bra, there was a click in the lock of the door to her room. Isla's head shot up and she let out a squeal as a man walked in. The shock registered on his face at the same moment as hers, and he blushed violently as he began mumbling confused apologies.

'I'm so sorry but...' He began to back out and peered at the door number to check while Isla hurried to pull her clothes back on. He turned to say something else, covering his face with his hands as she yanked her jeans up and fastened them. 'I think you might be in my room,' he continued from behind his hands.

'But I just got the key!' Isla said as she pulled her sweater over her head.

'Well I have a key too,' he said, though this much was obvious given he'd just let himself in.

Isla stubbed her toe on a chair leg as she crossed the room and cursed under her breath. She'd thought the room was a bit more luxurious than the one she'd booked – had there been a mistake? In anticipation of as much, she began to shove her belongings back in her suitcase. All the while, the man was mumbling from behind his hands, clearly unaware that she was now fully clothed. Or perhaps still too embarrassed to show his face. She was about to tell him he could look again when there was movement from the doorway behind him and the receptionist from downstairs raced in.

'I'm so sorry,' she said, looking shame-faced as Isla turned to face her. 'I'm afraid I gave you the wrong key! Your room is in fact number twenty-five...' She held up another key with the number on its fob. 'The key was missing from the hook for this room and I couldn't understand what I'd done with it when Sebastian checked in so I gave him the skeleton key... I thought I'd just misplaced it – I didn't realise what I'd done until it was too late… I hope it hasn't been too much of an inconvenience for you. I hate to ask, but I'm afraid you'll have to move…'

'Inconvenience?' Isla squeaked. 'I was nearly bloody naked when he came in!'

'Oh… my…'

The woman looked so genuinely mortified Isla thought she might have to hand her some tissues for when she burst into tears.

'It's an easy mistake I suppose,' Isla added, her tone softer now.

'I feel just terrible about walking in on you,' the man said, hands still over his face.

'You weren't to know. And you can take your hands away now, because I'm dressed.'

He did as he was asked, but his gaze went straight to the floor. In the semi-darkness of the room it was hard to make out his features. Which was probably a good thing because it meant he hadn't really seen much of her nakedness either.

'Give me a minute and I'll be out of your way.' Isla began to gather up the last of the belongings scattered across the room and fastened her suitcase.

'Let me take that for you—' the man began but Isla pulled the handle out of his way.

'I can manage,' she said, refusing to look him in the eye. The little contact they'd already had was awkward enough without prolonging the agony.

'Right…' he said, turning to go back out onto the landing. 'I suppose I'll go and get the rest of my bags then.'

In leggy strides he was already halfway down the corridor when Isla emerged from the room she now had to vacate for him.

Dragging her suitcase, she handed back the incorrect key and then followed as the woman led her to room twenty-five, opening the door to admit her. Isla couldn't do anything but be disappointed as she walked in; while this room was clean and warmly furnished, just like the first one, it was half the size, the window a tiny square of glass overlooking the street below and barely a mountain or a pine needle in sight. But this did, sadly, look exactly like the room she'd booked. Upgrade wafted under her nose and then snatched away again – story of her life. She tried not to let the feeling of disappointment get the better of her as she took the key from the receptionist.

'I'm so sorry – again; really, I feel just terrible. Please enjoy a complimentary drink at the bar when you're ready as an apology.'

'Honestly, there's no need,' Isla said, waving the offer away. 'No harm done in the end.'

'Well, if there's anything you need then be sure to shout. I'm Dahlia and I'm at the desk downstairs most hours, so call whenever you want me.'

'Thank you.'

The woman left and Isla closed the door behind her with a heavy sigh as she took a moment to appraise the room again. It wasn't high-end luxury, but it was cosy and it had bags of character. She supposed there were far worse places to stay, though it was hard to resign herself to the change when she'd been so utterly spoilt by the first room. Still, perhaps now she could get that shower…

It was hard to understand what had made Isla's eyes open at the exact moment they did. Something unknown had woken her from sleep, and she shivered as she noted that the blanket she'd draped over herself after falling onto the bed had slipped off. Pulling it round her shoulders, she yawned and made her way to the window. After the excitement in her original room, she hadn't felt like taking a shower after all and had ended up taking a nap instead, just in case the receptionist decided to accidentally give anyone else the keys to her new room. The street below was in the grip of a freezing but glorious dusk, cobalt skies scored by streaks of pink cloud, the first stars gleaming over the mountaintops while the ice on the pavements glinted in the street lights just winking into life. And it was in the light of one of those street lights that she saw the shadowy figure of a man, looking up at the hotel. Staring was more like it, because this was no idle glance – he seemed to be studying it, looking carefully for something.

'Dad…' Isla murmured.

How she could know this she couldn't possibly say. She couldn't even see the figure clearly and yet she felt it, deep in her soul, in a way she couldn't explain. Should she go down? He'd emailed again before she'd left home for the airport but they hadn't arranged to meet until the next day. Was she supposed to wait until the official meeting? Did it matter if they met before? What was the norm in situations like these? She'd never met anyone who'd been through it before and she didn't have a clue. Going to the lamp, she turned it on to look for her boots and coat. But when she went to the window again, just to check, the man had disappeared.

Pressing her nose to the window and craning her neck to check up and down the street, Isla decided that he was definitely gone. She let out the breath she'd been holding. It had surely been a silly notion. And if she was so desperate to see her dad before the meeting, then she only had to ask downstairs if the hotel receptionist knew where his hire shop was and she could find him there. She knew it was in town and the place didn't look all that big. But perhaps that would complicate things unnecessarily so she quickly decided against it.

Her growling tummy, however, reminded her of a far more pressing and practical matter. It was probably too early to get a table for dinner, but perhaps she could get a snack to keep her going down in the bar. She had a free drink to claim too, and right now a drink seemed like a tempting offer. If it could be alcoholic, even better still. After a quick splash in the bathroom to freshen up and a change of clothes, Isla locked her room door behind her and made her way downstairs.

The bar was empty, save for two couples in chunky sweaters in a corner drinking shots and laughing raucously every so often at some skiing anecdote and a man sitting at the bar with his back to the doors.

'I have to confess to feeling guilty about it. It was lucky it was so dark…' the man at the bar was saying to the woman who'd been on reception earlier that day but was now serving drinks. He sounded unnecessarily apologetic. Isla searched her memory for the name of the woman listening to him. Dahlia, wasn't it? Did that poor woman run everything in this hotel? 'Not that I would have looked even if I could, you understand…'

Isla frowned. The man wore a tweed jacket. The voice sounded familiar too. It took a moment to place him, and then her cheeks flared at the memory. She almost groaned out loud and turned to leave again, but too late. Dahlia called cheerily over.

'Ready for that drink now?'

Isla gave a stiff nod and made her way over, the man swivelling round to offer a warm smile.

There was a moment of shared recognition. Not only the man who'd caught her in her underwear earlier that day, but she now recognised him as the man from the airport with the errant suitcase who'd nearly sent her flying.

'Oh!' he said, his mouth forming a perfect circle of surprise. 'Hello!'

Isla forced a smile in return and tried not to make it obvious that she was already looking for an exit. Of all the places he could have ended up he had to come here and now, despite the briefest knowledge of each other, the fact was that they *did* know each other and they'd have to engage in some sort of conversation which recognised that. 'Hello.'

'Fancy,' he said. 'What a coincidence.'

'Yes,' Isla said. 'I didn't see you on my shuttle bus.'

'I hired a car. Handy to get about although the driving's hard work in the snow.'

'I can imagine…'

The conversation stuttered to a halt and Isla glanced up at Dahlia, who seemed unconcerned by their awkwardness. In fact, she was looking fondly between the two of them as if they were favourite nieces and nephews. Considering that their unnecessarily intimate knowledge of each other was Dahlia's fault, Isla thought she ought to wipe the soppy look from her face. Isla's gaze went back to the man. Sandy hair, quiffed up at the front and curling a little at his neck where it needed a cut. Perhaps he didn't worry too much about timely haircuts. Intelligent eyes, inquisitive and wondering, the blue of cornflower fields under a summer sun. And weirdly, the one thing that stood out was a smattering of freckles across the bridge of his nose. Isla had never considered freckles to be an attractive feature before but on him they just looked…

She shook away the thought. She was tired and feeling lost in a strange place and it made for odd emotions. He was still wearing that ridiculous bow tie and jacket from earlier and, in her book, nobody was attractive enough to get past that. Who did he think he was – Indiana Jones?

'I hope your suitcase is somewhere it can't get under my feet.' Isla sat on a barstool next to him. It wasn't that she particularly wanted to sit next to him but she didn't feel she had a lot of choice.

'I really must apologise for earlier… both occasions, in fact. I don't quite know what's going on today but all in all it seems to have been a bit disastrous. Please, let me buy you a drink to say sorry.'

'I'm already owed a complimentary one, so it's fine.'

'The one after that?'

'I'll be legless at this time of the day.' Isla gave her most courteous smile, the one she reserved for the lecturers at university when they patiently explained why she'd got something wrong when she was still convinced she'd got it right – the one that she gave to her mum when she looked over Isla's shoulder as she made *fufu* and told her to add more semolina – the smile that said she was listening though she had no intention of taking the advice. 'Really, it's not necessary; it was an accident and we all have them.'

'Well… you could let me buy you a drink as one lone traveller to another? As we're both alone in a foreign land it would be nice to see a friendly face around the place.'

'It's hardly the back of beyond.'

At this, he seemed to look hurt, and his expression was one of such heart-wrenching rejection, something almost childlike, that Isla instantly melted. 'Sorry,' she said. 'That was rude of me. I didn't mean to sound quite so brusque.'

'It's OK; I suppose I can hardly expect anything else considering the terrible start we got off to. I just thought…'

Isla shook her head. 'Honestly, it's not that. I've got a lot on my mind and I'm not myself. But a drink would be most welcome.'

He hesitated for a moment, and Isla wondered if he was deciding whether to probe her further on what was troubling her. But then his expression of uncertainty lifted into a bright smile. 'So, how long are you staying in St Martin?'

'Just a week. I want to be home for Christmas.'

'Me too,' he said. 'Although I expect to come back after the holiday season and stay for much longer. Oh… what did you want to drink, by the way?' He tilted his head at Dahlia who was ready and waiting to launch into bartending action. 'I think our lovely host is waiting to take your order.'

'A gin and tonic would be amazing,' Isla replied, smiling at Dahlia and wondering if she could manage to at least get their drinks order right.

'And how about you, honey?' Dahlia turned to the man. 'Another one?'

'Another beer please, Dahlia,' he said before turning back to Isla. 'I'm Sebastian by the way. Though everyone calls me Seb so please don't feel the need to stand on ceremony.'

'Isla.' She stuck her hand out and he shook it warmly, the relief that he appeared to be forgiven for his earlier mistake obvious on his face.

'That's a pretty name. Sounds a bit Scottish.'

'My father's choice. I'm often surprised he won that argument because my mother is formidable when she wants to lay down the law and I can't imagine how naming me would have been any different.'

'Maybe she liked it?'

'She must have done; she's never actually said.'

Dahlia set down the drinks and looked at Seb. 'On your tab?'

'Yes, please.'

With a nod she glided to the other end of the bar where one of the sweater-clad couples was waiting to order more shots.

'So,' Seb continued. 'Got any plans while you're here? Hiking, mountain climbing, skiing?'

Isla took a sip of her drink. The gin was dry and sour, just a splash of tonic over a generous wedge of lemon and a mountain of ice. Just the way she liked it and just the thing to wake her from the grogginess that still hung over her since she'd been disturbed from her sleep. It seemed Dahlia wasn't a complete loss after all. Perhaps Isla was being unkind – everyone made mistakes and she decided to give Dahlia the benefit of the doubt. The woman was no spring chicken and if she was always as busy as she seemed to be right now then she could be forgiven the odd slip-up. She glanced up at Seb's blue, blue eyes, the way his lightly freckled nose wrinkled with his quizzical smile – it was a friendly enough enquiry and yet there was no way she could answer it without getting into the whole tale of her father, something she had no intention of telling a stranger no matter how cute he was making himself look. She decided on a semi-lie. 'I haven't really planned anything yet – I thought I might just see what's available and decide.'

'Spontaneity? I like it. Never a dull moment when you tackle life like that.'

'Hmmm. If you asked any of my friends to describe me, spontaneity is not a word they'd use. My best friend, Dodie... she's the one you need to talk to about spontaneity. That phrase about where angels fear to tread could have been written about her.'

'She sounds like fun.'

'She is. I think you'd get along brilliantly.'

He raised his eyebrows slightly. 'You can tell that much already?'

Isla's cheeks suddenly felt hot. She'd based her flippant comment purely on his wacky wardrobe and Dodie's penchant for vintage clothes but it was hardly something she could say in reply to him now without sounding like she was making fun of his fashion sense. Or lack of it.

'Just a hunch.' Taking a bigger sip than she'd intended of her gin, she turned her face to the long windows hugging the room. Dusk had settled properly now and lines of yellow light shone from the buildings across the road.

'I don't meant to pry,' he said, pulling her back from where her thoughts had taken her. Thoughts of meeting her half-brother or sister for the first time, of seeing the father who'd abandoned her and yet cared for them, of hearing the will of a grandmother who had taken no interest in her up until this point... thoughts that seemed to consume her every waking hour these days. But now she turned to him with a silent question. 'It seems to me that you're not in the mood to share. I'm sorry, I should have realised... I was just trying to be friendly. I read the situation wrong.'

Isla shook her head. 'No need to apologise. Like I said before, I have a lot on my mind right now. I appreciate your sentiment but your efforts might be wasted on me.'

'You're travelling alone?' he asked. 'Nobody coming to join you? No boyfriend... girlfriend... family?'

'No,' Isla said, her mind going back to the family she had come to join. Or perhaps join wasn't the right word. She felt more of an inconvenience than a welcome addition – the daughter who had driven her father away.

'Only, I just wanted to say that I'm around if you need anything. I know you have the hotel staff and you're probably very capable but sometimes it's nice to know that. I mean, I might be missing some days but if I'm around and you're looking for someone just to have dinner with or ask about this or that mountain, I'm happy to help. That's all. But, of course, if you'd rather not then I'll leave you alone.'

'That's kind of you. You're a seasoned visitor then? To St Martin, I mean? You said if I wanted to know about the mountains…'

'Oh, yes, I've been a few times before. It's sort of what I do, you know.'

'What, like a mountain expert?'

He smiled. 'Something like that. But you don't need to know about any of that boring stuff.'

'I wouldn't find it boring,' she replied, forcing a smile. He was pleasant enough company now that they'd got over initial disasters and perhaps a distraction from her morose thoughts would be a welcome thing after all. Either way, she'd been a lot ruder than was forgivable and she probably owed him for taking that so well if nothing else.

He pressed the beer bottle to his lips and took a long slug before setting it back onto the bar. 'You say that but I guarantee your eyes would be glazed over within five minutes. Coma and death quickly follows for many. Alas I've seen it happen all too many times.'

Isla's laughter was now genuine and it felt like the first time in weeks she'd laughed properly. 'In that case you'd better not tell me! Death on the first day is definitely not in my itinerary.'

'That's what I thought. So instead, if you're not already bored of my company, and as you still have at least one more drink to get, maybe I can tell you about some of the best spots to visit in the area.'

'That sounds good. Nothing too scary, though. Hiking – as soon as I get some decent boots – and perhaps the odd après ski. That's about as adventurous as I get.'

'You don't ski? I thought more or less everyone who comes to St Martin comes to ski.'

'Have you come to ski?'

'I've come to study. Hand–eye coordination and I are uneasy bedfellows.'

Isla laughed again. It was already something she could get used to, and it wasn't often she met men who could make her laugh. As her friends often said, she was a tough nut to crack. 'So you can't ski?'

'Ah, I didn't say that. I can if I need to but I avoid it in situations where the demonstration of grace is required. That way lies humiliation.'

'It's more than I can do because I've never skied in my life.'

'Perhaps you'll learn this week?'

Isla cocked her head this way and that. Ski lessons were the last thing on her mind but she could hardly deny the little frisson of excitement now that she was here in this incredible and beautiful town. Who knew, in a couple of days, if all was sorted amicably with her dad, then she might be more in the mood to see what else St Martin had to offer. 'Maybe. If I have time. But I might just relax and enjoy the scenery, perhaps try some new fancy cuisine and generally soak up the atmosphere.'

'That sounds like a very good plan to me.'

'If you need any tips…' Dahlia cut in. Isla looked up, vaguely surprised to see her there when she hadn't noticed her return. 'I'd be glad to help out. There's more to this town than just skiing and it's a shame most folks don't see that.'

'I'd be glad of that,' Isla said.

'There's a surprising amount to see aside from skiing,' Seb agreed. 'It's a truly beautiful part of the world. Mont Blanc and Lake Blanc aren't too far away for a start. Then there's the Péclet glacier…'

Dahlia smiled and shook her head slightly. 'And if you'd like to see something that isn't recommended by a mountain enthusiast then you can always check out the Notre-Dame-de-la-Vie.'

'What's that?'

'It's a beautiful old religious building up on the rocks. A lot of people make pilgrimages there.'

'Oh, I saw that online when I was researching. It's not the village church then?'

'A lot of folks confuse it with the church but it's a completely separate thing, far older. Worth a look, though, if you like old buildings. And there's the neighbouring resorts if you don't much care for old things. Val Thorens has a lot more going on than we do here. There's a spa too, if you fancy a day of relaxation, and plenty of sports other than skiing.'

Isla gave Dahlia a grateful smile. Everything she'd suggested sounded good. If nothing else good came out of this trip, at least she'd have had this experience to take away with her.

Chapter Seven

Isla hadn't wanted to see her father before their officially designated meeting in the fear that he might influence her emotionally into making decisions about her inheritance before she knew what it was. She hadn't told him this during their brief email exchange and she had barely recognised the fact herself, but she knew it, deep down. It wasn't that she didn't trust him but... OK, so she didn't trust him, or herself. She couldn't risk the little girl inside her rushing to embrace him, promising anything he asked for in return for a crumb of fake affection. At least at a neutral venue she could maintain distance, have space and time to think logically and rationally before reunions of a more emotional nature could take place. And if she didn't like what she saw? At least she could maintain a safe distance until she was given the opportunity to run home and never come back.

That morning she got ready for the midday appointment, trying her best to remain composed and optimistic about what the meeting might bring. As she ate breakfast, she'd found herself looking around the dining room for Seb, despite her stout resolution that she wouldn't come to rely on his easy company. Even though she'd made excuses to leave early the previous evening, she'd enjoyed their brief chat as he'd talked her through the various tourist attractions and how to get to them. But there was no sign of him so she sat alone, hugging a hot black coffee that, on reflection, probably wasn't doing anything for her nerves. Though, after another restless night, she needed the caffeine. Too jittery to sit still, she took herself out to a shop on the main avenue recommended by Dahlia for some new and far more practical boots.

Isla hadn't really expected much in the way of shops. St Martin was a small town – a village, practically – and the tourist websites she'd checked out had shown only a handful of places in grainy photos. However, their variety and charm had been deeply understated. They were fascinating; far removed from the corporate chains she was used to in the high streets of Britain. Each one was unique and quirky, from the tobacconist that sold toys and postcards, the air dripping with the sweet, earthy scents of dried leaves and smoky flavours, to the *boucherie*, its window hung with cooked and cured meats and shelves inside crammed with honey, cheese and wine, the unmistakable smell of garlic on the air. Isla lingered there for a long time and looked carefully at everything, torn over a decision to buy that gift for her father after all, but in the end she decided against it. Instead, she settled on plopping a jar of mountain honey on the counter to take home for her mum, paying wordlessly for it as the shopkeeper chatted amiably in French that was too fast for her to catch the few words she might understand. All she managed was a sheepish *merci* and *au revoir* as she left the store, but the shopkeeper, a sprightly looking man who had to be at least ninety years old, didn't seem to mind.

There was a gift shop selling stuffed animals dressed in ski suits, quaint wooden toys and miniature alpine chalets, clocks and watches, sunglasses, silver jewellery and colourful beads and bright rustic-looking pottery. Isla wanted to buy almost everything she saw, despite having almost wiped out her budget for Christmas presents in Dorchester before she'd left. Then there was a glut of ski equipment and clothes shops, and even though she didn't ski Isla couldn't resist a peek inside. She knew one of them must belong to her dad, so she didn't linger long.

Eventually she reached the shop Dahlia had recommended and was delighted to find that the assistant spoke perfect English which, she had to assume, was the reason Dahlia had told her to go there.

'*Bonjour,*' the young assistant greeted brightly as she walked in. The floor and shelving were honeyed pine, row upon row of T-shirts, fleeces and ski wear hanging from them. There were racks of sunglasses and goggles and a radio was playing Christmas carols quietly in the background. Over by an oil-fired heater, a tabby cat lazily licked a paw and Isla vaguely wondered how on earth such an ordinary-looking cat managed in mountain terrain. In the corner of the shop, a grey-muzzled dog lifted its head and gave Isla the most cursory of glances before settling back to sleep again.

'I'm looking for some boots…' Isla lifted up a sodden foot, clad in her own wholly inappropriate fashion footwear.

'Ah,' the girl replied with a grin. 'Perhaps something more suited to our snow?'

'I hadn't expected it to be quite this… wet,' Isla said with a smile. 'I can't imagine why.'

'I am sure we can help you there. Please… come this way and I will show you what we have…'

'Almost everyone's out skiing or snowboarding,' Dahlia told her sagely as she polished a great brass bell that hung over the counter. Isla had returned to change into her new boots and grab a last coffee in the now deserted bar before heading off to the restaurant to make her appointment. It was tempting to get something stronger but perhaps being tipsy wasn't the best way to meet her dad for the first time in twenty-four years.

'I'm not staying long. I've got to be somewhere in an hour or so…'

'You want a drink?' Dahlia asked briskly as she rubbed at the bell.

'A drink would be great… What's the bell for?'

Dahlia stopped and blinked at Isla. 'It's not for anything,' she said. 'Belonged to my grandfather,' she added, as if that were explanation enough.

'Right,' Isla replied, none the wiser. But then, she barely had anything that belonged to the generations who had gone before her, so it was hard to imagine treasuring an old heirloom in such a way. 'Where's it from?'

'His boat. He was a fisherman.'

'What was he like?'

'Couldn't tell you – drowned in a storm just after I was born. This was in my grandma's garage when we cleared out the house and my mom let me keep it. Don't suppose she was going to do much with it.'

'What do you do with it?'

Dahlia grinned. 'Mostly clean it.'

'It must mean a lot to you.'

Dahlia stopped rubbing again and gazed at the gleaming brass. 'Well, I suppose it must. Never really given it much thought.' She smiled at Isla, stowing the cloth and polish under the counter. 'That's enough talk of my old junk… What will you have to drink?'

At 11.40 a.m. Isla stepped out into the bitterly cold street in her new boots and enormous, down-filled coat to make her way to the restaurant. People smiled and nodded as they passed, but though her mouth

automatically stretched in reply she could barely keep her mind on
her surroundings. It was a shame, and on a different day she might
have appreciated the drama of the mist rolling in apace to consume
the distant peaks while the egg-yolk sun fought against heavy clouds
to own the rest of the sky. Her mind was full of the conversation she'd
had earlier with Dahlia about her grandfather's bell. It wasn't the bell
that fascinated her, but the idea that Dahlia treasured it so much
without really understanding why. She hadn't known the grandfather
who'd left it behind and yet she was connected to him through it. Isla
barely knew her dad and she'd never even had that much to help her
keep hold of him. Would today have been easier if she had? Would
she have felt she'd known him, just a little better? Perhaps it wouldn't
have made any difference in the end and she tried hard not to dwell
on it now.

Not knowing how long it would take her to find the restaurant
where they'd agreed to meet, Isla arrived there early. She wanted to
stand outside to wait, nervous about going in first, but eventually the
weather got the better of her.

Inside, the restaurant was slick and modern with mood lighting and
chrome fittings. Not at all as she'd expected considering what she'd seen
of the town that day. The maître d' switched smoothly from French
to English as she returned his greeting and showed her to a table big
enough for five – Isla, her father, his wife Celine and… two others?
Children? She ordered a coffee and settled down to wait.

So she waited for her newly found family, trying to imagine how it
would go. They'd all sit politely around the table after brief introductions
and drinks orders and listen as her father divulged who was getting
what. Perhaps she was the only one who didn't already know? What if
she didn't want what was on offer? What if there were conditions she

didn't agree to and she let them all down? Would she agree to them anyway? Powerful emotions would be bubbling under the surface like a geyser ready to blow, but she'd have to keep them in check – keep a cool head.

After a quick glance at her watch, she turned her eyes to the windows. She'd had ten minutes waiting alone, long enough for the nerves to tie her insides in knots and she wished they would hurry up and get here because she didn't know how much more she could take. If they didn't arrive soon she might just leave some money for the coffee and make a run for it.

Outside snowflakes stuttered sporadically from a rapidly whitening sky. At least her hotel wasn't too far away to walk if the weather got a lot worse. How bad did it get up here? You saw things on the news all the time about snowstorms and avalanches, but did they really happen as often as it seemed? Did they get many here in St Martin? The residents she'd met that morning appeared relaxed and carefree enough, so perhaps not.

Her thoughts were interrupted by movement in the corner of her eye. From her table she had full view of the main restaurant entrance and the doors opened now to reveal a party of four – a middle-aged man, a woman of around the same age and a younger man and woman in their late teens or early twenties. Isla's gaze flicked across the four of them but rested in the end on the man. Her father. She didn't see anything of herself in those features – dark hair shot through with grey, strong-jawed and heavy-lidded – but she knew him. Like a sluice gate suddenly opened, the memories poured back; images she'd locked away for so many years, of him sitting in an armchair laughing at something on the TV, eating at the table with them, ruffling her hair, folding a coin into her hand for an ice cream, tucking her into bed with a kiss. Memories so at odds with the picture she'd built of him since he'd left that the pain and confusion were almost too much to bear. She stiffened in her seat and suddenly her grip on the cup and saucer she was holding felt weak. With a shaking hand she placed it on the edge of the table in front of her, certain she'd let it go crashing to the floor if she didn't.

The maître d' swung an arm to indicate Isla at her table and they made their way across the room. Isla wanted to stand up to greet them. She wanted to be composed and refined and sophisticated and nonchalant. But her heart was thudding with such a force she was certain she'd topple over. So she sat, shaking in her seat, staring at the group like a deer in headlights as they approached. The moment had come, and it was too late to back out now.

'Isla…'

Her father's first word to her in twenty-four years, the first time in all that time she'd heard his voice. There was a moment of uncertainty, during which she couldn't read what he was thinking as he silently appraised her and she didn't know how to react. But then he broke into a stiff smile.

'I'm glad you came,' was all he said.

His wife took Isla by both hands and leaned across the table to kiss her lightly on the cheek.

'I'm Celine,' she said. 'I am very pleased to meet you.'

Celine McCoy, Isla thought, *Mrs* McCoy. She was suddenly fired with a brief rush of anger. Mrs McCoy was *her* mother. Isla tried to calm herself. She'd promised herself she wouldn't get emotional. As she dragged in a breath, Celine swept a hand at the young man and woman who were now both regarding Isla with some curiosity as they took their seats. 'This is my son, Benet, and my daughter, Natalie.'

Both children were the spitting-image of their mother: honey-blonde hair, aquiline noses, intelligent eyes – perhaps hazel, perhaps greener in better light – slim and lithe and effortlessly at ease. Infinitely more at ease than Isla was surely looking right now.

'You're our sister?' Natalie asked, her words curled into a soft accent as she looked between Isla and her father, and in her voice Isla detected some incredulity. It was hardly surprising when they were as fair as Isla was dark.

'Half-sister,' Isla mumbled. 'My mother's Nigerian.' She looked at her dad. 'Do they know anything about my mum?'

'Well, no…' her dad began awkwardly.

Isla turned back to Benet and Natalie. 'I guess you were expecting me to look a lot more like Ian then – at least the same colour.'

Benet looked blankly at Natalie and then at his parents.

'Never mind,' Isla said, casting a glance at her father, who simply moved to pull out a chair for his wife to sit.

'Have you settled in at your hotel?' Ian asked.

'It's nice,' came Isla's vague reply.

'And how are you finding St Martin?'

'It's pretty.' She tapped a fingernail on the handle of her coffee cup. Small talk. In the midst of something this huge they were engaging in small talk? What about starting with the stuff that really mattered, like what he'd been doing for the past twenty-four years that was so important he couldn't even send her one single birthday card?

The waiter came over and they ordered drinks. As he glided away again, Ian turned his attention back to the table. He was silent as his gaze fell on Isla once more and his new family simply watched him. What was he thinking? Was he already regretting asking Isla to come? Did he approve of the way she'd turned out? Was he thinking she looked like her mother? Did that cause him pain, or sorrow, or regret? Did it make him realise he'd missed her? Did he feel like he'd made a mistake all those years ago? Did he feel like this was a mistake now?

Isla shot the briefest glance at his new wife and wondered whether the same questions were running through her head too. Was she looking at Isla and feeling a pang of jealousy? Worried that his first daughter would remind Ian of his first wife – perhaps remind him of the love they'd once had? Because Isla knew, no matter what had happened to tear her parents apart, they had been in love once. Anyone who'd seen the way Glory talked about him in the years since couldn't fail to understand that it had been deep and fierce. Did Celine know that? Had Ian told her what it had been like in the early days?

'You are well?' Celine asked, and Isla sensed in it the need to say something, anything, to break the silence. Perhaps the tension was getting to her too.

'Yes. Thanks.'

'The food is good here,' Natalie put in with a nervous smile. 'You will eat with us, Isla?'

'I think so,' Isla replied, throwing another glance at Ian, who was still staring at her. She wished he'd just say what was on his mind, but perhaps it wasn't something he could share in front of his new family.

'How long will you stay in St Martin?' Celine asked.

'A few days. I promised my mum I'd be home for Christmas.'

'Ah.' Celine's short reply hinted at relief.

'There's nothing to do at Christmas here anyway,' Benet said, causing Ian to throw him a sharp look and Celine to purse her lips. 'There's nothing to do any time,' he added belligerently. He looked to be in his early twenties but sounded more like a moody thirteen-year-old. Isla liked Natalie and Celine so far – as much as she could – but Benet was a bit off somehow. Was there a hint of distaste in the looks he gave her when he thought nobody was taking any notice? But then, perhaps that was to be expected a little in the circumstances.

'I'm sure it's lovely and peaceful here all the time,' Isla said. 'And there seems like a lot to do.'

'If you're a tourist and you have money filling your ski boots,' he replied, and this time she was sure Ian gave him a shove under the table that shut him up.

'Perhaps we should get down to business,' Ian said, in a sudden and unexpected change of tack.

Business? Was that all it was to him? Isla fought the urge to squeal in frustration. She wanted answers, to know what had kept him away for all those years. She would get them, but perhaps now wasn't the time. She pressed her lips into a hard line and faced him, forcing herself to pay attention as he continued.

'So, we all know that my mother's last will and testament contains some strange stipulations and some surprising gifts. I thought it fair to wait until we were all together to go into the details. I'm not sure everyone is going to like what's in here, but we have to respect Grandma Sarah's final wishes.' From a leather satchel he produced a wad of paper and laid it on the table, smoothing a hand over the pages to straighten them out. All eyes went to the document; in between those pages lay the answers – some of them at least.

Ian glanced up and eyed each of his family in turn, except for Isla. A moment ago he was staring, and now he couldn't look? Isla was aware that perhaps she was putting up a wall too, but surely if anyone was entitled to erect an emotional barrier, it was her. His job – the job of any decent father – was to break it down, no matter what it took.

And then he began to read – phrases and words Isla had never heard before and barely had the concentration to start unravelling the meaning of. She wasn't interested, because all she could think about was the proximity of the father who had scarcely given her a second look. The little girl still locked inside her was desperate for him to notice her, to tell her he'd missed her, that he'd been wrong to leave her. The same little girl who had bought Christmas presents he would never open. For so much of her adult life she'd hushed that little girl, hid her in the cupboard and pretended to the world that she didn't care. But she did care – had always cared. He was breaking that little girl's heart, all over again.

Natalie and Benet were attentive, nodding at various points, and every so often they and Ian would glance at Celine for approval or in a silent cue for any questions to be aired before he continued. When she gave an encouraging smile or nod they would continue. Despite the tumultuous emotions running through her head, Isla had to be impressed that they were keeping up with the words of this hellishly complex document in a language not their own.

Isla's gaze strayed to the windows where the snow was falling faster now. She pictured herself bolting from the table and running for the door. What was she doing here? What had possessed her to come? She should have listened to her mum, who'd known this was never going to end well. Glory had been right – her dad didn't want her; he only wanted his inheritance.

Isla was catapulted back into the room when she heard her name along with the words *holiday home* followed by a collective sharp intake of breath from Natalie and Benet. All eyes were now on her.

'Serendipity Sound?' Natalie asked, turning to Ian, who nodded, and then to Celine. 'She left her holiday home to… to Isla?'

'Yes,' Celine replied, not in the least flustered by the clear disbelief in Natalie's voice.

'That was supposed to be ours!' Natalie cried. 'It was supposed to be given to Benet and I!'

'It's just a cabin,' Ian said in a dull voice.

'It is worth a lot of money,' Benet replied indignantly.

'I don't want it.' Isla spoke into the gap, surprised to hear her own voice. 'What's the point of me owning that?'

'Perhaps your grandmother wanted you to spend more time here,' Celine said. 'Owning a vacation property would allow you to do that.'

'But why? She'd never even met me. What did she care whether I ever came to St Martin? Nobody at this table actually wants me here, and they certainly don't want me to come back…'

Celine opened her mouth to argue, but Isla continued across her. 'Isn't it enough that I came this once? I thought that was what Sarah had wanted. So here I am, and now I can go home and I never have to bother again. I thought that was the deal.'

'Some questions will never be answered,' Celine said simply. 'But your grandmother left you this house. We may never know what was going through her mind when she wrote this will; all we can do is enact it now she is gone.'

Isla flicked her gaze over the McCoy family. The *other* McCoy family. 'I can see this bequest is going to cause issues and I really don't need anything that's going to tie me to France in any way. No offence – I mean, it's a lovely place and everything – but there's just too much here that would have a negative impact on my life. I don't understand why she'd give me this.'

'It's not an unconditional gift,' Ian said, looking at her properly now.

'Even more reason not to accept it.'

'But the problem lies,' he continued, 'in that if your part of the stipulations are not met, then the other beneficiaries may not inherit their portions of the estate either. Every party must be in agreement to abide by the terms my mother has set.'

'And what are those?' Isla asked, holding back an impatient sigh. She wished she'd never come now. She wanted this to be over, and yet it seemed her grandmother had decided to make things as difficult and complicated as possible. Like she was goading her from the grave, as if she hadn't been cruel enough to Isla during her lifetime.

'That if either of us refuses to come to an arrangement regarding our future father–daughter relationship and the maintenance of that relationship, then neither of us will inherit the property she has bequeathed. Or more specifically, I have to make amends and you have to forgive me. We have to become father and daughter again.'

'What's your property then?' Isla asked, skipping over the most pertinent part of his statement. How could she acknowledge their fractured relationship when she couldn't even deal with the fact that he was sitting in front of her after all these years?

'My mother's house back in Scotland.'

'Do you need it? I mean, you don't want to live in Scotland, do you?'

'But it is our right,' Celine said. For the first time her voice had risen in something other than a friendly assured tone. 'It is your father's right to own it, whether he wants to live there or not.'

'And if I don't play ball you won't get it?'

'We could sell it,' Celine said. 'The money from the sale would help us to have better lives here in France. Our business—'

'You want me to help you have a better life?' Isla hissed. 'When you already live in a mountain paradise with your perfectly manicured nails and your perfect hair while my mum has struggled to bring me up in a tiny house where she can't even afford to go to a proper hairdressers?'

Ian turned to her and smiled tightly. 'It's not like that; this would help you too. We could make it work, couldn't we?'

Isla stared at him. For a moment she couldn't speak. But then it came from nowhere. 'You're joking?' she asked haughtily. 'You must be. I don't want anything to do with you. I came here thinking maybe I wanted to know my family, but this has shown me everything I need to know about you. The only reason you want me back in your life is so you can get your hands on your mother's money? And I get a shitty little shack in the middle of nowhere as a consolation prize? No dice.'

'But nobody will get anything if you walk away!' Celine squeaked as her two children watched in stunned silence.

'I'd like to say I care, but I don't.' Isla snatched up her handbag, blood roaring in her ears. 'I don't want any part of this, so you can do what you like with my cabin!'

The next moments were a blur. She made her way through the restaurant, tears stinging her eyes. She recalled yanking her coat from a stand and bundling it under her arm as she rushed for the entrance, and then she was running, slipping and sliding down the icy pavements as snowflakes pelted her hair. It wasn't until she realised how cold she was that she stopped to put her coat on. She spun to look back up the street but nobody had followed her. Ian McCoy didn't even care that much.

The sooner she could get a flight back to England the better.

Chapter Eight

The same phone number had shown up four times now. Unrecognised and unknown – it could only be Ian trying to call her. Ian, as he was to her now forever, because Isla now knew for certain that she would never call him Dad. She had no intention of picking up and he knew where the hotel was if he wanted to speak to her so desperately. Not that she'd have given him any more time if he'd arrived there in person, but surely he wasn't so stupid to believe that she was going to answer the phone to him after what had happened in the restaurant?

Isla pushed the phone across the table and flipped it over so she wouldn't have to look at the flashing screen. She was currently sitting in a quiet corner of the hotel bar – still as deserted as it had been that morning. Presumably it didn't really come alive until later in the evening when all the winter sports enthusiasts returned with tales of adventure and bravery on the snowy slopes, alcohol making each tale bigger and bolder as the night stretched on.

For now, it was just her and a brandy. The first had been at Dahlia's insistence as Isla flew through the hotel reception fighting back tears and Dahlia – sweet, apple-pie grandma Dahlia – had called her back and taken her gently through to the bar, observing that she looked like she'd seen a ghost and insisting she needed something medicinal to calm her nerves. Isla had been too distracted and too emotional to argue, and the first brandy had slipped down nicely, instantly warming and soothing her frayed emotions. So Isla had asked for another, and when Dahlia had to go to the reception to check in a new arrival (seriously, Isla thought, does anyone else actually work at this hotel?) Isla had nipped around the counter, at Dahlia's behest, and helped herself to another, leaving a little IOU on the writing pad by the till.

As she swished the liquor around in the glass, staring into its depths, she suddenly became aware of Dahlia at the doorway, a dark-haired man in his mid-twenties standing alongside. Dahlia's usual benevolent smile was gone, and she looked uncertain and confused.

'I'm sorry,' she said, wringing her hands. 'He says he's family and it's very important he speak to you.'

Isla frowned. She'd never seen this man before in her life.

'I don't know—' she began, but he cut across her.

'You don't know me,' he said, his French accent rich, softening the sharp edges of his words. 'My uncle – your father – asked me to come. He thought it would be easier to talk to someone other than him.'

'Your uncle?' This just got better and better. How many other doting family members were going to come out of the woodwork to torture her? 'So, you're my cousin? What did you inherit – the outside toilet?'

The man looked confused. But he didn't question any further and simply nodded towards the empty seat at her table. 'May I sit with you?'

'I can hardly stop you – it's a free country.'

Dahlia hovered for a moment, then took herself behind the bar to give the old brass bell its second vigorous polish of the day. She was clearly listening and trying very hard to make it look like she wasn't.

'I am Justin,' Isla's cousin said, taking a seat and offering his hand. Isla looked at it, and then up into his face. She didn't want to acknowledge the warmth and humour in his eyes, but it was there. She considered herself to have a good instinct when it came to reading people, and he might have thought he was doing good by coming, but that didn't mean he was.

'Why hasn't Ian come himself? I'm not that scary.'

'He knew you wouldn't talk to him.'

'Right. So he's not completely clueless then. What makes him think I'm more likely to talk to you?'

'I will not inherit anything… no house, no outside toilet…' A slight smile cocked the corner of his mouth. 'So, if I'm here you know it is because we are family.'

'Not exactly impartial family, though. You're going to be on his side rather than mine, so anything you say or try to persuade me to do will be biased to benefit him.'

'I'm not on anyone's side, but I know he is unhappy about what happened today. In fact, I know he regrets deeply a lot of things over the years, including not trying harder to see you. He doesn't say it, but I know it.'

'Is he your uncle by blood or by marriage?'

'I do not understand…'

'How is Ian your uncle?'

'My mother is Celine's sister.'

'Right. So you're not my cousin at all then.'

'Not exactly,' he replied, shifting uneasily in his seat.

'Look, Justin, I appreciate the sentiment and it's very noble that you've come, but I'm even less inclined to talk to you now that I know you're Celine's family. I'm sure you're all very nice, but essentially Celine is sitting where my mum should be and no matter how nice you are, that's how I will always see it. You can be the sweetest and kindest family member on earth and I won't like you. I'm programmed not to like you. Sorry, but I might as well get that out there now.'

'You don't need to like me – or my family.' Though his words were spoken with a casual air, Isla could tell that he was a little taken aback by her tone. 'I came because my uncle asked me to and I agreed that it was a good idea. My aunt Celine is sad for what happened too. They understand your anger and pain but they want to put the past behind them and build some bridges with you, if you'll let them.'

'The only reason they want to build bridges is so they can get their mitts on Granny's gold,' Isla said. She tipped the brandy glass to her lips and took a slug – probably bigger than was sensible – and it burned satisfyingly as it slipped down her throat and took the edge off her rage. 'I don't mean to take this out on you, but you're the only person here right now. I'm sorry Ian sent you in his place, but I think it's best you go.'

'Won't you listen? Can't you just give me one more minute?'

She folded her arms tight across her chest. 'Fine.'

'Meet them again. Go to dinner with them and do not talk about the inheritance. Get to know them as people, as your family, and you may find you have more in common with them than you thought.'

'I don't see the point.'

'The point is you've come a long way to be disappointed. At least if you've tried you can say it was worth coming to St Martin. As it is now, you may fly home with regrets.'

'I doubt that,' she replied, but somewhere in the back of her mind, Isla already knew he was right. 'But I suppose my flight back is days away and I don't have anything else to do. I may as well make sure Ian's an arse before I write him off as one. And I don't think I could stand the look of satisfaction on my mum's face if I went home early.'

'She didn't want you to come here?' Justin gave a brief glimpse of a smile again, but this time it was more assured. They were moving onto sturdier ground, and they both sensed it.

'You could say that.'

'Isla, I do not pretend to know much about what happened in your past, and I think my uncle must have caused you great pain. But it doesn't have to make things bad between you and me. I think we could be friends, if you'd let me try?'

'I'm not sure you do. I can be a little… um… spiky, I've been told.'

He raised his eyebrows. 'Spiky?'

'Difficult,' she clarified, taking another sip of her brandy. 'I'm not really a people person.'

'Everyone is a people person.' He smiled. 'Some of us only need to find the right people.'

Isla couldn't stop the smile that stole across her face.

'Let me go back and talk to my uncle and aunt. If you want me to set up the meeting I can do that, but it might be more sensible for you to talk it through and fix something up.'

'I'm not sure I can trust myself to be civil just yet. Maybe it's better if you act as go-between – for now.'

He gave a brief nod and stood up. '*Bon*. And by the way, could you please answer your phone next time I call?'

'That was you?' she asked. 'All the missed calls today?'

'Ian gave me the number. But it's not much use if you don't pick up.'

'Sorry,' she said. 'I'll store it as a contact so I know it's you. And yes, I will pick up.'

He turned to go with another brief nod, but then he spun back to face her. 'Have you ever seen Serendipity Sound?' he asked.

'No. The first I knew about it was this afternoon. Why?'

'Maybe you should see it. Maybe you should see what you want to throw away to be sure you're making the right decision. I'm sure Ian would take you there if you wanted to go.'

Without another word he left, and Isla was left wondering whether he might have a point.

A brief phone call from her mother had found Isla shamefully lying about the meeting at the restaurant, reassuring her mum that it had all gone to plan and doing her best to fend off further interrogation about her inheritance by saying she wasn't exactly sure what it was yet, and that Ian was busy sorting things. She would let her know as soon as she could. It was more than Isla could deal with right now to admit to her mum how badly things had gone. Her mother had been right to warn her off. She was always right, and it was bloody infuriating.

Isla had spent an hour exploring the town again, just for the want of something to take her mind off things. However, not in the mood for shopping, and with the grandeur of the peaks lost beneath heavy snow clouds, there hadn't been much to see.

Her thoughts wandered frequently to the meeting at the restaurant and the subsequent visit from her cousin, Justin. And the more she thought about it, the more she wondered whether she was letting her emotions get the better of her. She had never seen this house, but it had to be worth a decent amount of money. Perhaps enough to make a real difference to her life. There was a clause in the will that said she had to make good the relationship with her dad, but if she'd stayed to listen to the whole reading, would there have been another one that said she wasn't allowed to sell the property she'd been gifted? Could she be denying herself a golden opportunity?

By early evening she was ravenous, suddenly realising that she hadn't actually eaten anything since breakfast, which was very unlike her. So her afternoon walk had taken her into an unexpected Italian restaurant for the best spaghetti and meatballs she'd had for many years, and she returned to Residence Alpenrose fuller, happier, and ready for a drink before she retired to her room to assess what the day's events really meant for her.

As she walked into the cosy lobby of the hotel she passed the entrance to the bar and saw that Dahlia was behind it, pouring a drink for Sebastian.

'Isla!' Dahlia called. 'Come on over! Tell me how your afternoon has been!'

Isla gave her a small smile and peeled off her coat as she made her way over. Seb watched her with a broad, welcoming smile of his own; his nose wrinkled, his freckles barely visible now against the flushing of his cheeks. It looked as though he'd only just returned from a day out in the cold winter air himself. He still had walking boots on and a heavy coat was slung across a neighbouring barstool, but even though he'd clearly been mountaineering or something equally rugged and outdoorsy, today he sported a blue shirt and a red bow tie, which peeked out from beneath an argyle tank top. Isla wanted to laugh at the absurdity of it. Dodie would have called him delightfully eccentric, but Isla was more inclined to use the word bonkers. But he was harmless enough and pleasant company now that they'd got past the suite-stealing, peeping-Tom, suitcase-jeopardy phase of their relationship.

'I guess you were up and out early,' she said as she took a seat next to him.

'Oh, yes, with the cockerel,' he said cheerfully. 'I had a long drive and I wanted to get started in plenty of time.'

'Oh.' Isla wanted to ask where he'd been but she didn't want to appear nosey so she refrained. Instead she answered Dahlia's questioning look with a request for a beer. 'And I'm fine now, before you ask. I'm so sorry about before,' she added, and Dahlia broke into a broad grin.

'I'm glad to hear it. Then I won't pry any further on that matter. Just bear in mind that I'm always here if you ever need to get anything off your chest.'

Isla nodded, and as she turned back to Seb, she could see that it was now his turn to burn with a question that he was just too polite to ask.

'So you've enjoyed exploring the town this afternoon?' Dahlia asked as she placed a beer on the bar in front of Isla. 'We're not exactly New York but I wouldn't live anywhere else.'

'It's very pretty,' Isla replied. 'Though it's a shame the weather has moved in and made everything so murky. I was going to take some photos of the mountains to send to my mum, but it was just grey skies by the time I got around to it. The town itself is lovely. I can see why you like it here.'

'Been here thirty years now running this place and never regretted moving one single day.'

'Where are you from?'

'Chicago.'

'That's quite a move.'

'Sure is. But we wanted mountains and peace, not sidewalks and noise, and we'd always been in love with Europe so the minute we could get enough money together we bought this place and gave up our old jobs to run it.'

'You and your husband?' Isla asked.

'Yes, me and Jerry.'

Isla wanted to ask about this mysterious Jerry. She hadn't seen a single other person working in the hotel apart from Dahlia but she was convinced there must be someone else.

'Does Jerry love it as much as you?'

'He did,' Dahlia said. 'Right up until he died.'

Isla clapped a hand over her mouth and Sebastian bit his lip, throwing Isla a sympathetic look.

'Oh, I'm so sorry to hear that.'

'Tsh!' Dahlia waved a hand. 'We're talking ten years ago now; I've had plenty of time to get used to life alone.'

'You've never wanted to go home to Chicago?'

'Not for a second. This is where my Jerry is buried, and this is where I'll stay until I join him.'

Isla gave her a small smile. It was a sad story, but she wanted Dahlia to keep talking because, in a strange way, it was making her feel a lot less stressed by her own worries. She wanted to ask so much more about Dahlia and her brave move with Jerry, about how they'd found life in a small alpine town, which must have been so very different from the city they'd been born in, about how Dahlia had coped without him when he'd first passed on. Dahlia was a woman she could happily sit and listen to all day. And it also meant that Sebastian wouldn't be able to ask any questions about her own day, which she definitely didn't want to talk about. At least, not the first bit.

'You were wonderfully brave to carry on here,' Sebastian said. 'And just imagine how much poorer my life would be without you in it.'

Dahlia flushed and giggled. 'Oh, you British guys are all the same – always know just what to say to flatter a girl; always such a beautiful way with words.'

'You wouldn't say that if you'd ever met some of the guys I know,' Isla said darkly. 'Unless your idea of a beautiful way with words is: get your coat, you've pulled!'

While Dahlia laughed, Sebastian looked genuinely confused.

'I've *never* said that to a girl,' he exclaimed, looking deeply wounded.

Isla found herself wanting to laugh now too. Looking at him with his dippy bow tie and ridiculous argyle tank top, she didn't doubt for a minute that he'd never said anything like that to a girl. He probably wrote them love poetry or long letters of flowery prose and took them to art galleries and foreign language films. Or else proclaimed words of affection under the dome of a planetarium as the stars whirled above them. Or wrote complex equations that described the beauty of his love for whoever the lucky cow was. What sort of girl dated a man like him? Did *any* girl date a man like him? Sebastian was a relic, like someone had plucked him from a PG Wodehouse novel and dropped him into the twenty-first century. Even his name sounded like something from a bygone era and Isla couldn't quite decide if it was faintly ludicrous or the coolest thing ever.

'You've clearly never been to the sort of clubs I've been to then,' she said. 'Not that I'm recommending them in any way. Full of tossers.'

'Tossers?' Dahlia asked, looking puzzled.

Now Isla did burst out laughing. 'It's English slang,' she said once she'd managed to catch her breath. 'It means... well, we won't go into the literal meaning but it's what you might call a douchebag... you know, a lowlife.'

'Oh...' Dahlia nodded sagely. 'I get it. Most of the people who live here are good types so I'm lucky not to run into too many of those.'

'Then you're lucky indeed.' Isla turned to Sebastian. Now that her low mood was beginning to lift, for the first time since she'd arrived in St Martin she was enjoying herself. *Truly* enjoying herself without the threads of worry and angst that the reasons for her visit wove into her mood. 'So, you're being very cagey about your research, and I think we know each other well enough that I can ask. What exactly is it you're doing here?'

'I'm studying glaciers and snow,' he said, and Isla thought she caught the hint of a blush. 'I mean, that's what I do. I'm a glaciologist.'

'That's cool!' She leaned forward and smiled. 'I have no idea why anyone would need to study them and I didn't even know it was an actual job, but it sounds very impressive.'

Perhaps he wasn't used to getting this sort of reaction, because for a moment he seemed uncertain and surprised, but then he gave a small smile and sat a little taller on his stool. Then Isla glanced at Dahlia and saw the expression that she imagined Sebastian usually got when he told people about his glaciers, because she just looked blank.

'There's a lot more to it than people imagine,' he said, clearly buoyed by Isla's interest.

'Like what?' she asked, and from the corner of her eye she noted Dahlia drifting off to do something at the other end of the bar. Most people she knew would probably do the same, but the most unexpected things often piqued Isla's interest and she was in the perfect mood to be distracted by something, or someone, who didn't constantly remind her of Ian. She took a long pull at the bottle of beer, never moving her expectant gaze from Sebastian.

'Oh.' He flushed again and dropped his eyes to the floor. 'It's all very technical and probably boring if you're not into it. Mostly lots of measurements and sample-taking. I spend a lot of time just staring at snow and ice.'

'I'm sure I can understand some of it if you try,' Isla insisted. 'And I might be into it if you gave me a chance.'

He looked up and his expression flickered into life, as if some internal flame had just been lit. 'Really?' he asked. 'You're really interested?'

'I wouldn't be asking if I wasn't.'

Sebastian broke into a broad, grateful smile, and then he began – bombarding Isla with terms like ablation, fracture, stratification, moraines and drumlins, he explained about the different disciplines like meteorology and ecology, geology and geography, and how glaciers came in many different shapes and sizes. He talked about how he hoped, one day, to study in Antarctica if he could get the funding and how in the future it might even be possible for study on the ice caps of Mars. As he spoke he became more animated and more hopelessly enthusiastic, like a boy with his first train set. There was something so captivating about it that, even though Isla didn't have a clue what most of it meant, it was difficult not to get swept up in his fervour. This was true geekdom and it was infectious in a way that Isla completely understood. Because, while she often played it cool, there was a small part of her that revelled in that kind of obsession too. It was how she'd approached her own studies back home, and why she was on course to get a fantastic grade in her final exams, even though she'd never say so for fear of looking boastful.

He stopped for a moment to draw breath and they both seemed to realise, at the same time, that while they'd been talking the bar had slowly been filling up. There was now barely a chair left unoccupied and the room was filled with laughter and gossip. Sebastian looked around, surprised to see the transformation, as if he'd been dropped into a parallel universe and couldn't figure out how he'd got there. And he blushed again as his gaze turned back on Isla.

'Sorry,' he said, fiddling with his tie. 'You must wish you'd never asked.'

'Not at all – it's fascinating. You want another beer?' She nodded at his empty bottle.

'If I have another beer I might move on to geomorphology, and you really don't want that.'

'I might.' Isla smiled. 'Let's give it a try.'

He was silent for a moment, gazing earnestly at her as if sizing her up, his cheeks now flushed from the beer and his excitement rather than the cold. 'I could do better than talk to you about it. I could show you?'

Isla held back a frown. 'Show me a glacier?'

'The Péclet glacier is a bit of a drive, and obviously it would involve a little hiking, but it's doable, if you wanted to go and see.'

'We can walk on it?'

'Yes.'

'But…' This was all suddenly real. Chatting with an interesting man to distract herself was one thing, but going up to a glacier with him?

'I'm sorry,' he mumbled. 'That was very forward of me and of course you wouldn't want to…'

'I mean, I'm sure it's amazing,' Isla said, feeling awkward and guilty and wishing she hadn't led him on quite as much as she now realised she had. 'It's just that I don't think I'll have time…'

'Of course.' He shook his head forcefully. 'I quite understand. Please forget I mentioned it.'

'I'm sorry. I mean, any other time I'm sure it would be amazing but…'

'I shouldn't have asked. Please don't apologise; it's completely my fault.'

They were silent again, the space between them filled with the conversations and laughter of the room while Isla supped at her bottle of beer, now wanting to drink it as fast as was practical without getting drunk. From the way Sebastian was attacking his, he was trying to achieve the same thing. It was a close race, but he won, and he sat his bottle back on the bar with a tight smile that was a world away from the warm enthusiasm of only five minutes before.

'It's late and I have another early start tomorrow,' he announced. 'I should…'

'Me too,' Isla said, feigning tiredness. Perhaps, she reflected ruefully, it was for the best though. She'd gone and done it again – ruined a perfectly nice evening by saying and doing the wrong thing. She'd encouraged him when she shouldn't have, and it was her fault he'd been emboldened enough to ask her out. Sebastian was cute and she supposed that some girls might have found his foppish, hot-nerd-mad-professor guise wildly attractive, but it wasn't for her at all.

He stood up, and the smile still plastered to his face looked more desperate than before. He was trying very hard not to let it crack.

'It's been a lovely evening, Isla,' he said. 'Thank you.'

'God, no… thank you!' she said, a little too fervently. Followed by a smile that was just a little too bright and wide and almost as desperate looking as his was. If someone had looked up the word mortification in that great big virtual dictionary of life, they would have found an A4 picture of her face. 'I've really enjoyed our chat. Goodnight.'

'Goodnight, Isla.' He nodded once more and made his way out of the bar without another word.

Chapter Nine

Isla was about to head up to her room when Dahlia came over and sat next to her with a long sigh.

'These old legs don't hold me up the way they used to.'

'You need some help around the place,' Isla said. 'I only ever see you working here. Do you have staff?'

'Of course I do!' Dahlia laughed. 'Mostly doing the invisible jobs people don't think about. But I don't have the money to hire too many folks and the place is small so I can manage on a tiny crew. It's pretty seasonal work too so at times I have more help than at others, depending on how many guests I have booked in.'

'It must be hard work running this place.'

'It is, but I love it and I wouldn't do anything else. For a start, with so many interesting visitors I never get bored. I have breathtaking mountain scenery in my back yard, incredible wildlife strolling through the town and white Christmases every year. Why would I need anything else?'

'When you say it like that it does sound idyllic,' Isla mused with a faint smile. 'Perhaps I ought to offer my services.'

Dahlia patted her on the hand. 'You'd be welcome any time.' She paused, seeming to appraise Isla more carefully before she spoke again. 'You know, if you ever want to talk about anything I'll always spare a minute to listen.'

Isla had the feeling that, after the drama of earlier when she'd run out of the restaurant and been chased up by Justin, she'd become Dahlia's pet project. She couldn't blame the old lady for being intrigued, she supposed, and she'd probably be the same in her shoes. But she also realised that Dahlia had a sweet, kind soul, and she genuinely wanted to reach out. 'Thank you; that's good to know.'

Dahlia nodded. 'You seem perkier after your drink with Sebastian. He's a nice boy.'

'He seems it,' Isla replied carefully.

'So clever. Sweet too. His mamma must be so proud of him. He's stayed with us a couple of times now – never a bit of bother and always buys me a gift when he checks out.'

'Does he? Wow, that's lovely.'

'Oh yes. And one time he took me out to the glacier to show me his research. I didn't understand a thing he was saying, but it was a wonderful day. Even took me to lunch afterwards. Most people wouldn't have much time to spare for an old lady like me. Such a sweet boy.'

Isla was silent as she held in a groan. How badly could she have misread the situation? Of course Seb hadn't been trying to get off with her. He'd been offering the hand of genuine friendship, just like he had with Dahlia. He was just a regular, lovely bloke who was so passionate about what he did that he loved to share it with anyone who took a passing interest. Now she felt worse than ever for turning him down. She cursed herself. Perhaps she needed to start taking people at face value a little more instead of living in a constant state of suspicion. Through the years her friends had told her as much, and even as they both approached the back end of their twenties Dodie sometimes had to remind her every now and again that not everyone was out to trip her up.

Perhaps coming to France was no coincidence – perhaps it was part of fate's plan to help her take a new path. Perhaps everything began and ended with her father; he'd started the rot, but maybe he could halt it too, if only she could trust his motives.

She took a deep breath. Perhaps the first step was opening up to Dahlia now. It was as good a place to start as any and if there was any judging to be done, at least Isla didn't have to stick around past the end of the week to be on the receiving end of it. She badly needed to sound off about her dad and sometimes talking to someone who was completely neutral was a good thing – or so people said. She opened her mouth, was about to begin, when Dahlia almost leapt from her stool.

'Well,' she announced airily, 'I guess I'd better get back to work. This place won't run itself.'

Isla clamped her mouth shut again. Just like always, she'd held back, hesitated too long, and the opportunity had passed her by. Of course it had. Why change the habit of a lifetime?

The following morning started with a phone call from her father, and this time she picked up.

'Ian. I suppose you're going to say we need to talk.'

She could almost hear him wince at the other end of the line. 'Isla, I know that it looks bad. You think I'm out to get my money and I'm not going to deny that it matters to me. In fact, it would make a huge difference to our lives here in St Martin… might even be the difference between being able to stay and having to sell up and live somewhere cheaper. But that doesn't matter to you, and I realise that. I have no right to ask you to care what happens to me and Celine and the kids. And I know you won't believe this but I care about what you stand to gain from this too, and I seriously think you should consider what you're throwing away. You don't trust me – hell, you almost certainly don't owe me any love or loyalty – but I truly think you'd regret any decision to turn your back on your inheritance. And though you don't have to believe anything I say, I hope too that I might be able to make you see I'm sorry for all the years you lived without me. I can't make that up to you, no matter how long I try, but I'd like it if we could at least make a start.'

'I don't know,' Isla said. 'I don't know if I'm strong enough to cope if you let me down again.'

'I won't let you down again.'

'How can I know that? How can *you* even know that? Let me ask you this: when you first got together with my mum did you intend to run out on her? When she gave birth to me did you look down into my cot and think to yourself that you wanted to leave me fatherless for the best part of my life?'

'Of course not, but—'

'That's what I'm saying. You don't even have any control over it yourself. You say you want to make it work, but that's until the next event changes your mind.'

'I tried to stay in touch and your mum—'

'Don't you dare blame her! Whatever it is you think you did, you obviously didn't try hard enough. Mum's life ended when you left. She had hopes and dreams and you took all those with you, and she was left with a kid and a mountain of debt while you ran away across the globe to start another family. And before you start, I don't even want an explanation because whatever you say will never excuse what you did and it will only make me angry again. So please, spare me the details. If I say yes to the inheritance it's not because I forgive you or because I want you to be my dad again, it's purely mercenary. Do you understand?'

There was silence. 'Isla, I—'

'I hope that's not the beginning of an explanation,' she cut in. 'I mean what I say. I don't want to get close to you and I'm not even saying a definite yes to the inheritance yet. I'm saying that I'm willing to give it some more thought.'

There was another pause. 'You know where to get hold of me when you're ready,' he said finally. 'And for the record, Celine really liked you. Until you took off that is.'

That was one vibe Isla hadn't got from any of her stepfamily. Perhaps her state of mind at the time had blinded her to the signals. 'Is there a time limit on this? A cut-off date or something?'

'I don't know. But I suppose you'll be going home soon, so it's going to be very difficult to start any sort of meaningful relationship when you do.'

Meaningful relationship. It was hard to know what he expected that to be and even harder to pretend it was a realistic possibility. She had to keep reminding herself of the promise she'd silently made the night before to start opening up a little. But it was hard to break the habit of a lifetime, just like that.

'I need a couple of days,' she said.

'OK, sure. Whatever you want. Like I said, you have my number so call me when you're ready.'

'I will. And I suppose I should say thanks for phoning. I appreciate that it probably wasn't easy.'

'Harder than you could know. What are your plans for the day? I could—'

'No. If you're thinking of saying we can meet up then I'm sorry but no. I appreciate the sentiment but it's not going to help. Sorry.'

He was silent for a moment. Then: 'How about Justin?'

'Justin?' Isla repeated.

'He mentioned that you two had got on pretty well. I think he said he'd offered to take you out to see the chalet.'

'Actually he didn't, but he said you might.'

'Do you want me to?'

'It's OK... I know you're busy with the shop.'

'Right,' Ian replied, seeming to understand that what she was really saying was that she wasn't ready for that yet. 'Justin did tell me he'd be more than happy to take you over there...'

Isla raked her teeth over her bottom lip, deep in thought. Would it hurt to take a look? She had nothing else to do and it did make sense to her rational brain that she should see just what she'd be giving up. 'You're asking on his behalf? I don't know, maybe he wants to phone me himself if he wants to go.'

Ian let out a sigh. 'God, I know you don't want to hear this from me, but you remind me so much of your mother – quick and clever and stubborn as hell.'

'She taught me everything I know,' Isla replied with a wry smile.

'I could see it in you, even as a baby.'

'Is that why you left us? Because you thought I might be hard work?' The sentence was out before she'd meant it to be and immediately she wished she could take it back. He was trying, and she was giving him nothing. She just couldn't help it.

'It's complicated—' he began, but Isla cut across him.

'Forget it; I don't need to know and I shouldn't have said it.'

'I suppose I'll have to expect that for a while,' he said. 'I understand it's going to be hard for you and I don't want to push things.'

'I'll be in town all day if Justin wants to get in touch,' she said.

'OK – I'll tell him. Hopefully I'll speak to you soon then.'

'Yeah. Bye.' She went to end the call and then another question occurred to her. 'Ian…' she added quickly.

'Yes?'

'The first night I arrived in St Martin, were you standing outside my hotel looking up at my window?'

'Well, I…' he began, but he sounded flustered, confused and guilty all at the same time.

'I thought so,' she said with a slight smile. 'I just wanted to be sure. Bye, Ian. I'll let you know what I decide.'

Whenever people told her that anxiety about something or other had stopped them from eating, Isla was mystified. Far from stopping her eating, any sort of anxiety or sour mood had her racing for the fridge to eat everything in there. Her mother had often expressed amazement that she wasn't the size of Belgium, and Isla didn't know whether to laugh or feel deeply insulted. So she had no problem tucking away the stack of fluffy pancakes Dahlia put in front of her at breakfast the next morning.

'I'm going to miss these when I go home,' she said as Dahlia hovered over her with coffee. 'Can't you come and live with me? The hotel will manage, won't it?'

'Maybe.' Dahlia beamed, clearly enjoying the praise. 'I'm expensive to hire, though.'

'Worth every penny!' Isla cut into another pancake and popped a large wedge into her mouth, just to show Dahlia how worth it she thought the money would be.

With a tinkling laugh, Dahlia went to serve at another table while Isla went back to her breakfast. Now that she'd had time to reflect on her conversation with Ian that morning she felt strangely positive about the whole thing. Perhaps it was the syrup-drenched pancakes or the excellent coffee, or perhaps it was just that she'd reached some sort of unconscious decision – as yet unknown even to her. But an unexpected sense of contentment had stolen over her.

It might have been helped by Sebastian's absence too. She'd entered the breakfast room with some trepidation after the way they'd parted the evening before, knowing that she'd feel awkward about it and he probably would too. Not to mention the guilt she felt for getting it so wrong. But it looked as though he'd taken off on one of his early starts because there was no sign of him.

Her gaze went to the windows and above the hazy blue lines of the mountaintops she could see pockets of cloudless sky. It was probably freezing, but at least the weather was settled enough to go out. She just had to decide where it was she wanted to go. She made a note to pop down to reception after she'd had a post-breakfast freshen-up to take a look at the rack of visitor leaflets next to the desk and ask Dahlia what she would recommend. It wouldn't hurt to finally get to see a bit more of the town as a tourist; there was the pretty village church to view and the Notre-Dame-de-la-Vie perched on an outcrop that Dahlia had told her about, various walks and husky sledding in the neighbouring resorts. She'd learned from the girl she'd bought her new boots from that there was even a goat farm open to the public. It wasn't exactly high-octane excitement, but peace and quiet was what she needed right now and it was different to anywhere she'd travelled to before. Not that she'd been far.

As she was taking a slurp of her coffee, the mobile she'd left on the table next to her began to buzz a call. Justin's number flashed up on the screen and she couldn't help a small smile. Ian hadn't taken long to employ his secret weapon.

'Good morning,' she said as she swiped to take the call. 'I take it you've been talking to Ian already.'

'Ian?' he sounded confused. 'Not today. Should I have done?'

'Well, no, but… Then why have you called?'

'I thought… well, I thought a little persistence might pay off. So I was wondering if you wanted to make that trip out to your grandmother's chalet. I have a day off, so…'

'You're offering to take me?'

'If you would allow it. It's not so far, and it's a good day to walk.'

Isla chewed her lip for a moment as she stared in the direction of the windows again. It *was* a good day for a walk. Would it be so bad to take that walk with Justin? She'd make sure to tell Dahlia where she was going because… well, you never knew. She had a feeling Justin would be good company, plus, she'd already made the mistake of turning one well-meaning man down because of her stupid suspicious nature. Justin was easy on the eye too, which certainly helped make a day with him a more appealing prospect.

'Sod it!' she exclaimed.

'Is that a good thing or a bad thing? What you just said?'

'I'll come. You're right – I should go and see the chalet. Plus, I still don't know a lot about my new family and perhaps you can fill me in on a little history.'

'I'd be glad to. So, what time can you be ready? The weather looks OK now but at this time of the year it may change very suddenly.'

'Give me an hour? I just need to finish my breakfast.'

'Great. I will wait outside your hotel in one hour's time.'

One hour later Isla stepped out of the hotel entrance to find Justin leaning against the wall, staring ahead at the line of distant mountains.

'Boo!' she said, and he twisted round with a start, looking sheepish as he realised who it was.

She laughed. 'I didn't mean to make you jump.'

'You know I'm not a tough guy now.'

'That's OK – I don't particularly like tough guys.' She smiled, unable to help herself. The sun was still shining and although the air was cold, knifing her lungs as she breathed it in, she was now almost excited at the prospect of seeing the chalet her grandmother had gifted to her. Nobody had ever left her anything in a will before, let alone a house. It was probably a tiny shack, hardly worth the wood it was built from, but it could be hers and it would probably be the only property she'd own for a good many years to come. 'Do we have far to walk?' she asked, zipping up her coat.

'About ten minutes. It is a pleasant day but you would be well to keep your jacket on.'

'Don't worry I intend to – it's freezing.'

'It is a good jacket... very *big*...'

Isla's smile turned into a broad grin. 'It might not be the most elegant item of clothing, but I'll have you know this coat represents a good portion of my student loan. I'll be eating cheap beans for the whole of next term because of this. But at least I'll be warm.'

He offered his arm. 'Shall we walk?'

She hesitated for a split second before taking it. And even as she did she glanced up, her breath hitching as she noticed who was emerging from the hotel in her wake. Their eyes met at the same time and blood rushed to her face. Sebastian stood at the step with his perky little bow tie peeking out from beneath a huge coat, his foppish hair dipping over one eye and his freckles stark against his skin in the sunlight. He looked from her to Justin, and then his whole figure seemed to visibly sag. Isla hadn't counted on the fact that he might have been having a late start, rather than an early one, and she'd assumed she wouldn't see him at all that day. There couldn't have been a worse moment to bump into him. Why did he have to come out of the hotel at this precise moment? Now she felt like an absolute bitch for turning down his offer of a day out only to be caught going out with someone else. There was no law against it, but still… He didn't say a word, only heaved a metal case from the pavement where he'd rested it and turned in the direction of what Isla had to presume was the hire car he'd mentioned the day before.

'Shit,' she muttered.

'Is something wrong?' Justin asked.

She faltered, torn between calling Sebastian back to explain and just making a run for it. In the end there didn't seem any point in trying to explain. She didn't even know what it was she was supposed to be explaining. She wasn't doing anything wrong, so why did it feel like she was?

She shrugged and shook her head and they began to walk. Knowing she shouldn't, she risked a glance back to see Sebastian return to the hotel doorway, pick up another metal case and hurry back to his car, head down as he walked.

'You know that man?' Justin asked.

Isla turned to him. 'Huh?'

'You know him?'

'Oh, he's staying at the hotel. British. We got chatting one evening, that's all.'

'I could guess he is British. He couldn't look more British if he stuck a flag in his hat.'

'He's harmless enough,' Isla replied, immediately realising just how patronising she sounded.

'He has an… interesting sense of fashion. I think somebody should talk to him.'

'He does,' Isla said, and she turned to see Justin laughing. It might have been funny, but she didn't feel like laughing at all. She just felt mean and cruel and thought that right now she probably looked a lot like the girls at school who'd made her own teenage life a misery. It wasn't a nice feeling. She simply wanted to go before he came back again for the third case she could see on the hotel steps.

'I wonder what is in those suitcases?' Justin continued, now deeply interested in Sebastian's comings and goings.

'I think it's his scientific equipment. He studies glaciers.'

Justin gave a low whistle. 'He is a scientist, or perhaps just boring?'

She forced a smile and tried to look like she didn't care. 'So,' she announced, 'shall we pay attention to where we're meant to be going? If we're going to make the chalet by nightfall maybe we'd better stop worrying about Sebastian's suitcases.'

He shot her a sideways grin. 'Of course.'

Isla risked one last glance over her shoulder. Sebastian was making his way back along the pavement, his eyes still trained on the ground. She winced as he nearly walked into a lamppost and then looked up as if shocked to see one there. She glanced at Justin and was inexplicably thankful to see that he hadn't noticed, his own eyes now on the way ahead. She wanted to look back again to see if Sebastian was OK, but she didn't dare, and so she looked forward and tried not to dwell on the squirming, uncomfortable feeling in her gut that had nothing to do with her enormous breakfast.

As they trudged along glittering lanes overlooked on either side by the roofs and gables of colourful wooden houses Justin explained that Grandma Sarah had mostly used her holiday home during the summer months. He hadn't known her that well, not being direct family, but he had met her on one or two extended family occasions. Towards the end of her life she hadn't been well enough to visit more than once or twice a year, but even when she was ill she still came. She wouldn't let anyone else use the house when she wasn't there – not paying guests and not even family. Isla imagined her to be a rather cantankerous old woman and thought it was no wonder young Ian McCoy had been attracted to the beautiful but stubborn Glory.

She listened to Justin carefully as he went over details and descriptions of family members and events, habits and traditions, alliances and enmities, silently trying to get a handle on the family dynamic. She wondered where on earth she might fit in if she did decide to become a part of it, how her mum might take the news, and even how her mum might fit in too. Because whether he'd realised it or not, if Ian was serious about bringing his eldest daughter back into the fold, he was going to have to deal with his ex-wife at some point.

Justin talked and Isla listened; he had an accent like melted chocolate dripping from a spoon, a charming turn of phrase and the most perfectly imperfect words that came from speaking a language not his own. It was soothing, like a water feature or the steady gurgle of a mountain stream, and Isla let it wash over her. They passed through winding streets, beneath the hanging eaves of houses, through snow-snagged alleyways and wider boulevards where the snow had been cleared. Past the church with its stone walls and delicate steeple and a frosting of snow on its roof, receiving friendly nods from passing groups of skiers making their way up to the slopes. Trees and evergreen shrubs were dressed in Christmas glitter, every shop and hotel had decorations and strings of lights in windows and hanging from porches, and every restaurant doorway sent tendrils of sweet and spicy aromas out into the frosty air.

After a time, Justin stopped and smiled, nodding towards a sharp incline. 'The house is just up there.'

It took another couple of minutes before they could see fully the cluster of chalets at the top and he guided her to one standing apart from the others. Isla glanced at him as she followed. Surely that wasn't it? She waited for him to realise his mistake, to change course for the actual chalet that was going to be hers. But he slowed to a halt outside it and turned to her with a broad grin.

'Here it is: Serendipity Sound. You like?'

'You're kidding?'

'Why would I joke?' He gave a slight frown. 'This is your grand-mother's house.'

'It's *incredible*! Are you sure I'm not supposed to be looking at some shed or annexe at the back? This is actually it?'

'It is not what you were expecting?'

Isla gazed up at the building. Like the church, it was built from solid grey stone, with hardwood eaves and a steeply sloping roof, a wooden veranda and balconies at every upstairs window, of which there were many. It was three or four times the size she'd imagined it would be, and instead of looking like a cute log cabin with maybe a bed and a washbasin, it was more like a mansion.

'Not at all. I was expecting it to be a tiny wooden hut. You know, like the ones you see in horror films all dusty and falling to bits, with moose heads hanging from the walls and people getting chopped up in the cellar.'

'*Mon dieu!*' he laughed. 'Your imagination is crazy!' He shot her a wicked grin. 'You were worried? Did you think I was bringing you here to chop you up in the cellar?'

'I hope not because I'd have a devil of a time running away in this snow.'

'You are quite safe with me. My uncle would not be happy if I chopped you up.'

Isla raised her eyebrows. 'Well, that makes me feel better.'

'Come,' he said, still laughing. 'Let me show you around.'

She followed him up to the porch where he took some keys from his pocket. 'Is that the only set?' Isla asked, angling her head at them.

Justin held the bunch up. 'There are two sets. One is with Monsieur Rousseau in Scotland – he will keep them until you decide what to do. This set belongs to my uncle, but he has given them to me today so I can bring you here.'

Isla wondered whether Grover Rousseau knew about the spare set. She was pretty sure that the lawyer was supposed to have everything relating to the property if it was part of an as yet un-administered estate. But what did she know about it? And why did she care? The bigger puzzle was still why Grandma Sarah would have left this magnificent house to her. She'd been vaguely determined not to be swayed by anything she was shown today but it was becoming increasingly difficult to hold onto that resolve.

She looked up at the weathered hardwood eaves, the delicate lead patterns of the glass in the front door, the loose gathering of trees that shaded it from the worst of the elements and the shadow of the mountains at its back, and already she could feel the house working its magic, could almost picture a life in which she owned it. The air was fresher and cleaner here than any she'd breathed before and it was tranquil like nothing she'd ever experienced. She pictured herself sitting on the porch in the summer, bugs hovering in the long grass as the sunset burnished them gold, the gentle sounds of birdsong and the chirruping of crickets replacing the car horns and engines of her home back in Britain. Grandma Sarah had been canny; whatever her motives, she hadn't underestimated the power of this place. She must have known it would lure Isla in and persuade her to spend more time here.

Justin twisted the key in the lock of the front door. As it opened wide he stepped back to allow Isla to enter first.

When she looked back on this day, the one thing she'd remember about stepping inside for the first time was the smell of waxed wood – warm and mellow. They walked straight into a cosy living room, almost bigger than her mum's entire flat back home. The sunlight filtered in through the slats of closed blinds, throwing subtle stripes of light and shade onto the opposite wall. Justin stepped round her to open them up, washing the room in glorious lemon light and revealing detail in every corner: a plump red sofa with soft woven cotton throws, gleaming hardwood floors with patterned rugs in earthy tones dotted around them and modern art prints on the walls. A cavernous stone fireplace dominated the far wall, so large and wide that Isla half expected to find a grizzly bear hibernating in there. A few feet away stood a mahogany piano. Surprisingly nothing was dust-sheeted and it was free from the musty smell of a place neglected. Either the house had been in use recently, or someone had made an effort to go in and air it especially for Isla's visit. She was betting on the latter, though she still didn't trust any of this branch of the McCoy family.

Justin closed the front door. 'Do you wish to see the kitchen?' he asked.

Isla nodded and followed him through. The kitchen was more modern in feel than the living room, with gleaming white units, stainless-steel accessories and a light wooden dining table with storm lamps hanging above. The large windows behind the dining table looked out onto a stunning mountain view.

They went upstairs. Three bedrooms, all en-suite with showers, apart from the master bedroom which had a bathroom that contained a huge free-standing bath and a large window looking out onto the same mountains as the dining table below.

'That's some bath time,' Isla murmured, and Justin grinned.

'You like it?'

'Grandma Sarah must have been minted.'

'Minted?'

'She must have been rich.'

Justin shrugged. 'She did OK. Your father paid for some refurbishment shortly before she died. He loaned a lot of money.' He looked squarely at Isla. 'He wanted his mother to be comfortable, but also I believe he and my aunt thought they would inherit this place when she died. But they need money now… things are not so good for them since that.'

Isla nodded. She'd been determined that the house wouldn't influence her decisions regarding both inheritances and she was still determined now. If she agreed to anything, it would be on her terms. Instead, she simply folded her arms and looked up at Justin. 'Well, that backfired.'

'Yes.'

'Perhaps he should have just kept his money safe instead of splashing it out here with no promises that it would become his.'

'I do not know if it was promised or not. Perhaps it was.'

'And then Sarah changed her mind?'

Justin inclined his head. 'Perhaps.'

'Was he angry?'

'Perhaps, at first.'

'I'm surprised they didn't contest the will – see if there was some way to freeze me out. They could have done and I would never have even known about this place.'

'My aunt may have done that – she did not know you,' he replied, and Isla was impressed by his refreshing frankness. 'But my uncle... I think he would not let her do that.'

'I can see why she was upset to be honest.' And she could, even though she hated to admit it. The place was fantastic, and it must have cost a fortune to refurbish. She couldn't even imagine how much it must be worth. And she didn't feel she deserved it, now that she was here. How could she take this gift with the new strings attached? Ian and Celine had borrowed money to do it up in good faith and then Grandma Sarah had bypassed them without so much as an explanation or acknowledgement. Her gaze wandered the bathroom again and then turned once more to Justin. 'You knew I'd feel guilty about it if you brought me out here.'

'That is not the reason we're here. I wanted to help. I wanted you to see what you were throwing away, and Ian did too.'

'Surely he'd have been better off fighting the case in court to claim all of his mother's estate instead of jumping through hoops with me to get it.'

'Maybe, and maybe he could win. But that is not his plan.'

'You believe he genuinely wants me back in his life?'

'I know it doesn't seem that way. Perhaps he did not even know it himself before your grandmother died and left the condition in her will, but I believe he does. Even more now he has met you.'

'What about Celine and her kids?'

'When they heard that you had to come and meet him…' He scratched his head and frowned. Isla guessed that he was feeling he'd already said too much.

'They didn't want me to come?'

'They didn't think you would. They wished that Monsieur Rousseau wouldn't be able to find you.'

'I bet they would have wished a bit harder if they'd known what Grandma had put aside for me,' Isla said with a wry smile.

'They thought it might be a little cash, maybe some jewellery. They would have been unhappy about that. But this house…' He glanced around and shook his head. 'I did not know her well, but I heard Celine say many times that your grandmother could be strange and mischievous. Maybe she left this house to you because she thought it was funny. She and my aunt did not always like each other and things got worse in the last few years.'

'Why are you telling me all this?'

'Does it matter if you know? I don't see what difference it makes – it does not change the facts. This place is yours, if you want it.'

'You know all about the deal?'

'Yes, that my uncle inherits his mother's house in Scotland and some of her money.'

Isla appraised Justin silently for a moment. 'And what do *you* get?' she asked finally.

'Me?'

'You've gone to an awful lot of trouble to get me here and onside. So, what's in it for you?'

'Nothing. I'm here because Ian asked me to talk to you.'

'He could have persevered and I would have talked to him eventually. Why did you need to be involved?'

'I wanted to help.'

'Him, me or yourself?'

He turned his back on her and began to make for the stairs. 'Are you hungry?' he asked in a dull voice. 'It is not fresh but there are tin cans and dry goods in the kitchen. We could use our imagination to make some lunch?'

Isla hung back. There had to be more to it than he was letting on and yet he'd looked so mortally wounded at her accusation that perhaps she was wrong? But when she followed him into the kitchen, an apology on her lips, he didn't look round and he didn't acknowledge her. He began to rifle through the store cupboards, placing packs and tins out onto the counter.

'OK, so we have beans, vegetable soup, pasta and sauce, rice, ketchup…'

'Pasta sounds good. Justin – I'm sorry about what I said. I didn't mean to infer that you were trying to pull a fast one or anything, it's just… You have to understand that it's hard for me to trust Ian. And, unfortunately, as you're on his side, it's hard for me to trust you too.'

He straightened up and closed the cupboard door. 'I'm not on anyone's side. I was trying to help, that's all.' Then he broke into a small smile. 'And I thought you were nice… good-looking. I thought I would like to spend a little time with you.'

Isla narrowed her eyes. 'Are you flirting with me? We're cousins, don't forget.'

'That's not what you said when we first met. Do I need to remind you that you were the one who said we're not really cousins at all?'

'Ah, fair-weather cousin? Cousin when it suits you.'

He grinned now, the tension of earlier easing again. 'What is your saying? All is fair in love and war.'

'We're not in love.'

'Not yet,' he said, and before she'd had time to reply he strode out of the room, muttering something about firewood.

Isla frowned. Was he coming on to her? She wasn't sure whether she should be appalled given his connection or deeply impressed by his efforts. He wasn't a blood relative, true. And he wasn't bad-looking either. Good company – witty, smart, gorgeous, and with the most dreamy French accent. And he seemed nice. She *had* kept telling herself how she needed to let go of all this distrust that poisoned every potential relationship. Maybe Justin wasn't such a bad place to start.

She shook away the idea. It was the most stupid one she'd ever had. A relationship with him would never work – not even a casual fling. Things were complicated enough without adding sex to the mix. Especially sex with someone who, even though he wasn't actually related to her, was close enough to it. She couldn't let anything cloud her judgement, and it was more important now than ever that she kept a clear head. She didn't know what she wanted, but she knew that when she made the decision, it had to be hers alone, without any influence from anyone who might not have her best interests at heart. First Sebastian and now Justin – what was it with her and men this week?

Letting out a sigh, she took another long look at the kitchen. Her gaze was drawn to the mountains beyond the vast windows. Imagine being able to sit every day and look out on that majesty. Imagine owning that view. Even if you only made it over once a year it would be worth the wait. But this was crazy, surely? She was a practically penniless student and, in reality, what would she do with a house like this? How could she afford the upkeep, let alone the regular flights to come and visit? Grandma Sarah must have been out of her tiny mind. Or else, she really did have a mischievous streak a mile wide. The sensible decision would have been to give it to Ian and Celine, who could look after it and use it. Isla could sell it, she supposed, but that hardly seemed fair now that she knew just how much Ian and Celine had invested in it. She could give it to them. But was she allowed to do that? She looked around again, and it was so achingly beautiful, so beyond her wildest dreams that she could ever hope to own something like this that, when it came to the crunch, could she really bear to give it away? She may never have an opportunity like this again – this was life-changing stuff. If she could find a way to make it hers and keep it, the idea of bringing friends over, even her mother (once she'd forgiven Isla for ever coming to St Martin in the first place) was a wonderful dream. She could have such amazing times here, and she could gift equally amazing times to those she loved, give them the sort of holidays they could never afford otherwise. And one day, maybe she'd even think of relocating more permanently. Perhaps the day would come when she'd want to say goodbye to England and move out here. She couldn't imagine it, but the idea that she had a choice was a nice one.

Her thoughts were interrupted by the return of Justin carrying an armful of firewood. 'It's cold. I thought you would like a fire.'

'That sounds lovely,' Isla said, wondering vaguely how long he was planning for them to stay. She'd assumed that it would be a jaunt out, a quick look around and then back to her hotel, and so she hadn't asked. But then she hadn't expected much of the house either. 'You want me to start lunch while you do that?'

'You'll be able to find everything you need?' he asked.

'Probably not, but I might as well have a go rather than stand here like a prune.'

'Be my guest,' he called over his shoulder as he stomped through to the living room with his wood. 'I will help as soon as I have done this.'

Isla turned back to the pile of food he'd laid out on the counter. She wasn't entirely sure what to do with the pasta and sauce that wouldn't be pure student fare. Unfortunately, student fare was about her level so he was going to have to lump it. She stuck her head back in the cupboard and came across some tins of tuna. Now that was more like it. It wasn't going to be gourmet cooking, but it would be a tasty warming meal to keep them going until they headed back.

A small smile stretched her lips, despite the warnings in her head. She was cooking in her own kitchen for the first time ever. *Not yours yet*, she kept on telling herself, but she couldn't shake the tiny kick of excitement deep inside. Not yet, but it could be.

They sat with their bowls of pasta in front of a roaring fire in the living room and it was perfect, like a Christmas music video where they laughed and joked and ate in the warm glow. Only the decorations were missing, and when Isla mentioned this Justin broke into a grin.

'I remember being here once near to Christmas time and I helped your grandmother bring some decorations up from her basement. Perhaps they are still there. We could look.'

Isla glanced around the room. 'It sounds like fun, but is there any point? It's not like I'll be here to see them after today.'

'But you are here today. And if you like I can come here to pack them away after Christmas. I pass by often and it would not be too difficult.'

'Sounds crazy to me.' Isla shook her head slowly. 'Though I suppose I *am* quite curious to see what's in the basement.'

'*Bon*. You will enjoy it. Afterwards, if the sky is still light, I will show you more of the garden.'

Isla frowned. 'I didn't see that the house had a garden…'

'That is because the house does not need one. The mountains and valleys are your garden. The most wonderful garden you could have.'

'I don't doubt that,' Isla smiled. 'It sounds good to me.'

He leapt to his feet and held out a hand to Isla. 'Let us go to the basement!'

He said it like it was an offer to a luxury spa day. It wasn't exactly the most attractive proposal she'd ever had but she was curious nevertheless. After the briefest of hesitations, she pushed herself from her corner of the sofa and followed him.

Once her eyes had adjusted to the gloomy light of a single dull bulb they took in the racks that lined the walls, full of tools, old appliances, snowshoes, wooden skis, mouldering tarpaulins, rusting snow chains and even tins of paint.

'This needs a good clear out,' Isla said, wrinkling her nose. 'It's all very well refurbishing upstairs, but when was the last time anyone came down here?'

'I don't know,' Justin said. 'I have been down here only once.' He gave the space a thoughtful once-over. 'But I will tell my uncle and aunt that it should be done. You are right.'

'I don't suppose they'll care about a house that won't end up being theirs,' Isla said. 'If I had more time I'd have a go myself. Perhaps that's a job to put on a list for when I take ownership.'

'You are going to take the house?' Justin said with an expression of mild surprise. 'Will you live here all the time?'

'I haven't actually decided for sure I'm taking the house,' she said. 'Because I haven't decided if I can forgive my father. And as for living here all year round, that's impossible. If I visit at all it would be once a year maximum.'

He nodded before rummaging in some boxes on a shelf. 'It makes you sad,' he said.

'What does?'

'That your father left you and came to live in St Martin.'

'Wouldn't you be? And not sad, but furious. Especially when I see him with a new family. He loves them and it's hard to take.'

'He loves you too.'

'Don't be ridiculous.'

Justin turned to her and gave a vague shrug. 'You do not believe me, but he is your father. All fathers love their children.'

'Has your dad always been there for you?'

'Yes.'

'Then you couldn't possibly know what it's been like for me.'

He looked as though he would argue, but then he turned back to his search. 'I am sorry; you're right. I do not know what it has been like for you. But I believe he loves you.'

'Can we not talk about it?' Isla said, pinching the bridge of her nose and squeezing her eyes shut. The room was beginning to close in on her and she wanted to get back to the glorious light-filled spaces of the house above. 'If you're struggling to find the decorations then maybe we should just forget the idea. They might not even be here now – although I don't see how that could be the case if all this other crap has been kept.'

'Ah! Here is one… and there is another.'

Isla made her way over. He handed her a box before taking hold of the second one and then gestured for her to go back upstairs first, flicking the basement light off as they emerged into the natural light of the main house again. In the kitchen they placed the boxes onto the counter. Justin blew the dust off the lid of the first one and opened it up.

'I think these are old,' he said, taking a painted glass bauble out and holding it up to the light.

'Perhaps they're Grandma's spare ones or something, old ones she brought from home and left here. They're still in a good condition though.'

'My aunt says she cared for things very well. But I think she was really saying that she was mean.'

'She doesn't strike me as someone who was mean. After all, she left me this house.'

Justin shrugged as he retrieved another bauble from the box and laid it out on the counter next to the first one. 'She had a lot of money because she didn't spend it. She would not pay for repairs on this house because she said none were needed, but the roof was leaking and many things were old and rotten.'

'But it's huge. She must have paid a lot for it.'

'Not so much. It was a low price because the family who owned it wanted to sell quickly.'

'Didn't she find it annoying that Ian and Celine wanted to make changes if she was happy with the house?'

'Maybe.' He scratched a hand through his hair. 'Maybe that is why she decided to give it to you. *Mais*, she is not here to tell us so we'll never know.' By now there was a row of shining baubles on the counter. Justin glanced down at them and back up at Isla. 'There is no tree. Where do you want to put these?'

'They're pretty,' Isla said, tracing a finger over the bevelled surface of one of the baubles.

'Unless you would like to take an axe from the basement and find a tree outside?' Justin asked.

'God, no! I wouldn't want to do that, especially as we won't even be here to enjoy it.'

'We could decorate one outside.'

'Wouldn't the bears eat the baubles or something?'

Justin laughed. 'There are no bears. Just tourists and skiers.'

Isla shook her head. 'I'm happy for nature to be natural. Let's just decorate in here with the tinsel and then go for that walk.'

They used every scrap from the boxes and draped it wherever there was a hook or a space throughout the ground floor. It wouldn't win any style awards but it was suitably twinkly and festive by the time they'd finished. And there had been moments that Isla couldn't ignore – a brush of the hand here, a lingering look there, a proximity as they passed each other in the kitchen – that had her heart beating a little faster. As much as she'd wanted to deny it, the chemistry was most definitely there. What was the protocol around dating cousins that weren't really cousins? Never mind dating, what was the protocol about mindless, rampant sex on the living-room floor? It had obviously been far too long since her last man because by the time they'd begun to pack away the baubles it was all she could think about. Which was ridiculous and had come from nowhere. Why would she even be having these thoughts, if not for the fact that she was alone in a gorgeous house in the middle of an idyllic town, with a handsome and charming man and starved of sex to the point where she might have forgotten where her bits were? Was this why she'd said yes to him when she'd said no to Seb? Because she fancied him and Seb was... what was Seb? Slightly less of a sex god? Justin had nothing to hide – his fitted T-shirt showing the goods in full and very attractive view.

She chided herself. This, whatever *it* was, was not going to happen. So she dashed for her coat the minute they were finished and waited on the porch, certain that the freezing air outside would do something to cool her ardour. But when he came out to join her and they made their way down the steps, like an idiot she tripped. He caught her as she fell, grinning down into her face as if he thought that this was a game designed to get his attention. She had to wonder if, at some unconscious level, it was. But she shook the idea off. She wasn't that sort of girl.

'I'm fine,' she snapped as she righted herself, and as she glanced back she saw his smile widen. 'Which way are we walking?' she added, annoyed more with herself than him. He was a bloke, so he had an excuse, but she didn't.

'As we have walked through the town perhaps you would like to walk away from the town a little?'

'Perfect,' she said before stamping off ahead. Laughing, he caught her up and fell into step alongside.

'Why are you unhappy?' he asked.

'Am I? I don't think so.'

'Is it because you fell down the steps? Or because I might have persuaded you to love your grandmother's house and you don't want to admit it?'

'Both,' she said, and the sound of his laughter echoed across the frozen clearing.

'*Bon*. Perhaps if I try harder you will decide to stay.'

'Stay where?'

'In St Martin of course.'

'Would that matter?'

'It might.'

'Why on earth would you care if I stay or not? It wouldn't change your life.'

'Maybe.'

'Is that all you can say?'

'In answer to that particular question, yes. What do you want me to say?'

'Nothing.'

'Can I speak when I need to give instructions?'

'Yes.' She bit back a smile. 'But only in a life or death situation.'

'OK.' He was silent for a moment. 'You are a mystery.'

'Am I? In what way?'

'I cannot tell whether you hate me or want to make love to me.'

Isla's head whipped round and she stared at him. 'I can assure you it's not the latter,' she replied haughtily.

'So, you hate me?'

'No…' Isla shook her head forcefully. 'I didn't mean that. I only meant I don't want to do the other thing.'

'Make love?'

'Yes, that one.'

'Not even a little?'

'No. And I think it's a very arrogant presumption on your part.'

'Then I am sorry. I had a very different idea.'

'I'm afraid you did.'

'If I kiss you now you will not like it?'

'I'd punch you in the face and run back to my hotel.'

'Perhaps I will not kiss you then.'

The smile itched at Isla's mouth.

'You like the house?' he asked.

'Of course I like the house. I mean, who wouldn't?'

'You will talk to your father about the will?'

She let out a sigh. 'Yes, you played your part well. You can tell him that your little ruse worked.'

'It wasn't a ruse. Yes, the plan was to make you fall in love with the house but that was not all I wanted. I wanted to spend some time with you.'

'I should double any reward you've been promised for that hardship alone. It wouldn't be the first time I've been told I'm not an easy woman to live with.'

'I am not living with you. But I would like to know you better.'

'Was this part of the plan?'

'No, but the plan changed when I met you.'

Isla mused silently as she cast her gaze over the frozen ground. It wasn't yet evening but the sun was already low in the sky, a blazing brass orb sinking quickly below the horizon, and with it the temperature dropping by degrees as they spoke. She could no longer tell with him what was genuine and what was artifice. He'd been in cahoots with Ian, that much was obvious, and he must have been promised something for his efforts, despite his denial. But she couldn't have read the other signals wrong. He was interested in her beyond the inheritance and she was interested in him too, but where did that leave them?

'It's freezing,' she said, hugging herself.

'It can become cold very quickly when the sun goes down,' he said. He pulled her close and wrapped an arm around her shoulders. 'Don't worry,' he said in answer to her silent question, 'I'm just trying to keep you warm. You want to go back?'

'We've only just got out.'

'But you're cold.'

She nodded, unable to deny it.

'We can come back if you want to take a longer look. Perhaps you can spare the time before you fly home.'

'I suppose I could. I have a couple of days yet.'

'Tomorrow then?' he asked.

She paused and then nodded, wondering at the wisdom of the reply she was about to give. 'I don't know. I'll let you know how I feel.'

'If you want to see something new tomorrow that's easy to do,' he added, ignoring her vague response. 'Do not answer now. Whatever you want we can do. You have my phone number.' He offered an arm and she took it. 'We will return to the house now.'

Chapter Ten

Ian had sounded thrilled when she'd phoned him with her thoughts on Serendipity Sound once Justin had walked her back to the hotel. But then Isla supposed he probably was; it looked as if he was going to get his inheritance after all. Back in her room after a quick drink with Dahlia, she stood in front of the mirror and straightened her shirt over her jeans. She'd agreed on the phone to another dinner with Ian, Celine and her half-siblings and was worrying now whether it was the right decision. It was a shame Justin couldn't come – he was about as close to an ally that she had here in St Martin and she would have felt better with him there. As steadily as her shaking hand would allow, she carefully applied a slick of claret lip gloss and stepped back to appraise her reflection. It wasn't exactly high glamour but considering her limited travel supplies it was as good as she was going to get.

'Come on,' she told herself, rolling her shoulders like a boxer about to enter the ring for the fight of his life. 'You can do this.'

And in many ways, a boxing match was what she felt she was walking into. Only she didn't stand a chance as one against four. Celine and Ian had invested in Grandma Sarah's house and surely they weren't going to let it go without a fight? Was that a fight even worth having? Isla didn't blame them one bit and she'd rather deal with it all openly than have them scheme and trick behind the scenes to reclaim the inheritance they must have felt was rightly theirs.

'You have yourself a good evening.' Dahlia smiled as Isla passed the reception desk. 'Going out to dinner?'

'Thanks,' Isla replied. She paused. She'd wanted to talk to Dahlia the day before about what was going on with her dad. Something about her invited trust, and Isla didn't doubt that she had a stock of good, sage advice to hand out too where family matters were concerned. And perhaps sharing it might simply lighten the burden. She glanced at her watch; she had ten minutes to spare and perhaps that was enough. But then a movement from the corner of her eye made the decision for her as she looked round to see Seb coming back in. Judging by his red nose and ruddy cheeks he'd been out in the snow for some time.

He shot an awkward smile at Isla.

'Sebastian… Did you have a good day?' Dahlia asked.

'Very good,' Seb replied, pulling off thick gloves and rubbing his hands together. 'Perfect conditions really.'

'You were working?' Isla asked. She wasn't sure she was meant to ask after the last time she'd seen him but it seemed rude not to. Besides, she'd since decided the easiest way to deal with a mortifying moment was to pretend it didn't exist.

'Yes,' he replied. 'I've got a lot to do before I go home for Christmas.'

'You're still leaving us on Christmas Eve?' Dahlia asked. 'I can't persuade you to share a turkey with me here?'

Seb smiled. 'I'd love to,' he said. 'But my flight is booked now and I'm not sure the university would be happy with me wasting their research grant on empty plane seats.'

'Well, I tried.'

'And a valiant effort it was too,' Seb replied. 'If you'll excuse me, I think the shower is calling my name.'

With another fond smile for Dahlia and a courteous nod to Isla he made his way to the lifts.

'He's one in a million,' Dahlia said in a low voice as she watched him go. 'Good breeding always shows, and he has plenty. His parents must have thought they'd brought an angel down to earth when they got him.'

The way Isla saw it, there was no such thing as good breeding, only lucky breaks where some kids got dealt a good hand and some kids got the shit one. Seb had obviously been brought up in a loving, stable, affluent home and he'd reaped the rewards of that by being a stable, affluent and successful member of society. If he'd been subjected to her childhood, maybe he wouldn't be quite so bow-tie-wearing clever-clogs chipper. Breeding had nothing to do with it – and angels even less so.

She thought all this, but it was best to keep it to herself. Instead, Isla gave Dahlia a tight smile. 'I'm eating out if that's OK so I won't need a table for dinner.'

And with Dahlia's acknowledgement, she headed out into the night.

Barely fifty yards from Residence Alpenrose, Isla was regretting not having something more positive to say to Dahlia about Seb. Sometimes she couldn't help being snappy and, what was worse, she knew it. Her current mood didn't bode well for the meeting she was heading off to, although the meeting did have a lot to do with her mood in the first place.

As she made her way to the restaurant she tried to force some positive thoughts. The only thing worse than a head full of bitter thoughts was a mouth full of bitter words.

Five minutes down a surprisingly busy street and Isla stopped in front of a glowing frontage. The building was a traditional alpine construction, like so many in St Martin, the signage neat and subtle and the windows dressed in tasteful Christmas décor – a richly jewelled garland on the front door and ice points of lights threaded along the eaves. Above the door hung a picture of a cow wearing a ski jacket and holding a knife and fork. A final brief pause, where she glanced up and down the street and considered her options for escape, and then Isla went inside.

It was a fairly traditional steakhouse, like so many that she'd seen back in England. She stood at the doors and took a deep breath. A waitress scooted over with a broad smile.

'I'm with the McCoy party,' Isla said, hoping the waitress spoke decent English. If she was going to be visiting more often, then she was going to have to improve her language skills.

The waitress flung a hand towards the far end of the restaurant. 'They're right over there,' she replied in perfect English, much to Isla's relief.

'Thank you,' Isla said, looking to where the waitress had pointed.

It took a moment of searching but then she saw the table. They hadn't yet noticed her come in, and not for the first time that evening she was half tempted to turn back towards the hotel, especially given the way their last meeting had ended. But she knew that, as much as she craved the amiable chat and ready supply of booze of Dahlia's bar right now, she had to do this.

Ian looked up and met her gaze with an anxious half-smile. He got up from the table and the rest of the family watched as he made his way over.

'Thanks for calling me today,' he said, swinging awkwardly towards her as if he might kiss her on the cheek before backing off again at the last second. 'And we're all really glad you've agreed to meet us again. I think maybe this will be easier than the last time – more relaxed. I mean, we would have asked you to dinner at our place but...'

Isla forced a smile. 'Don't worry – I think this is perfect. A neutral venue was a good idea.'

He indicated the table with a sweep of his hand. 'So, shall we try again? Have another crack at getting to know each other?'

'We can certainly try,' Isla replied carefully, making her way over as he followed. At the table Celine stood up and kissed her lightly, her daughter Natalie doing the same while Benet pulled out a seat for her. Isla had to wonder if their greetings had been discussed and staged, particularly when she thought back to the way they'd reacted when they'd first met her. Benet looked far from comfortable with his act of chivalry and he sat back in his own seat with a thud as soon as he could. Isla reached for the carafe of water in the middle of the table to pour a drink, her mouth already dry.

'Have you enjoyed your day?' Celine asked.

Isla nodded. 'The house is beautiful.'

'So you went with Justin?' Ian asked.

'Yes. He showed me around – the place is amazing.'

'It is,' Celine said. 'We love it very much.'

All eyes were on her, waiting for something else. What did they want her to say? That she was sorry she was getting their gorgeous house? The one they'd spent a small fortune on in the assumption that it would one day be theirs? Perhaps she might as well get it out of the way now or the question would hang over the gathering like a storm cloud.

'Look,' she began, 'I know things aren't how you'd imagined they would be. God knows I'm more surprised than anyone. If anyone had asked me a month ago whether I could imagine sitting at the table with you all, I would have laughed at the ridiculousness of the idea. But we've been forced into it and we have to deal with it. So I want to propose something…' She took a deep breath. She'd thought long and hard about this decision once Justin had left her that day, and it probably wasn't the one they'd been expecting. 'I'm happy to fulfil the conditions around the inheritance to the letter, but no more. And when all the property is handed out and Mr Rousseau's happy that Grandma Sarah's wishes have been carried out, then I'm going to hand the chalet to you and go home. I don't wish you any ill – any of you – but I don't need the extra complication in my life. I can't afford to keep a house like that and I certainly can't afford to visit it. However, I don't see the point in stopping your inheritance coming to you and, in fact, even I can see that would be downright mean. And I don't want to profit from the house you've spent so much on.'

Ian exchanged a look of confusion with Celine.

'Well, that's noble of you, but—'

'I don't want to hear you say you don't want it, because I know you do. I know you spent a great deal of money renovating it and even if you don't want it perhaps you need it.'

'Justin told you this?' Benet asked, suddenly bright with interest. At least, if not bright, certainly the most animated Isla had seen him. 'He told you about the renovations?'

Isla nodded.

'You are a good and kind person.' Natalie beamed, and she looked across at Celine for agreement. But the smile Celine returned was strained.

'You would regret this decision,' she said.

'I wouldn't. What you never had, you never miss – that's what they say, isn't it? Well I never had it to miss, but you did. Sort of. So I'm giving it to you.' Isla pressed the glass of water to her mouth again and took a gulp. Why did they insist on making this more difficult than it had to be? The decision she'd taken hadn't been made lightly but it was still hard. Of course she wanted Serendipity Sound – who wouldn't? But it wasn't rightfully hers and she wanted to do the right thing.

'That's just it,' Ian said. 'You can't give us Serendipity Sound. Part of my mother's deal is that you can't give it to us.'

'But I thought I could do what I wanted with it?'

'You can. Almost anything. But not that. I guess my mother knew how it might go. We've checked with Grover – believe me, we've checked every line of that will – but there's no way around it. I think she meant to make amends for the past and that's the only way she knew how.'

'I can sell it then?'

Ian shrugged. 'I'm not sure. Maybe.'

'Then I can give you the money from the sale.'

'I'm not sure how that works,' Celine put in. 'It might void our claim on the rest of the estate if it came to light. I will not lie, we are unhappy about losing the house, but there's just no way around it. You have to accept the terms of the inheritance if any of us are going to get our share.'

Isla nodded slowly. So much for noble sentiments. She supposed she ought to look at it as an amazing, life-changing gift but it felt more like a shackle, tying her to a place and a family that she just wanted to put behind her. St Martin was beautiful and so was the house, but her grandmother's gift, in real, practical terms, represented nothing but worry and responsibility.

'Are you saying that you're going to come on board?' Ian asked. 'You want to try to fulfil your grandma's wishes?'

'I think it would be pretty unreasonable of me not to. It doesn't have to mean anything anyway…' She glanced at Natalie and Benet, who were listening, silent and attentive, to the conversation. Probably weighing up their own part in the arrangements. Natalie was smiling sweetly and Benet was doing his best not to wear the glower she was becoming used to seeing on him. Could she be family to these people? Would the day come when spending time with them was as natural as breathing? Right now it was impossible to know but Isla was sure of one thing – she didn't want to be the cuckoo in the nest. They had their family life and it seemed from the outside like a good one; she had no desire to get in the way of that. 'We can go through the motions but you don't have to feel as if you should be inviting me for Christmas dinner or anything. As long as we convince Grover, right?'

If she hadn't known better, Isla would have said that Ian looked hurt by what she'd said. Celine replied for him as he reached for his beer.

'If that works for you,' she said. 'But we've been thinking too and we don't want to stand in the way of you spending time with your father if you feel you'd like to. It might not be so bad. We must not forget that you are also Natalie and Benet's half-sister and maybe you would like to get to know them a little while you're here.'

'I suppose it's not every day you find out you have two new siblings,' Isla said. She turned her gaze to Natalie and Benet and forced a smile.

'Exactly,' Natalie said. 'We are willing to try if you are. Perhaps while you visit we may see you again? For dinner? Now that we have the business completed, we can get to know each other as family…' She turned to Celine and Benet, who both gave a short nod.

'One thing,' Isla said, 'and I'm not going to get upset if you tell me the truth, I just want to know... Did you know about me? Before this all came out in the will, did you know you had a sister in England?'

Both Natalie and Benet looked uncertainly at their parents for guidance. Ian shook his head slowly.

'They didn't know.'

'I did,' Celine added. 'And I know that your father tried to reach you many times over the years. Birthdays and Christmases would go by and your mother refused to grant him access.'

Isla should have been shocked by this news but she wasn't. Deep down, she must have always suspected it but her loyalty to her mother wouldn't allow her to acknowledge those suspicions. And knowing her mum, it made sense. Glory would deny it, of course, until her dying breath. But it was exactly the sort of thing she'd do, and she would believe that it was for all the right reasons. 'He could have gone to court,' Isla insisted, but she didn't really feel the conviction of her words as she spoke them.

'We lived too far away; it was not practical. And your mother forbade it. All your father wanted was to send you a letter and get a reply. Perhaps a phone call from time to time.'

'Glory said that it would upset you and rake up old feelings,' Ian cut in.

'And Ian thought,' Celine continued, 'maybe she was right, and the kind thing to do was to disappear. So he stopped.'

'I'm not proud of that,' Ian said. 'I should have fought harder and I'll always regret that I didn't. But you have to understand how hard it was. I thought it was the right decision at the time, and the longer it went on the tougher it was to contact you. Being straight with you now as one adult to another – we want the house in Scotland, of course we do. But I want you to have what's due to you too. It's only the first step in making amends for all the years I was a terrible father, and I want to do it properly. I want to do whatever it takes to make it at least half way right.'

Isla could have chosen to believe that his words were all about the inheritance. But something in his eyes told her that they were true. The years she'd spent apart from him weren't all his doing.

'We can't fix it now,' Isla said. 'So there's no point in dwelling on it. If you're willing to make peace then I am too. All I'm saying is it might not be easy to build a real relationship, but we can have something that satisfies Grandma Sarah's will and maybe even one day we'll be friends. It doesn't matter now how it all happened, the fact is that I grew up without you and I'm a product of that. What I'm proposing is the best I can offer right now.'

Ian nodded gravely. 'Of course; I wouldn't expect anything else.'

'Now that we have that out of the way,' Celine said with forced brightness, 'maybe we should try to have some fun. We have a lot to discuss, but it doesn't have to be hard work, does it?'

'I suppose not.' Isla shot Ian a small smile. She wanted to believe that they'd soon be chatting like long-lost friends, but she had a feeling it was going to be a long and difficult evening.

If not exactly pleasant, the evening had at least been reasonably cordial in the end. They'd parted with an agreement that Ian would contact Grover Rousseau back in Scotland again and explain where they were at and find out what they needed to do next. Plenty of wine at the dinner table had helped things along, of course, and Isla had crashed into her bed back at the hotel with her mind racing, fully expecting to lie awake for the next few hours thinking over what had been said. But she'd woken the next morning hardly even remembering her head hitting the pillow.

She'd woken early, though, and rather than lie in bed mulling things over, she got up and showered so she could make breakfast early and get out to see some of the country she had only a few days left in. Making peace with Ian had, at last, given her an appetite to treat her last few days in the Alps as more of a holiday than she had before. Her day with Justin had helped too, and she craved more of the magnificent scenery and clean air he'd shown her. There were mountains and fresh air aplenty not far from where she was, not to mention more than enough interesting sports and activities, and if she couldn't find something to keep her occupied for the day, then it was a pretty poor showing. She would ask Dahlia for some tips and a packed lunch to take with her.

As she was applying a modest layer of make-up, the phone lying on the bedside cabinet flashed to alert her to a text. Justin's name appeared on the screen. It was not yet eight, and Isla mused on the possibility that Ian had already been in touch with him to tell him how the meal had gone the night before. She wasn't sure what to make of that, but crossed the room and snatched up her phone to open the message. Sure enough, Justin knew.

I am glad to hear it went well last night. How do you feel? Are you happy?

Isla clutched the phone for a moment as she gazed out of the window. The streets were still cloaked in dawn's grey light. Was she happy? Was that the thing she was feeling right now? It wasn't a kind of happiness she recognised, but something had changed between her and Ian. Perhaps the most significant was that at times that morning she'd even thought of him as *Dad* rather than Ian. She felt positive and full of new energy and she felt as if she could see an end in sight that might be a good one. But there was still too much uncertainty to call it. She began to tap out a reply.

I think it did. Don't know how I'm feeling. Early days yet.

Would you like to talk about it?

I don't know.

Today? I can pick you up.

Not today. Spending time alone today.

Why alone?

I need to collect my thoughts. Sorry.

Tonight? Dinner? I would like to pay.

I don't think that's a good idea.

Please? I would like to hear all about it.

Was that friendly dinner to chat, or was that *dinner* dinner? Either way it looked as if he wasn't taking no for an answer. Was this something she wanted to get into? She was ready to go home in a few days, and though she'd agreed that she'd come back to St Martin as soon as she could to build on the progress she'd made with Ian (and make it very obvious to Grover Rousseau that they were making a concerted effort to get along), it wasn't exactly a permanent arrangement and certainly too tenuous to build a romance on. As for one night stands, she'd learned that they never ended well and were best avoided. Even two or three night stands for that matter. So what, exactly, did Justin want from her? More importantly, was she willing to give it to him?

As if he'd sensed her reticence through the ether, the phone bleeped again.

No funny business, I promise.

She couldn't help but smile. Of all the English phrases to know! How many times had he needed that phrase before? She supposed there must be a lot of British tourists passing through the resort in a year – young, pretty female tourists. Still it didn't diminish his attractiveness, even though it probably ought to.

You'd never get away with it anyway. Dinner sounds good in that case.

I'll pick you up at eight?

Eight is perfect.

Putting her phone down, Isla crossed back to the mirror and finished applying her mascara before scraping her wild hair back into a sturdy hairband. Though Dodie had often expressed awe and envy at the magnificent volume of Isla's curls, Isla herself found them uncontrollable and an absolute pain. Most days it was easier to pull them back out of the way and secure them with something of industrial strength. Her bathroom at home housed a ton of products to tame her locks, but it had been too much hassle to carry them onto the plane so most days here she'd been tying it back. But now, the prospect of dinner with Justin was making her wish she'd brought some with her so she could look her best. Maybe there was a shop nearby where she could get something. But then, with a sharp click of her tongue, she shook her head in exasperation as she gazed at her reflection.

'Silly cow,' she muttered.

With a final check in the mirror, she snatched up her room key and headed down for breakfast.

Dahlia was in the dining room, already racing around from table to table with a pot of coffee for the early risers getting a head start for a day hiking, climbing or skiing. But today she had a teenage girl work-ing with her setting tables and clearing them again.

'I thought you were making it up when you said you sometimes had help,' Isla said as Dahlia showed her to a table with a broad smile. She looked bright and cheery, despite the fact that she'd probably done half a day's work before Isla had even woken up. Before she could respond, however, both women's attention was drawn to Sebastian ambling into the dining room wearing a rather sombre dark blue bow tie and a plain navy cardigan over his powder blue shirt. His gaze caught Isla's, and she tried to fight the blush that spread through her, especially as she recalled how she'd mentally compared him to Justin in the shallowest way. He was such a sweet guy and that ought to matter more than any physical attribute.

'Good morning!' Dahlia called, the silent and mortified exchange of her guests apparently passing her by. 'Give me a minute and I'll find you somewhere to sit.'

Sebastian, if possible, looked more awkward and mortified than ever as he realised that every table in the tiny dining room was already full. He'd have to stand around and wait for someone to finish. But Isla quickly realised that she was sitting alone at a table for two, and no matter what had happened between them it was churlish to deny him a seat. Maybe she could even use the opportunity to clear the air. She forced a carefree smile.

'There's room here, if you care to join me.'

'Oh, yes, what a wonderful idea!' Dahlia exclaimed. 'Come on over and sit down.'

Whether he wanted to or not, the decision had been made for him. And Sebastian looked very much as though he'd rather be anywhere but there as he made his way over to the table and sat across from Isla with a stiff smile.

'Thank you,' he said. 'Very kind of you.'

'Not really – it's just a seat. I was hardly going to let you stand there while I ate my breakfast.'

Dahlia poured him a coffee and he gave her a grateful nod as Isla continued.

'You're up nice and early. I suppose you're out at the glacier again today?'

'Yes.'

'Only, I was maybe going to take a look at the mountains and I wondered if you could give me some advice on where to go… What was it I read about online earlier… a gondola up through the peaks to a neighbouring resort?'

'The gondola will take you through to the Méribel slopes but you'd struggle to walk back – it's better suited to skiing,' Dahlia cut in. 'I could put you in touch with an instructor if you wanted to learn.'

'I don't think there's really time for that.'

'Perhaps if you come again then. But I wouldn't go up on the gondola in the hopes of getting down any other way.'

'Right…' Isla watched as she bustled off to tend to another table. 'That's a shame. Maybe I could just go out to a neighbouring village? Do you think there'll be transport? A tour or something?'

'I don't know much about it to be honest,' Seb replied.

'It's just that I'd like to see more of the area and I daren't go walking around mountains alone. You hear of people getting caught unawares all the time, especially if they're inexperienced in the snow.'

He was silent for a moment. 'So does today's lack of a plan mean you've done what you need to do here and have free time?'

'Sort of. I have a couple of days left and I didn't want to go home having seen practically nothing. How many people dream of coming here? And yet, here I am not even making an effort to explore what's right on the doorstep. But I don't want to take any unnecessary risks.'

'Would you feel better if you had a guide?'

'You can hire someone to take you up? Wouldn't that be expensive?'

He tipped his head slightly. 'Not necessarily. I know the peaks quite well so we could take a look. I wouldn't be able to get you right up top, of course, but I'll show you as much as I can.'

Isla's eyes widened. 'You'd come with me? But I thought you had to work today.'

'I can work any time I like as long as it's done. But I thought… Actually,' he added, seeming to be struck by a sudden idea, 'perhaps you'd like to drive out to Lake Blanc? I mean, it's a couple of hours' drive but it's pretty spectacular and it's got everything you want from the Alps – gorgeous lake, beautiful mountains and clean air.'

'I'd love that!' Isla said, and she meant it. The strength of feeling that his offer had stoked in her came from nowhere. She couldn't understand it, and yet she was suddenly thrilled. There was also a measure of undeniable relief that he seemed to have put her previous rebuff behind him. 'I'd get to see a lot more with you than on my own because you know what to do and what everything is,' she added, trying to temper her excitement for his sake, not wanting to give him the wrong impression. But if she was giving the wrong impression, it wasn't an act at all. Where the hell had these feelings come from?

'We'll have to leave very early,' he said.

'Perfect! We can go straight after breakfast if you're OK with that.'

He shot her a smile that wrinkled his nose and she couldn't help but laugh at it, pleased to see he was feeling more comfortable with her again. 'Nothing would make me happier.'

It seemed it hadn't taken long for Sebastian's hire car to fill up with the detritus of his work as he shoved aside a mound of folders and graph paper so she could sit in the passenger seat. On the floor sat a selection of empty coffee cups and chocolate bar wrappers. He gave a sheepish smile as Isla glanced at them and then up at him.

'Sorry about the mess. I was meaning to clear it all out before I gave the car back. Not many rubbish bins out on the glaciers, you know.'

'But there are lots of coffee shops, apparently.' She cocked an eyebrow.

'In town at least,' he said, his smile widening. 'I'll shout up before we pass the last chance to get one.' He was bouncy, full of nervous excitement, like a little boy showing his favourite teacher a pet project. It was probably a little bit like that, Isla mused, as his pet project happened to be his job. 'Have you been to the toilet?' he asked.

Isla's eyebrows shot up her forehead this time. 'Yes, Mum. Thanks for checking, though.'

'Sorry,' he said, blushing. 'Just that it's a good two-hour drive and not many stop-off places along the way.'

'I'm sure I can control my bladder for two hours. Or I could just use one of your extensive collection of empty coffee cups if I get really desperate.'

'I didn't mean anything... sorry.'

'Sebastian,' she said, and he looked up from where he was slotting the key into the transmission.

'Yes?'

'I'm just kidding.'

'Right,' he said, relaxing again into a boyish grin.

'I'm told my sense of humour is an acquired taste, so don't worry if you don't always get it.'

'I'll try to remember that,' he said. 'So we're taking the N90. It's a spectacular highway – at least in my opinion. You should keep your eyes peeled for wildlife along the way.'

'Will you be giving me a running commentary as we go? Like when I went on a guided tour to the Tower of London?'

'I could, but you might get very bored of the sort of facts I'd be spouting,' he replied as they pulled away from the kerb.

'Would it be lots of glaciologist stuff?'

'More or less.'

'You could try me and let me judge. Or we could just put the radio on.'

He laughed. 'Put the radio on. I don't want you to slip into a coma.'

'That would make for some very awkward silences,' Isla agreed. She turned to the window as he chuckled and the town began to move across her vision. There were thick clouds on the horizon, but they looked harmless enough and there was even the occasional chink of blue. Her mood was lighter than it had been for days and now that she was out she was looking forward to her trip. Seb promised to be good company too, better than she'd anticipated, and already she could see a wicked sense of fun lurking beneath that nerdy and eccentric exterior. If she could see past the mad bow-tie collection he might even be considered attractive. She'd have to remember to get his number at some point, just so she could pass it on to Dodie.

Isla fiddled with the tuner on the radio; the stations were quite predictably in French but she managed to drop onto one playing contemporary pop songs she knew from the charts back home. She flicked a glance at Seb.

'I suppose you hate this sort of music,' she asked. Though she thought she detected a tiny grimace he shook his head.

'It doesn't bother me; I'm happy to concentrate on the roads and I doubt you'll find any of my taste on the commercial stations anyway.'

'So, that's a yes.'

'No,' he said with a slight smile. 'I don't hate it – I just don't listen to it given a choice.'

'So what do you listen to... hang on – let me guess. Classical? Swing? Jazz?'

'A bit of all of those,' he said. 'I don't really listen to a set genre, I just like real music with heart and feeling.'

'Boring music then?'

'Some would say that I suppose,' he laughed.

'I could turn the radio off—'

'Please...' he cut in. 'Don't do that. Honestly, I'm happy to listen to whatever you want to listen to.'

They were silent for a moment as Seb kept the speed low while they were in the village. After a brief period he spoke again.

'I was hoping to get away with it, but in the end I decided to put the snow chains on,' he said. 'I hope they're not too distracting for you.'

It was only then that she registered the gentle bump of the car along the road. It wasn't annoying, and she only felt grateful that at least they were guaranteed some traction. Isla had never actually had to use them before – when it snowed at home she just did her best not to go out in it – so she was glad she hadn't been driving out here alone or she would have ended up stuck for sure. She was also glad that Seb seemed to know what he was doing. He handled the car so deftly that she felt safe in the knowledge they'd reach their destination in one piece.

The low wooden farms and chalets clinging to the slopes began to give way to open vistas of majestic snow-capped peaks, their flanks scored by rivers of rock and ice. It was hard not to feel overwhelmed by the sheer scale of them, an endless stretch of giant after giant unlike anything she'd seen before. As they drove Seb pointed out things of interest, like a lone ibex standing sentry on a terrifying-looking outcrop and a frozen waterfall like something from a fairy tale. He talked her through geological features, myths and legends of the region and the origins of place names and soon she'd stopped noticing what was on the radio. She was enjoying his company, and strangely, she was beginning to realise that his company alone was enough. She didn't need to see lakes or glaciers or mountain goats – she was happy just chatting to Seb.

'So you went out yesterday? With that chap I saw you with in the morning? Somewhere interesting?'

'Justin,' Isla said, thrown by the abrupt change of subject and suddenly feeling it was a question to make her squirm. 'He's my cousin,' she added, feeling that such an answer would fend off any more awkward enquiries. The fact that he wasn't really her cousin, and that she'd almost snogged his face off at Serendipity Sound was something she wasn't about to add to what little information she was volunteering.

'Oh. Is that why you're here? To visit family? I thought you were travelling alone.'

He sounded relieved. Isla tried not to think about what that might mean.

'I am travelling alone. It's sort of complicated but, yes, I am sort of visiting family. But sort of not.'

'There seems to be a lot of unexpected variables there.'

'I suppose so. To be truthful I don't know myself what to tell you about it.'

'Do you want to tell me anything? I don't want to pry if it's going to cause you discomfort. But at the same time, I'm happy to listen if it makes you feel better to talk.'

'That's sweet of you. I suppose when I say it all out loud it doesn't sound like as big a deal as I'm making it in my head. Besides, I think we're close to sorting it now. Let's just say my father and I have been separated for a long time and this trip was to see if we could mend things between us.'

'And has it?'

She nodded. 'I think so. We're making progress at least.'

'So if your father's here then how did you end up living in England?'

'Ian's Scottish. He moved around a lot, or he seemed to, because he met my mum when he was working away from home on the south coast. Then he moved here when... well, he moved here and that's why I haven't seen him for such a long time.'

'Ian?'

'My dad.'

'You don't call him Dad?'

'Not yet.'

Silence enveloped the car for a moment. And then Seb spoke again.

'I didn't mean to pry.'

'You didn't. I volunteered the information – remember? And actually, I feel weirdly lots better for sharing it.'

'My shoulders are broad if you want to share some more. Anything I can do to make you feel better still would be my pleasure.'

Isla looked across at him. His gaze was trained straight ahead, concentrating on the icy highway, his brow creased slightly, one mischievous lock of hair curling across an eye. He blew it away, but it simply dropped back again. His eyelashes were incredibly long, and she'd never really noticed that before. And the freckles across his nose and cheeks had a distinct symmetry to them that was sort of handsome. She'd never considered freckles to be handsome before. She didn't doubt for a moment that he'd do anything in his power to bring happiness to the people he encountered – instinctively anyone who met him would be able to tell he was that sort of a man. Kind and sweet and generous. It wouldn't be so bad to share her woes with him, and she was certain she'd feel a lot better afterwards. And then she realised she was staring silently at his profile and that she probably ought to say something.

She shook herself. She really must remember to get his number for Dodie before they parted – he'd be the perfect man for her sweet-natured friend.

'You're sure you want to hear it?' she asked. 'There's a lot to tell and not all of it makes us look like a nice family.'

'Absolutely. I'm very open-minded and I'm sure it's not nearly as awful as you might think it sounds.'

Isla shook her head and smiled. 'OK. You asked for it.'

*

By the time they reached the outskirts of the lake Isla had pretty much told him the whole story. Far more, in fact, than she'd planned to, going right back to her childhood and ruminating aloud on her mother's part in the events that had ultimately altered the course of her life. But something about Seb invited trust – he made her feel comfortable, unjudged, listened to and taken seriously in a way that few people did. He didn't interrupt and didn't offer counsel unless she asked for it – he simply let her talk.

When they finally reached a rather mundane and uninspiring car park, they left Seb's car behind to take the Flégère cable car, and from there it was a hike long enough to finish Isla off before she'd even begun to explore. But despite the blisters beginning to form nicely on her heels and a severe shortness of breath due in part to her lack of fitness and in part to the altitude, it was worth it. As they stood on an outcrop overlooking the lake with the shadow of Mont Blanc beyond, Isla could do nothing but stare.

The waters gleamed turquoise as the clouds parted to allow chinks of vibrant blue through, snow-dusted peaks crowding in beneath heavy blankets of thick white cloud, dark spines of rocks sweeping the shoreline. It was so perfect it was almost as if it couldn't be real.

'Wow!' Isla took in a lungful of cold air. It might have been the cleanest she'd ever breathed.

'Was it worth the walk?' Seb asked.

She turned to him. 'Yes. It's like Narnia or something.'

'Let's hope we don't find any wicked witches. I wouldn't fancy my chances with a lion either, come to think of it.' He zipped his coat up high around his neck and the funny little bow tie he always wore disappeared. Isla suddenly missed it, as if he somehow didn't look like himself any more without it. 'What do you want to do?' he asked. 'We could walk for a while – spot some wildlife? There's a circular walk we can do that will take us round to Lac des Chéserys and we should be able to see the Argentière Glacier that way too.'

'Well, I can hardly argue the need to look at a glacier with a glaciologist, can I?'

He shot her an adorably boyish grin. 'I don't need much encouraging. It's all rather sad I suppose.'

'You're lucky. Lucky you love your work so much – not many can say that.'

'I suppose so. If you're happy with that arrangement then shall we make a start? Tell me if you get tired and we can always turn back. Sound OK?'

Isla nodded and they began to trudge through the snow. It was hard going – they often lost the path, such as it was, and divots and bumps underfoot hidden by the blanket of white sucked in boots and turned ankles when they least expected. She was thankful that she'd ended up buying a decent pair of winter boots, even if they weren't quite as elegant as the gorgeous, fashionable ones she'd left in the wardrobe of her hotel. But Isla didn't mind the fact that she was sweating, or the fact that the ground wanted to break one of her ankles, because she was mesmerised by the glittering landscape, decked out for Christmas in nature's own finery and making her feel that if she ever had a moment where life felt like too much once she'd left France, all she had to do was visualise this silent, frozen beauty and she would always find peace.

Every so often Seb would look back and grin as he led the way and then turn his long legs back to his task, like a puppy straining on a leash. Isla couldn't help but catch some of his enthusiasm. If the scenery was making her happier than she'd ever thought a few mountains and a lake could do, the company wasn't doing such a bad job either.

'OK back there?' he asked after five silent minutes of struggling through the drifts. He turned to check.

'I'm still on my feet, if that's what you mean.'

'Care for a piggy back?'

'And have you flat on your face in the snow with me on top of you? I don't think so.'

'Just don't struggle. I'm stronger than I look and you wouldn't be the first girl I've carried through snow.'

'Very chivalrous of you. Was that your girlfriend?'

'She was,' he sniffed. And then he was silent. Isla sensed the mood suddenly shift. It was slight, almost imperceptible, and as soon as she'd recognised it things seemed to shift back to normality again.

'Not now then?' she asked.

'No. Not now.'

'So you're single? Footloose and fancy free?'

'I suppose you could say that. My job takes me away from home a lot so it's hard to maintain a relationship.'

'That's a shame; you'll make someone a good husband one day.'

He turned to her and laughed, more his affable self again. 'I'll make someone a terrible husband and everyone knows it. Unless my future wife is passionate about rocks and soil and permafrost. In which case it would be a match made in heaven. But if she's out there, I haven't found her yet.'

'Surely the right woman will learn compromise, even if she doesn't love what you love. Being *in love* is what counts – with each other. The rest will follow, even if it needs a bit of work.'

She watched the back of his head move as he nodded slowly. 'I suppose so. Perhaps the problem lies with me then. Perhaps I'm not ready to compromise.'

'There's time, right? How old are you?'

'I thought it was quite impertinent to ask someone their age.'

'That only applies to women because we're all neurotic about it. We're allowed to ask men.'

'Twenty-eight,' he said. 'Do I get to ask you now?'

'No,' she said. 'But I can tell you I'm in that range.'

'That's all I'm getting?'

'Yes.'

His head tilted again. Then he stopped and waited for her to catch up. 'It's a bit more difficult underfoot here – you might want to hang onto me.'

'What makes you think you're more likely to stay on your feet than I am?'

'I don't. I was hoping you'd hold me up.'

She broke into a broad grin as she threaded her arm through his. 'You know exactly the right thing to say, don't you? I can't believe you're still single.'

'Not through lack of effort, I can assure you. I take it you're single too?'

'What makes you say that?'

'You haven't mentioned a man – at least romantically – all day. Most people with a significant other will bring them up pretty early in the proceedings.'

'Maybe I like to keep my private life private.'

'So there is someone?'

There had been outrageous flirting with Justin, of course, but did that count? 'No,' she decided, almost as if confirming it to herself. 'Not at the moment.'

He offered no reply, his eyes fixed firmly on the horizon, and Isla found herself wondering just what was going through that strangely intriguing brain of his.

*

They were still marching, their gazes everywhere, silently drinking in the intense and captivating beauty of the scenery, when Isla's attention was drawn to the banks of the lake. A dark shadow slinking through the undergrowth suddenly caught her eye. She stared, trying to work out what it looked like and was about to call out to Seb when she slammed into a warm, padded mass.

Seb flew one way and she flew the other and when she looked up they were both on their backsides on the ice, laughing uncontrollably at one another.

'Sorry!' Isla giggled. 'I thought you were further ahead than that!'

'I thought I ought to wait for you – as you were so slow and everything.'

'Cheeky bugger!' Isla squeaked, which only made Seb laugh harder.

Isla hauled herself to her feet and staggered over to him. She held out a hand.

He shook his head. 'I'll pull you over again.'

'You won't. I'm stronger than I look. And you wouldn't be the first man I've helped up from the floor where I'd knocked them.'

'Touché,' he said with a wry smile.

He took her hand, but as he stood upright, she stepped back onto a sharp rock and wobbled. As she lost her footing, his arms were suddenly around her and he pulled her close. She looked up, wrapped in an embrace that felt strangely right and good. His nose wrinkled as he smiled down at her. 'I've got you,' he said, his voice husky and low.

'You have,' she said, feeling all at once reassured and confused by his sudden and unexpected sex appeal. His arms were still around her, and without even realising hers had slipped round his waist in return.

And for some reason she didn't want to let go. 'You're a regular Clark Kent, aren't you?'

He laughed, blushing, which only served to make him more attractive. He cleared his throat and stepped back. 'I think they were serving hot chocolate somewhere near the cable car building,' he added, his face still burning, and he turned away to look back in the direction they'd just come from. 'Would you like one?'

'Does that mean you've conceded defeat on the hiking?' Isla asked, oddly deflated by the idea that their morning might be coming to an end.

'I have to admit, I'm a little concerned about the weather,' he said. 'It doesn't look quite as promising as it did earlier and we don't want to get stuck up here if it turns.'

Isla nodded slowly as he cast her a furtive glance before turning away again. She couldn't deny that the clouds were moving in apace, even though it seemed they'd both been trying to ignore the fact for some time now. 'Perhaps that's not such a bad idea.'

Two hours later they had settled at picnic tables overlooking the incredible vista of the mountains with cups of steaming chocolate clasped in freezing hands. Isla was now grateful for Seb's suggestion that they head back; she was exhausted and it had taken far longer to return than she'd anticipated.

'I forgot to say, I saw something by the lake,' Isla said. 'That's why I bumped into you – not because I'm a klutz.'

'Are you sure that's the reason you bumped into me?' Seb smiled, his composure recovered and his good-natured and unassuming ease now returned. 'Sounds very much like an excuse to me.'

'I did!' Isla laughed. 'Some sort of animal but I only got a glimpse so I couldn't tell what it was.'

'What did it look like? From what you saw?'

She shrugged. 'Like a dog, I suppose. Could it have been a wolf?'

He nodded. 'It's rare but not impossible to see them. Lynx have been seen in these parts too. They usually stay away from the tourist trails though.'

She fell silent for a moment, gazing out at the peaks.

'You don't have to worry,' he said into the gap. 'There's no reason to be afraid – they're generally happy to keep out of our way if we keep out of theirs.'

She turned to him with a smile. 'I'm not worried.' It was strange, but she meant it. She wasn't worried at all. Having Seb there made her feel safe, even with his nerdy bow tie and ridiculous face full of freckles and the nose that wrinkled boyishly when he smiled.

'Good. So this is your day. What do you want to do now?'

'To be honest, now that I've sat down my legs are stiffening up and my boots are taking chunks out of my feet.'

'You'd like to go back to St Martin?'

She nodded. 'If that's OK.'

'Of course,' he said, and he took a huge gulp of his drink. It was impossible to miss the tone of disappointment in his voice, no matter how he might be trying to mask it.

'I could show you Serendipity Sound,' she added.

His forehead creased slightly.

'My grandmother's house. The one I'm supposed to inherit. It's not too far from our hotel.'

He smiled and instantly he seemed brighter. 'I'm happy to do whatever makes you happy.'

'It's not often I get an offer like that so I'll take it. Serendipity Sound it is.'

They'd got lost, of course, but eventually the paths and back alleys started to look familiar and they finally stood before what had been Grandma Sarah's second home.

'This is all yours?' Seb stood with his hands in his pockets, staring up at the house.

'Not yet, but it will be.'

He let out a low whistle. 'That's some gift.'

'Especially from a woman who didn't want anything to do with me when she was alive. I only wish I had the keys so I could show you the inside too.'

'If it's anything like as impressive as the outside then I can imagine it must be fantastic.'

'It is,' Isla said with a smile. For the first time since learning of its existence and the fact she was set to own it, there was more than a hint of pride in her voice. 'I still can't believe it's coming to me.'

'I'll bet. I'm quite sure I'll never own anything as beautiful as this.'

'That's what I thought. Just goes to show you never know what life's got in store for you.'

'It's a shame we can't go in.'

'We can't get in but I can show you around the outside. And we can sneak a peek through the windows so you'll get some idea.' She nudged him. 'Come on.'

Snow had fallen overnight and in a few short hours the path she'd taken with Justin up to the house had been buried. But they trudged through, ankles disappearing into the drifts, until they made it to the sheltered veranda where they stamped the snow from their boots. With hands cupped around their eyes, faces pressed against the window, they peered into the living room. It was as warm and welcoming as Isla remembered it to be, and she itched to go inside, wishing now she'd persuaded Justin to give her the keys before they'd parted.

'It looks nice,' Seb said from beside her.

She was about to suggest that they try another window for a view of the kitchen when she stopped and frowned.

'That's weird.'

'What is?'

'Yesterday when I was here we put Christmas decorations up. They were just crappy old ones but they were all over the place. Now there's nothing.'

'Someone's taken them down?' Seb moved away from the window and Isla followed his lead. She stared up at him.

'Yes, but who?'

'Your cousin, perhaps? Before you left here?'

'We left together; I would have known if he'd done it then because it would have taken a while to do.'

'So he came back to do it later on?'

'He could have done, but the question of why still remains. Why would he feel the need to strip it back to normal? Nobody's coming in here, so what's the point? And it's Christmas anyway so why take down the decorations before Christmas is over, even if he felt he needed to?'

Seb opened his mouth to speak but then closed it again.

'Come on,' Isla said. 'Whatever you're thinking you can say it and I won't be angry.'

'Perhaps your cousin is using the house. Bringing guests up here? You said he had the keys.'

'I still don't see the need to take down the Christmas decorations. And we're assuming it's him.'

'Who else could it be?'

Isla narrowed her eyes slightly. 'I don't think it's a passing bear, that's for sure. I'd put a fair amount of money on Ian.'

'Your father? But why would he need to do that?'

'I don't know,' she replied, folding her arms tight across her chest and staring out at the snowy wilderness beyond the veranda. 'But I intend to find out.'

Chapter Eleven

Isla was quiet and preoccupied on the walk back to Residence Alpenrose. Seb had asked her on more than one occasion if she was OK, and she'd given him a vague smile and reassured him that she was just tired from all the fresh air and exercise. In reality, her mind was full of thoughts of the strange and perplexing absence of the Christmas decorations. Who'd been in to take them down? And why would they bother? What did it matter that there were a few strings of tinsel around the place – it was almost Christmas after all. She hadn't wanted to make the phone call to her father with Seb there, so she'd have to wait until they'd arrived back at the hotel and she was in the solitude of her own room again.

Seb had seemed a little disappointed that she hadn't wanted to top off their day out with a drink in the bar, and though she felt a little kick of something like regret deep inside, her mind was simply too focused on the mystery at her grandmother's house to recognise it.

Ian answered on the third ring.

'Isla!' he greeted. Despite the years of living all over the world, the hints of a once strong Edinburgh accent were still recognisable – and more so whenever he said her name. 'How are you?'

'Fine,' she replied, her tone brusque enough to warn him that she hadn't called for a cosy chat. And though her tone might have been a warning signal to anyone who didn't know her, in reality, Isla was fighting to keep control. She didn't want to believe that there was some sort of conspiracy, some scheme to trip her up. She didn't want to feel like everyone else knew something massive that she didn't. That the willingness to form a new relationship the McCoys had shown since she'd been in St Martin wasn't real. Her tone might have been harsh but it hid the fear of heartache, of a second rejection by her father, that the words of regret he'd spoken to her had meant nothing.

'Fine? It doesn't sound that way to me. What's going on?'

'I could ask you the same thing, Ian. I went to take a look at Serendipity Sound yesterday, as you know, and while I was there with Justin we put some Christmas decorations up.'

'That's nice…'

'So today I went back and they'd been taken down. It just struck me as weird.'

'I don't understand.'

'Who would need to do that?'

'You think I've done it? What would I do that for?'

'That's what I was wondering.'

'Isla, I haven't been anywhere near your grandmother's place – not for weeks now.'

'Then who has?'

'I've no idea.'

'Are you sure?'

'I know my own mind, if that's what you're suggesting,' he said, and his tone had hardened a little. 'I'm not lying either – I've no need to. I haven't been to the house and I certainly don't have time to mess around taking your Christmas decorations down. The place is yours now and if you want tinsel up until July it's got nothing to do with me.'

'Well, could Celine have been in? Or Benet or Natalie?'

'Celine has been with me since yesterday. Benet and Natalie were both working in the shop yesterday and today, and I don't see why they'd go to the trouble of walking all the way to your gran's house to take down some old tinsel. Besides, they don't have keys.'

'But you do.'

'I've told you it wasn't me.'

Isla raked her top teeth across her lip. 'Do you have the keys?'

'You were there yesterday. How do you think you got in? Don't you have them now?'

'No, Justin...' Isla's forehead creased into a deep frown. Justin still had the only set of keys outside Grover Rousseau's office, then. But why in the world would Justin feel the need to go back without her and take down the decorations they'd put up together? She was missing something, and she didn't like the feeling that, in the background, someone was taking her for a mug. Was that someone the seemingly amiable Justin? 'Justin has the keys,' she finished. 'At least he did yesterday.'

'I thought he was leaving them with you when he was done. Want me to call him and have a word?'

'It's OK, I'm seeing him later.'

There was a brief silence at the other end of the line, and Isla could almost imagine the cogs working in Ian's head. 'You're seeing Justin. Again?'

'It wasn't something you'd worked out between yourselves then? You know, like all the other times you asked him to schmooze me into agreeing to this stupid will condition?'

'Isla...' He let out a frustrated sigh. 'Justin offered to be a neutral voice because you wouldn't talk to us and it seemed like a good idea. There was no plan to trap you or manipulate you or anything else. Although, to be honest, there doesn't seem any point in me telling you this because you'll believe what you want to believe regardless of the evidence.'

She guessed that he was tempted to ascribe that particular personality trait to her mother but to his credit he held back.

'I'm sorry,' she said. 'It's early days, you know.'

'I know that. But you need to start trusting me a little if we're going to make this work. I realise that I haven't given you much cause, but I'm trying very hard now. You need to give me some wriggle room if I'm going to make any progress.'

'I know, and I'm trying too. I'm sorry I accused you.'

'Thank you, but I'm not sure what I was being accused of. If you don't mind me saying, your decorations being taken down is hardly the crime of the century. If you couldn't get in how did you discover this?'

'Through the windows.'

'Did it look as if anything else was missing? Furniture or such?'

Isla gazed at the window where the streets were already bathed in dusk. 'I don't think so,' she replied uncertainly. 'You think a burglar would have taken the tinsel as well?'

'I just can't think of an explanation otherwise.'

'Me neither.'

'I can ask Celine but I think she'll say the same as me. Are you sure you didn't just miss them? They could still be up and if you only managed to see a corner of the room through the window you could have not noticed them there.'

'They were definitely missing,' she said. She sat on the bed and began to kick her boots off. 'I don't suppose it matters – it was just weird, that's all.'

'I can only suggest you ask Justin when you see him.'

She was silent for a moment. Was there anything else to say? It didn't look as if Ian knew anything and if he did he wasn't sharing it with her. Something didn't sit right with her still but she didn't know how to tackle it without antagonising him further. And if he was genuine in his desire to fix their relationship she didn't want to jeopardise that.

'Right; I'll do that. Bye, Ian.'

'Before you go,' he cut in as she went to end the call, 'I needed to talk to you anyway and I didn't want to send this by text. About Grover… You know, we have to let him know about the inheritance and what we agreed.'

'Oh, sorry, yes. I'd almost forgotten about that.'

'I'm not sure *what* we have actually agreed, if I'm honest. And I want to make sure we're singing from the same hymn sheet before I call him. So maybe you could come by tomorrow and we can talk more.'

'Come by? To your house?'

'Yes. Or you could come to the hire shop if it makes you feel better? Somewhere a little more public and neutral. I'd completely understand and Celine could hold the fort for a while.'

Isla chewed her lip for a moment. 'Sure,' she said finally. 'I'll come to the shop tomorrow.'

She'd thought about phoning Justin to ask him about Serendipity Sound but she wasn't sure how to frame the question. Neither was she sure how she felt about seeing him for dinner now. Part of her wanted to seek out Seb's opinion, though she couldn't even say why, but her logical inner voice told her not to be so stupid. Even if she wanted to, she couldn't talk to Seb about it, because talking to Seb would mean revealing that she and Justin weren't exactly cousins in the way she'd described to him earlier that day. For reasons she couldn't fathom either, admitting that to Seb mattered even more than getting to the truth.

With one thing or another, it seemed Isla wasn't sure about very much that evening as she got ready to be picked up for dinner, and all she could think to do was stick to the original plan and see how the night panned out. Whether she would find the moment to broach the subject with Justin in person remained to be seen, but there was a small part of her that wondered whether she had been mistaken after all, as Ian had suggested. She could have been, but the more she thought about it, the more she was convinced she was right about what she'd seen in the house.

So, if not Ian, and not Celine or Natalie or Benet, as Ian had asserted, then who? It left only Justin, but why would he have done that when he'd spent so long with her putting them up? And it meant him having to return at some point after he'd seen her back to Residence Alpenrose and before she'd returned to her grandmother's chalet with Seb. Had he banked on her not returning to the house again before she left St Martin? She supposed she probably wouldn't have gone back if not for her trip out with Seb. That still didn't explain why he'd do such a weird thing, though.

At eight Justin sent a text to let her know he was waiting outside. As she stepped onto the pavement she saw him wrapped in a quilted coat and woollen hat. He stamped his feet and blew into his hands as he glanced up and down the street, spinning round to face her at the sound of her voice.

'Sorry to keep you waiting in the cold.'

'That's OK,' he smiled. 'I hope you like fondue.'

'I don't really know,' Isla replied as they began to walk. 'I assume you've booked it already.'

'Yes, but we can change our plans if you don't want to go there. I thought—'

'It's fine. I'll give it a go.'

A pause.

'You are unhappy, I think,' he said.

'What makes you say that?'

'You are the ice queen again – like when we first met. Yesterday I thought we were friends but today you are colder than the depths of Lac Blanc.'

'And I suppose I should be insulted by that colourful simile. Well, I would be if I cared enough. Which I don't.'

'Oh,' he said. 'Would you prefer to go back to your hotel? We do not have to eat dinner tonight.'

'Do you want me to go back to my hotel? Because you were the one who asked me out to dinner but then didn't even bother to find out what I liked before you booked on my behalf.'

'I thought you might like a surprise.'

'I never like surprises. If you'd been paying any attention at all you'd have worked that out. I like predictability and logic. And I like to be asked about things.'

'OK…' he replied slowly. 'Where would you like to go for dinner? Very predictable Italian? Pizza with a side order of safety?'

'If you're going to take the piss then we can call this off right now and I'll go back to my hotel.' Her voice was rising, and perhaps she was being unreasonable, but her doubts about Justin, coupled with her attraction to him, had her emotions tying her common sense in knots. She didn't know whether she wanted to slap him or kiss him.

'I thought that's what you were doing anyway. Don't make idle threats if you cannot act on them.'

'Urgh!' Isla squealed, causing several passers-by to stare. 'I don't know why I ever liked you!'

'That is the same for both of us!' Justin hissed back. 'What's the matter with you tonight? No wonder your father ran away from your mother if you're anything like her!'

Isla halted and stared at him, her nostrils flared and rage in her heart. 'How *dare* you even mention my mother! You don't get to talk about her, not in any context at any time. You know nothing about her, or me for that matter!'

'I know she was crazy! I know she drove your father crazy too! He had to run before he was driven to suicide!'

'That's not true!' Isla cried, fighting back tears. She wasn't even crying because he'd hurt her, but because in her heart she knew that some of what he'd said was true. Her mother had never been an easy woman to live with, even for her daughter, and she could only imagine what she'd been like as a wife. But she loved Glory despite her flaws, and more painful than anything else was admitting to herself just what sort of woman had brought her into the world – far from perfect and far from selfless. Isla wanted to ignore those aspects of Glory's personality but it had become harder as the years had gone by and Isla had grown to see her through the eyes of an adult rather than a child.

But then the tears came, and there was nothing she could do to stop them. Rubbing a gloved hand beneath her eyes, she spun on her heel, almost losing her balance on the ridges of ice coating the pavement, and turned to walk back the way they'd come.

'Where are you going?' Justin called after her.

'Where do you think? You told me to go back to my hotel you pig, so that's where I'm going!'

Her step quickened and she became vaguely aware of his echoing on the street behind her as he followed.

'We have not finished!' he shouted.

'We're *so* finished.' Isla walked faster still, head down.

'I'm sorry!'

'You sound it. Tell it to someone who believes your bullshit.'

'Isla… wait!' His hand was on her arm and he pulled her to face him. 'I mean it, OK? I'm sorry; I shouldn't have said what I did but you do strange things to me, you…'

There was a second of charged silence. And then he pushed her against a nearby wall and kissed her hard. Shock and anger turned to fierce desire as an explosion of conflicting sensations coursed through her. All at once she was appalled and enraged, but the electricity of those feelings sent sparks through her entire body. She wanted to push him off and yet she wanted him more than she could understand. This was a man she could barely trust but she couldn't deny the force of their attraction. It couldn't go anywhere, could it? If she were thinking straight she wouldn't even want it to go anywhere. But she wasn't thinking straight.

He pulled away and leaned his forehead against hers, his breathing harsh, still pulling her desperately close so she could feel the heat of him, even through their jackets. 'You're so hot when you're angry,' he said. 'I want you. I want to make love to you so much I'm going to explode.'

She was silent, her hold on his gaze almost a challenge, desperate not to melt in it.

'Won't you say something?' he asked.

'I think you should get off me,' she said quietly.

He shook his head slightly. 'I cannot do that because I know you want this too. You can lie but your body does not.'

And then he pressed into her and their mouths met again, all her logic and predictability captive in the molten lust of his touch. She needed to walk away from this before it got out of hand, but she was powerless.

'Please…' she whispered between his hot, urgent kisses. 'Please don't…'

And yet her words that came out like a sigh only seemed to spur him on. Now his hands were beneath her coat, travelling the length of her body and stirring her to desperate new heights of need.

'No…' she murmured. 'Justin, stop…'

'Let's go back to your room,' he said, kissing her again. 'I am so mad with desire I must have you…'

And something clicked into place. Pushing him away, she side-stepped out of his reach. 'No. This is not happening.'

Rather than anger at her refusal, he threw her a sardonic smile. 'Do you think either of us can stop it?'

'You think I'm not strong enough?'

'That is exactly what I think.'

'You caught me off guard and you know I find you attractive. But…'

'What?'

'I don't know what I think about you but I do know this is all too fast. If you had any respect for me you'd slow it down.'

'You are looking for love? Marriage?'

'I'm not looking for a one night stand, and if you thought that you're sadly mistaken. I might look vulnerable and in need of a friend, but I'm not.'

'I never said that.'

'But you thought it. Perfect situation to get a desperation shag, right?'

'There is no need to complicate things. You want me and I want you – why do we need anything else? Passion is life and everything else is unnecessary.'

Isla wrapped her arms around herself and stepped away as he made another move towards her. 'Justin – why did you go back to Serendipity Sound yesterday and take down all the Christmas decorations?'

The mocking, patronising smile slipped from his face. 'I don't know what you mean,' he replied, but it wasn't quick enough and Isla knew he knew something about it.

'I went there. Today. I just wanted another look. I couldn't get in, of course, because besides Grover Rousseau you have the only keys, so I looked through the windows and you know what I saw?'

He shook his head slightly.

'I saw a perfectly tinsel-free room. How do you explain that? More to the point, why would that happen?'

'I thought I would tidy it for you.'

'So you went back? And you tidied it out of the goodness of your heart? Wow, you must really have wanted sex, though it's an unusual seduction technique by most standards. I'm not bothered that you went back because you had some weird compulsion to tidy some old tinsel away, but I don't know why you just felt the need to keep it from me and then lie when I asked.' She stared at him for a moment more, and then shook her head. 'You know what, it's not even worth the hassle. Forget dinner, I'll ask Dahlia to fix me a sandwich.'

She turned and began to walk.

'I was wrong!' he called. 'Isla! Come back and let's talk!'

But she didn't stop and he didn't follow.

Chapter Twelve

Isla paced the room as she waited for her mum to pick up the phone. She didn't even know what she was going to say to her. Above all else, she was angry with herself for letting Justin get to her – both with his jibes and with his damn sexual magnetism. She didn't need that jumped-up little shit to tell her what sort of woman her mother was, but that didn't mean she couldn't love her just the same. Glory was difficult and stubborn and prone to passionate outbursts, fierce in love and even fiercer when you crossed her. But what if all the years of her demonising Isla's father had coloured her view? What if, far from being the perpetrator of the hurt, he'd been a genuine victim of it? What if he really hadn't been the bad guy? Her mother had blamed her father for just about everything that had ever gone wrong in their lives, but was that fair? Who was Isla supposed to believe? She couldn't believe her mother was the villain of the piece, even if she now doubted her father's guilt. Marriages ended all the time and sometimes it was just nobody's fault. Isla wanted to believe that of her parents' marriage. Right now, she didn't know what to think.

'Finally she decides to phone me,' Glory said in prim tones as she answered. 'I'd almost forgotten I had a daughter. I suppose you're having such a wonderful time with *him* that you'd almost forgotten you had a mother.'

'It's been a bit busy. I've been out and about, taking in the scenery, you know… I probably won't ever get the chance to come back here. And the phone signal has been pretty bad,' she added. Not quite the truth but easier than admitting that she just hadn't felt like talking to her.

'They don't have landlines in France?'

'I suppose so, I just never seem to catch the hotel owner to ask.'

Glory gave a sharp click of her tongue. 'So, you're coming home tomorrow?'

'The day after.'

'Your aunts have arrived for Christmas with your cousins. They're helping me to get the house ready.'

A deliberate dig designed to make Isla feel guilty for not being there. She wouldn't rise to it, not when so much else needed her attention. 'That's nice. It'll be good to catch up with them when I get home.'

Silent tears began as she sat on the bed. Why did life have to be so complicated? Why did she have to feel so disloyal for giving her father a chance? Why couldn't she have normal parents like other people had? Covering the phone, she sniffed hard and dried her tears.

'Are you OK, though, Mum?' she asked in a gap between sobs.

'I'm always OK,' Glory said. 'I've always had to be.' There was a pause. 'What's his new wife like?'

'Ian's? She seems nice enough. She's hardly new, though, they have two grown-up kids.'

'You know what I mean. Have you seen a lot of them?'

'Not particularly,' Isla said, which was the truth. Considering how long she'd been in St Martin-de-Belleville she hadn't really seen much of them at all.

'But you're all happy families now I suppose?'

'We're getting along, if that's what you mean. But we have to – it's a condition of Grandma Sarah's will.'

'For what? What has she left to you?'

'A house.'

There was silence at the other end of the phone.

'Mum?'

'A house?' Glory repeated in a husky voice. 'Are you serious? You inherited a house and this is the first you're telling me?'

'It didn't seem that important.'

'It's a house!' Glory cried, and Isla could hear the blind panic in her voice. 'Does this mean you're staying in France?'

'Of course not.'

'Then what is the point in having a house there? Tell them you don't want it!'

'I did, but Ian and Celine can't get their inheritance if I don't accept mine – it's a condition of the will.'

'What does that matter to you? It's their problem, not yours! You owe that man nothing!'

'I know, but that doesn't mean I shouldn't help. What's the point in us all losing out?'

'Why do you care what happens to him? He's got to you – I knew he would!'

'Mum, nobody has *got to me*! You sound hysterical and you need to calm down.'

'Is this how you repay all the years I spent alone raising you? Telling me I'm hysterical like I'm the bad person! What has he said about me? I suppose he's told you I was awful, how cruel and mean I was—'

'No, as a matter of fact he's been very diplomatic—'

'Diplomatic! This can't be the same man I was married to!'

Isla pinched the bridge of her nose as she held the phone away from her ear and looked at it. Glory was still yammering away at the other end of the line. She could press a button and end this call. If she'd hoped to get comfort from hearing her mum's voice, it looked as though she was going to be disappointed.

'Mum…' Isla took a deep breath. 'I love you and you know that. I'm not going to move to France but I'm not going to give up my inheritance or my new relationship with Dad.'

Dad. She hadn't yet felt right calling him that but somehow, as she said it, it sounded perfectly natural for the first time since she'd arrived here. And then another realisation hit her. She liked him. A lot. She couldn't say she loved him yet like she loved her mother, but she liked him and right now that was easier to deal with, because love and like were sometimes very different things.

'But all those years! Don't they mean anything to you?'

'You were as responsible for the rift as he was and don't try to deny it because there's no point.'

'That's what he's been saying?'

'Actually, no. He had more dignity than to blame you for everything. But I know about the letters you refused to give me and the phone calls you wouldn't allow me to take. I know it all, Mum, and I forgive you, but you have to let me forgive him too. I need some balance in my life and this is the way I can finally get it.'

Glory was silent again.

'You're sulking now?' Isla said. 'I'm a bad, ungrateful daughter, I know. Just let me do this and I promise I'll be home and all yours again in a couple of days, OK?'

'I miss you,' Glory said, her voice cracking. Isla couldn't remember the last time she'd heard that sort of emotion in it.

'I know you do. And I miss you too. I'll be back before you know it and we can talk things over properly.'

'I hope so.'

'You don't need to hope because it's happening. A couple more days, OK? You've got a houseful of sisters so I'm sure you can keep yourself busy until I get back.'

'Of course. I can't help worrying.'

'I know. I love you, Mum.'

'I love you too. You're the most important person in the world to me and...'

Isla didn't need her to say it. Glory was terrified of losing her daughter, even though she knew she couldn't have that little girl forever and hadn't really had her for a long time now. But what she couldn't seem to understand was that she didn't need little girl Isla any more when she had a grown woman who would love and support her no matter what she did. Isla might have known what sort of woman her mum was, but she was her mum nonetheless and she always would be.

Half an hour had passed since she'd ended the call to her mum and now that she'd worked through that part of her emotional turmoil, she found herself wholly absorbed by thoughts of Justin. Regret and shame filled her heart as she relived their encounter that evening. She'd been weak and pathetic and she was angry with herself more than him for what had happened between them. The signs had been there but she'd chosen to ignore them, dazzled by his charm and good looks, that delicious accent. Had she been so desperate for the hand of friendship and mediation he'd offered? Did her dad know what he was capable of? He'd certainly sounded surprised by the news that they were meant to go out for dinner together that night, so perhaps he didn't. At least, she wanted to believe that he didn't.

Dialling Dodie's number, she chewed on a thumbnail as she waited for her friend to answer. But it rang out and she hung up. She needed to talk to someone, even if it was about something and nothing to take her mind off things. Someone she could trust not to judge her. Someone who was a friend.

Putting the phone to one side, she pulled on her boots and cardigan and snatched up the keys to her room. She was halfway down the corridor to Seb's room when she stopped. What would she say? What if he was busy? Would it seem like she was intruding on his privacy, turning up unannounced at his door? Then he wouldn't be able to turn her away even if he wanted to, and he'd be too nice to do that anyway no matter how much of an inconvenience she was. Not only that but in a tiny corner of her mind she was afraid she couldn't trust herself, not after her disastrous encounter with Justin. Hadn't there been a moment with Seb too, back on the lake? She'd tried to deny it but now, with distance and reflection, she had to recognise it for what it was. Seb was a world away from Justin, of course, but still…

She turned on her heel and made her way back to her own room. Whatever troublesome thoughts were running amok in her mind right now, it looked as if she'd have to round them up and deal with them on her own.

The combination of emotional overload and clean mountain air had knocked her spark out, just when she'd least expected it. Returning to her room, she'd collapsed onto the bed and nodded off, on top of the covers and still in full make-up.

She awoke the next day to find Justin had left a raft of missed calls and text messages on her phone. In every message, a thinly disguised attempt at blame dressed up as an apology. Like how she drove him crazy because she was so unobtainable, like a prize he just had to win, how her beauty and self-sufficiency made him act in ways that were not like his usual self, how she got under his skin and made him lose control. Nobody had that much power over someone else, Isla reflected, and if he couldn't show any self-restraint then what was the next step? She didn't want to find out. Though the messages were meant to win her over, they were having the opposite effect; she didn't want to spend time alone with a man who had no self-control in her presence. She decided not to reply.

Still groggy from her deep sleep, she splashed some water on her face to wake herself, put on some fresh clothes and headed to the breakfast room. She had an appointment to keep but couldn't help but feel disappointed not to see Seb there before she left. A quick look out of the window at snow falling thick and fast told her that he wouldn't have gone far if he was out studying. At least she hoped he wouldn't have because, although it was pretty, it didn't look very safe to be driving around in, especially up to a glacier.

'The weather's set to move in,' Ian said as she stamped the snow from her boots at the doorway of his sports hire shop. He was behind the counter with Celine at his side. Her two half-siblings, for the first time, were nowhere to be seen.

'You might want to check on the flights,' he added. 'We've got a blizzard on the way and you may find yours is delayed.'

'I'm sure it'll be fine,' Isla replied a bit shortly, but then she looked again and saw genuine concern in his expression. 'I'll check online when I get back, don't worry,' she said, softening her tone. 'Mum will kill me if I don't make it home for Christmas, though. I'm not sure if I'd rather risk flying in a blizzard.'

To her surprise, he chuckled warmly at her flippant comment. 'I think I'd have to agree with you on that. Subtlety was never her strong point.' He glanced briefly at Celine and then at Isla again. 'How are you planning on getting back to the airport?'

'Same way I got here,' Isla replied. 'On the bus.'

'I could drive you, if you liked.'

Celine looked at him sharply now and Isla couldn't help an inward smile, guessing this had not been in the script.

'Maybe. I'll let you know, thanks.'

'Don't mention it. And it has nothing to do with... you know, this...'

Isla raised her eyebrows. 'I never thought for a minute it had. But thanks for clearing that up.'

Ian gave a rueful smile, and in it Isla suddenly saw every moment of regret he must have had over the last twenty-four years. It took all her strength not to lean across the counter and hug him, but now didn't seem like the time. Perhaps it was already too late for it ever to be the time. Perhaps this progress, here and now, was the best they could ever hope for. Celine looked up with a forced smile as a party of skiers arrived with equipment to return.

'It might be quieter in the back,' Ian said, beckoning Isla to follow him to a private office behind the main shop.

Closing the door behind them, Ian bade Isla sit in a battered old armchair while he pulled up a spare seat across from her.

'Coffee?' he asked. 'Tea?'

'I'm fine.'

'Are ye though?' he asked. Isla couldn't help but smile at the lapse into his native accent. She'd never heard it that plainly before. 'Because I can't help feeling there's still a lot of hurt in there. And I'd understand why.'

'It's not easy,' Isla admitted. 'I don't know what happened between you and Mum, and maybe I don't want to know. All I know is that she was around for me and you weren't. Is it any wonder I'm having a hard time trusting you? I don't want to be this way but I can't help it. I'm rude and snappy and I don't like those qualities about myself any more than you do, but it's the only way I know how to be. It's a defence mechanism, you know? So I can't get hurt.'

Isla was almost taken aback to hear herself say it, as if somehow a sudden epiphany had gripped her, one she hadn't seen coming at all. But he simply gave her a patient smile.

'You're not rude or snappy. You're confused and hurting, and you've every right to be. If you're nasty that's my fault.' He was silent for a moment, searching her face. But then he got up and went to a cupboard. 'Do you mind if I show you something? I brought these here today from home, not knowing whether the time was right to share them with you. In fact, I wondered if the time would ever be right. But maybe it will help you make sense of the past.'

Isla nodded, uncertain of what it was he was about to reveal and even less certain that she wanted to know. But it was plain to her that his question had been a rhetorical one and he needed to do this as much as he thought she needed to see it, whatever it was. He turned back to her, holding a bundle of paper secured with a rubber band, and sat down again. Without a word he handed it to her. Isla unfastened it and found envelopes. Some had Glory's name on the front, some had her own. All of them had previous addresses from flats and apartments where she'd lived with her mum over the years. But none they'd lived at during the last decade. On each of them Glory's handwriting was scrawled across in red pen – RETURN TO SENDER. She looked up at Ian with a silent question.

'Birthday cards, Christmas cards, the odd letter,' he said. 'Most of them have money in too, though some of the notes are probably not legal tender any more. Maybe if Glory had opened them she could have done something with the bits that were inside. You've never seen any of these, I take it?'

'No.'

'They're all for you. If you choose not to open them I'll understand. But I just wanted you to know that I didn't forget you in the way it may have seemed. I gave up, and for that I'm truly sorry, but I honestly thought it was for the best.'

'Mum can be quite persuasive like that.' Isla clutched the pile of letters in her hand, gazing at the loops and swirls of his handwriting and the harsh lines of Glory's over-scoring it.

'I'm glad you said it and not me. I didn't want to show you any of this when you first arrived because I didn't want to make it look like I was laying blame. I know you love your mother and I know she did a cracking job of raising you by herself – I can see that just sitting with you now – and I guessed insulting her or laying blame by showing you these letters at our first meeting wasn't going to do me any favours trying to win your trust. But I think we're past that now. At least I hope we are. '

'Honestly, it was probably a wise move.' Isla smiled. 'So, these are mine now?'

'All yours.'

'Do you want me to open them?'

'Do what you want with them. Keep them, burn them, I don't need to know.'

'I wouldn't burn them.'

'I wouldn't blame you if you did.'

He looked at her, hopeful and yet hopeless all at the same time. She wanted to hug him, to tell him that everything was good and they were on the right track at last, but she couldn't. She wasn't there, not quite yet, but she could see a day when she might be and that was progress enough.

'I don't suppose you'd like to grab some lunch with us before you head back to your hotel?' Ian looked hopefully at Isla as she shrugged her coat on and they emerged into the main shop again.

'I'd love to but I think I ought to get packed for the flight back tomorrow.' Things had changed between her and her father, as the bundle of letters in her handbag would testify, but she needed time to process all that she'd learned that day before she felt ready to see them all again.

'Dinner then? Later?' He glanced at Celine, who was now in charge of an empty store again.

'I'd be happy to cook an extra portion at our place,' she offered. 'If you didn't feel like eating out. It would be an opportunity to see our home, get to know Benet and Natalie a little better before you go back to England.'

'It's very kind of you but I would really rather get sorted for tomorrow,' Isla replied, wondering if the offer was just lip service, given to show Ian that she was making an effort to get to know the stepdaughter she would probably feel happier about once she'd waved her back to England. 'Maybe we could do it when I come back? Whenever that is, of course. But when we have more time.'

Celine inclined her head, clearly a little relieved, though Ian looked disappointed. But then he nodded too.

'OK,' he said. 'But let me take you to the airport tomorrow. I'd feel happier knowing you'd got there safely.'

'I'm sure the bus is equipped for snow,' Isla said.

'It will be, but if for some reason you get stuck at the airport, at least I'd be there to help you out rather than you managing alone.'

'I've been managing alone for—' Isla shook her head and forced a smile. It seemed, despite her intentions, that forgetting the past didn't come so easily after all. 'I'm sure I'll be just fine and it seems pointless dragging you all the way to Grenoble when you might be unable to get back.'

'I've got plenty of experience driving in snow,' Ian said. 'I'm sure I'd work it out. Please…'

Isla paused, and then let out a sigh. 'Alright then. A lift to the airport would be great, as long as it's not putting you out.'

Ian looked at Celine. 'I can't imagine the shop will be all that busy with snowstorms moving in so you'd be able to spare me, wouldn't you? If you're busy, ask Benet to help; he could do a bit of work around the place for once.'

Isla's forehead creased slightly. It was a throwaway comment, but you didn't spend your whole life preternaturally attuned to unspoken sentiments and feelings without noticing the subtle hint that perhaps brother Benet wasn't quite the model son Isla had at first been led to believe he was.

'I'm sure we'll be fine,' Celine said stiffly. Isla almost felt sorry for her; it can't have been easy having her here like this.

'That's settled then,' Ian said, turning to Isla with forced cheeriness. 'I'll come by for you tomorrow.' He made a move towards her but then stopped and retreated again. Instead of the hug she felt he might have been working up the courage for, he gave a weak smile. 'Be careful going back to the hotel, won't you?'

Isla nodded. 'Don't worry – careful is my middle name. It probably explains why my life is so boring.'

Chapter Thirteen

There was something magical about the snow as Isla walked back to Residence Alpenrose. It represented trouble, but the steady silent fall, the muffling of the village as it built by degrees on the kerbs, eaves and windowsills of the streets like icing on a Christmas cake seemed to soothe her troubled soul. The skies were beginning to darken, muted tones over the distant peaks, the warm glows of shop and restaurant doorways enticing in the cold, snatches of Christmas music reminding Isla that it was close. When the winding lanes and roads looked so beautiful, how could anything be wrong in the world? After all, it snowed all the time in the Alps in the winter, didn't it? And airlines still managed to operate so it stood to reason that even if she experienced a slight delay she would still make it home for Christmas Eve.

Dahlia was polishing the counter in reception as Isla knocked the snow from her boots at the entrance. Isla was beginning to notice that Dahlia polished *a lot*. In fact, she was always on the go. Did that woman ever stop to breathe?

'How did your meeting go?' Dahlia asked, looking up from her task with a bright smile. Despite her intention, Isla had still never fully confided just what her toing and froing was all about. Dahlia must have been curious though. Isla had the opportunity to tell her now but suddenly she didn't feel able to share it. That other part of her – the bigger, guarded, fiercely independent side of her – was happier keeping it in and dealing with it herself.

'It was OK, thanks.'

'Snow's getting worse,' Dahlia added, turning back to her vigorous rubbing of the wooden counter. 'Did you check your flight?'

'Not yet; I'll do it when I get upstairs.'

'Wi-Fi is in and out,' Dahlia said. 'Weather's affecting it, I think. But you can always call the airport from the phone down here if you're struggling to get online.'

'I don't suppose they'll know about delays today really,' Isla said. 'I mean, a lot could happen between today and tomorrow so they wouldn't be able to tell this early.'

'They might have an idea. They have special weather reports for that sort of thing.'

Isla wasn't convinced but she didn't say so. Surely there was no need to worry about it until the following morning. And although it was snowing heavily now it was hardly a blizzard.

'Your room is booked after you leave us tomorrow. Couple from Spain. They're due to arrive as you leave and that's all my rooms occupied over Christmas.' Dahlia looked up from her task and Isla replied with a silent question. 'I'm just thinking if you need to come back here if the flight is delayed I won't have a room, but I could call some of my buddies to see if they have anything if I have some warning. If not they might let their spares go too.'

'I'm sure it'll be fine,' Isla said. It was just like Dahlia to want to ensure everyone was happy and safe, which was probably what made her such a fabulous hotelier.

Dahlia nodded shortly. 'You want anything in the bar?'

'A coffee to go up to my room might be nice,' Isla said.

'Sure thing,' Dahlia said, putting her duster to one side. 'Come on through and I'll fix one up. In fact,' she added with a grin, 'as it's nearly Christmas, how about you try my new eggnog recipe? I've been waiting for a willing victim and I think you might just be perfect.'

Isla laughed, her spirit instantly lifted by Dahlia's good nature and gentle humour. 'Eggnog sounds amazing and I'm more than willing to sacrifice myself for the greater good!'

'I don't suppose you saw Seb this morning?' Isla asked as Dahlia prepared her drink, watching with some fascination as she threw ingredients together that should have tasted disgusting but would undoubtedly be full of sticky, seasonal goodness, a glorious, rich combination of nutmeg, vanilla and bourbon spicing the air. 'I noticed he wasn't at breakfast. I mean, I know he might have come down early, but it doesn't seem like very good weather to go heading off for glacier study today so I wondered…'

'Seb?' Dahlia frowned. 'Oh, Sebastian? I haven't seen him, honey. Some days he doesn't even bother with breakfast – he just heads out, but I doubt he's dumb enough to go up to the mountains today. Sometimes he works in his room – that's why he likes the suite when he can get it – and he gets room service when he wants to eat. Come to think of it, he hasn't ordered room service today at all.'

'You think he's OK? He might be ill in bed and nobody would know. You think we ought to check on him?'

'You could knock on his door when you pass through, I guess.' Dahlia placed Isla's mug on the bar. 'Put your mind at ease.'

'Oh, I'm not worried,' Isla said quickly. 'I just thought it was the neighbourly thing to do. I mean, I'm here alone and I'd like to think if I was in trouble someone might notice and come to my aid.'

Dahlia gave her a half-smile and Isla didn't know whether to laugh or feel annoyed at the knowing look on her face. 'Would you like me to phone his room?'

Isla shook her head. 'I'm sure he's fine. Probably went out – I suppose he's a grown man and it's not like he needs to tell anyone what his plans are.'

'I'm sure he'd be happy to hear that you were worried about him.'

'No, it would sound silly and neurotic. Probably better not to mention it.'

'Whatever you like. You want a table for dinner tonight?'

Isla glanced at the window where the snow was soft and relentless as it covered the street. 'Might be a good idea.'

'What time?'

'Seven, I think.'

'Perfect. I'll save you a spot.'

Isla half expected some quip about reserving a table for two in case she decided to seek Seb out after all and she was ready to answer it. But Dahlia said nothing, she just gave a benign smile and made her way over to the reservations book at the back of the bar. With nothing more to say on the subject herself, Isla took her eggnog and headed up to her room.

At Seb's door she hesitated for a moment. It was tempting to put her ear to the wood and listen, but if he was in there and came out unexpectedly that might be a bit embarrassing for both of them. Or, if he'd been out and arriving back caught her snooping, equally awkward to explain. So she stood for a moment, cup clutched in her hand, wavering as she glanced up and down the corridor, sweating under the bulk of the coat she had yet to remove. Then, with one last look and an impatient sigh, she carried on to her own room. If she didn't see him at dinner later, then perhaps she'd give him a knock. Just to see if he was OK – nothing else.

She made her way down the hallway to her own room, and just as she turned the key in the lock, her phone pinged the arrival of a text message. She thought perhaps Justin had given up, but shedding her coat and dumping her coffee on the bedside table, she perched on the edge of her bed and read:

Please talk to me. I would hate us to part as enemies.

Isla gazed at the screen for a moment. She'd liked and trusted Justin at first, hadn't she? Should she give him another chance? She was beginning to feel she'd been very wrong about her dad, so perhaps Justin, too, was as truly sorry as he kept saying he was. But she didn't know what to say in reply to his message. She didn't want them to part on bad terms, but she didn't want to talk to him either. Putting the phone to one side, she wrapped her hands around her cup and turned her gaze to the window. Dodie had messaged her to say they'd had a little snow in Bournemouth, but she bet the snow back home wasn't nearly as dramatic as this. Maybe Dahlia had a point about checking the flights. Grabbing her phone again, she tried to connect to the Wi-Fi but, as Dahlia had warned her, the connection was patchy at best. Every time she attempted to get on the airline's website the little circle whirled round and round in aimless perpetuity and then crashed. With a sigh, Isla put the phone down again.

*

An hour later Isla looked out of the window again. She'd almost finished her packing, apart from what she needed to tide her over until she left the next day. The letters her dad had given her, unopened still, were tucked into her suitcase. Simply diving in and reading them was not an option – she needed to wait, to get a little distance from St Martin.

Isla was desperate to question Glory about why she'd chosen to send them all back to Ian and never tell her a thing about them. But that was a conversation for after Christmas at least, because this felt like the last Christmas when everything would be just the way she'd always known it. Then again, perhaps it was too late for that. Perhaps this Christmas was already altered beyond recognition – perhaps everything had changed the moment Isla had decided to come to St Martin, and perhaps now there was no turning back.

The snow, while still steady, seemed lighter now. It was early afternoon and the skies were already darkening, though the streets were well lit. It seemed a shame to waste her last few hours in St Martin stuck in her room. She had boots and a good coat and it wasn't as if she'd go far wrong if she stayed on the main roads and streets.

Rushing from the window, she pulled on her outdoor clothes, grabbed her room keys and the dirty cup to return to Dahlia and headed downstairs. If she went out now, she'd be back in plenty of time for dinner at seven. Once more she paused outside Seb's door, and once more she went on her way without knocking. If he'd wanted her company he would have sought it out and if he was working then the last thing he needed was hassle. She'd look for him at dinner as she'd planned, and if he still didn't show then she would have every right to worry about where he was.

'Thank you,' she said as she swung by the bar to hand Dahlia the cup. She looked up from the dinner reservation book and raised her eyebrows as she clocked Isla in her coat.

'Going out?'

'I thought I might as well. It's my last day and I want to make the most of it.'

Dahlia glanced at the windows. 'You'll be careful not to go too far, won't you?'

'I'm sure it'll be fine. I thought I might just wander, perhaps get a closer look at the mountains. I mean, I won't go up there, of course, just get a bit closer, maybe take some photos to show the folks back home.'

'It looks tame now, but the weather can turn in a heartbeat. It's hard to imagine if you're not used to the climate here.'

'I know. And I will be careful, I promise.' Isla turned to leave and raised a hand. 'I'll see you at seven!'

Her foray out into the mountains with Seb had given her an appetite to see more. If she'd had more time and better conditions, Isla would have liked to visit a lot more of the romantic-sounding resorts that rubbed shoulders with St Martin-de-Belleville: Chamonix, Méribel, Les Menuires, Val Thorens, Orelle – names she'd seen during her search for a hotel and had ignored, failing to understand the spell that this region of the Alps would cast on her. Now that she'd seen it for herself it was impossible to be anything but spellbound; she got tingles just thinking about the beauty of Mont Blanc and the lake that shared its name.

After her meeting with Ian that morning, when she'd eventually agreed to visit as regularly as she could to maintain the new relationship, she'd started to think that perhaps the notion of coming over to St Martin more often wasn't just about agreeing to the conditions imposed by Grandma Sarah's will. How she'd get the money for air fares was another problem, but she would already have a house to use when she did come and a ready itinerary of places she was desperate to explore.

In winter it looked spectacular, but Dahlia had told her stories of St Martin in the summer too, where the ski runs became lush pastures and the sun was hot and the quaint little church that formed the heartbeat of the village staged concerts that sent music ringing out across the valleys. Isla had decided she'd like to see chamois and wild sheep ambling across the hillsides, to take the roads out to the Péclet glacier or scale the nearby peaks and look down on the towns below. She'd hike in the day and drink wine on the veranda of Serendipity Sound in the evening as the sun set and the fireflies began to bustle in the long grass. She'd have no company but her own, and she'd love it. It was strange – a week ago she couldn't have thought of anything she'd rather do less than hiking in the wilderness, not a shop or bar or café in sight.

Pulling up her collar to keep out the cold, she picked up the pace, soft fresh snow yielding easily beneath her feet with that satisfying creak of a path not yet trodden. Snatches of heat and music rolled out into the frosty air from briefly opened doorways, the sounds and smells of packed restaurants and bars as people sought respite from the cold and to share a few hours of good company. But for Isla right now, the best company was her own, and although these bright, wood-smoke interiors were tempting, she was happy to go on her own way and leave the hikers, the après-ski crowds and the snowboarders to their revelling. She just wanted to feel small, to feel lost but not alone in a universe that was so much bigger than her, to lose sight of all the petty struggles that bothered her in the small hours of the morning.

At heart, she'd always considered herself a city girl, tied to civilisation and the modern comforts she barely gave a second thought to, but the Alps were changing her in a way she had never expected and could never have dreamed of. St Martin had crept up and burrowed into her soul, and now she realised that she could never forsake it.

In her jeans pocket she felt her phone vibrate. There was nobody she felt a burning desire to talk to right now. If it was Justin, she still hadn't decided what to say to him, and if it was anyone else they'd call back. Anyway, she wasn't going to be able to reach for it without taking off her huge cosy gloves so the decision was made for her. She ignored it.

Half an hour saw her at the town boundaries. For such a vibrant community it was sometimes easy to forget that it was actually a very small place. The buildings suddenly stopped and the horizon was lost in darkness, the mountains and forests shadows against the indigo sky. Isla halted and took a deep breath. It was possible that this was the furthest she'd ever really been from civilisation in her whole life – at least alone. She stepped forward, another inch from the twinkling lights of the town behind her. Then again, and before she knew it she was walking – away from the avenue. If she could face this then perhaps she could face anything and it made her want to try harder, to test herself, to see how much uncertainty she could take before she caved in and ran back to the safety of St Martin. If she could do this then perhaps she could go home a little braver, be able to deal with the inevitable onslaught from her mum, with the mistrust she still felt for her dad, the resentment she still felt towards Celine, Benet and Natalie though she desperately fought it. Perhaps this was the moment she finally took control of her life, and it started, here and now, with a walk into the dark.

She walked slowly, one uncertain step after another, scared but feeling more alive than she'd ever felt before. Ten minutes later she halted on the road. It seemed to be getting colder, though that hardly seemed possible, and the darkness now pressed in as the lights of the town faded behind her.

'Maybe that's enough bravery for one night,' she muttered, with a small smile at her lips. It may have only been small steps, but her journey had begun.

Justin was waiting outside the hotel. Isla knew his silhouette so well already there was no mistaking the figure propped up against the wall. Faltering, she stood and stared, momentarily thrown. While she had expected a few more text messages, maybe even a phone call or two, she hadn't imagined for a moment he'd turn up at Residence Alpenrose. She had to hand it to him, he had balls for daring to after the way they'd parted the day before. He was motionless, staring up into the sky, his breath curling into the night as the sodium yellow of a streetlight washed over him. He turned and saw her. Too late to duck behind a building and wait for him to go, Isla knew there was nothing else for it; she straightened her back, jutted out her chin and marched over.

'I suppose you've come to see me,' she said.

'Isla, I need a minute to explain—'

She held up a hand and then gave a brisk nod. 'OK. And then you go.'

He scratched his head and threw her a look that bordered on reproach. As if she was the one being unreasonable… but it faded fast and he took a deep breath and smoothed his features. 'We parted badly last night…'

'You don't say.'

'But I thought it was what you wanted. I mean, you were so…'

'I didn't have a lot of choice considering you launched yourself at me.'

'You did not fight me away.'

'You weren't exactly giving me a chance to fight. You took me by surprise and I'll admit that up until that point I fancied you. It doesn't make what you did right, though.'

'You want me, and I'm not wrong about that.'

Isla sighed. 'You're not wrong, but the way you went about things was wrong. If there was an attraction then you've killed it now.'

He was silent for a moment, his gaze cast to the ground, and Isla almost felt sorry for him. Almost. But if his behaviour last night, and his refusal to accept any blame since, were anything to go by, this was a relationship that would be filled with poison from the start. If he could adopt this tone now, what would he be like if they got closer?

Looking up at her he forced a bleak smile. 'Can we start again? Pretend we have never met and try to get it right?'

Isla shook her head. 'I've seen the real you and I don't think I like it much.'

'That's not the real me. That Justin is driven mad with desire, but I'm not like that. If you give me time I can show you.'

'Does desiring something give you the right to reach out and take it?'

'Of course not – you do not understand what I am saying.'

'Then what are you saying? Justin…' She paused. 'You can't even tell me the truth about Grandma Sarah's holiday home.'

'I told you what happened. What's wrong with you? Why do you always have to be so suspicious? Why can't you believe the truth?'

'I don't know, but I just know when something isn't right.'

'You're crazy.'

'Maybe, but it doesn't change the way I feel about you. I don't see a way forward for a relationship and it doesn't even matter because I'm going home tomorrow. What were you even expecting coming here tonight? To get a second crack at seducing me? To get me into bed tonight? I'm not a prize to be won and I don't do one night stands – not with anyone, ever.'

'We could see each other again. You will come back to St Martin?'

'I might, but it wouldn't be to see you. Go home, Justin. Go back to the girlfriend you probably have tucked away somewhere. '

She turned to the hotel doorway and he grabbed her arm, spinning her back to face him.

'You're wrong – there's no girlfriend in St Martin, I swear. Isla, I'll admit one thing – OK? I'll admit that I never meant to fall for you and the plan was always to help get our inheritance. I'll admit that Celine promised me a share if I could help to secure it. But when I met you, all that changed.'

Isla's eyes narrowed. '*Celine* put you up to this?'

'Not exactly. She was not cruel, only desperate. They are not as rich as they look and they need the money to keep the business running. It was less of a plan, more an understanding that perhaps I could influence things.'

'Does Ian know about any of this?'

'He knew that I was trying to make you see sense. But this you know; I never made a secret of it.'

'And the charm offensive that led to you lunging at me last night? Did my father know about that?'

Justin's mouth twisted into a grimace. 'Of course not! He would be horrified!'

'Unlike Celine.'

He threw her a withering glance that told Isla exactly what he was thinking. She'd been perfectly sweet and courteous, but in reality why would Celine have any reason to care about Isla? Ian's other daughter was nothing but an inconvenience, a reminder of a past he'd had long before they'd met and a threat to her own family stability. They were silent for a moment and then Isla recalled the feeling of his hand still gripped around her bicep. Even as she looked down at it with a silent signal to let go, she heard a familiar voice from the doorway of the hotel and her insides were suddenly colder than the air of the street they stood on.

'Isla! Is everything OK?'

She turned to see Seb on the hotel steps, his face a mask of concern.

'Seb…' she replied weakly. 'I'm fine, I just…'

'Who's this?' Justin asked, inclining his head at Seb.

'I'm the person who's wondering why you're grabbing her arm in such an aggressive manner,' Seb replied, stretching to his full height.

'It's not aggressive and it's none of your business,' Justin replied, letting Isla's arm drop anyway.

Seb ignored his reply and turned to Isla. 'Is he bothering you?'

Justin cut in before she'd opened her mouth. 'What are you going to do about it? I told you, this is not your business. Leave us.'

'I think I can answer for myself,' Isla said, throwing an indignant glare at Justin. 'Yes,' she continued, turning to Seb. 'He is bothering me, but I can handle it. Thank you all the same.'

'Are you sure?' Seb asked. 'Only… well, Dahlia said you had a reservation for seven and it's now twenty past and so…'

'Isla said she was OK,' Justin warned.

'She said nothing of the kind,' Seb fired back, the blush rising to his cheeks visible even in the dim glow of the street lights. 'She said you were bothering her, which is not the same as being OK.'

'Tell me,' Justin said, climbing the steps to square up to Seb now. 'What do you know about this? Isla is my family, and this is family business.'

'She's my friend and I know what I saw.'

Isla manoeuvred to get between them.

'Leave it, Seb,' she cried. 'I said I could handle it.'

'I know you did but—'

'I said leave it!' Isla repeated, a little more forcefully than she intended. The last thing she wanted was a fight breaking out.

Seb gave her a look like a wounded pup that made Isla's stomach lurch. This wasn't supposed to happen; she'd only meant to get him safely out of the way. He nodded and said curtly, 'I understand. I just wanted to tell you that Dahlia was worried because she knew you were exploring on your own and you hadn't come back in time for dinner. But now I see you're OK, I'll let you get on. Excuse me.'

He slipped past them both, down onto the street, and walked away. As much as Isla desperately wanted to run after him, to explain that she hadn't meant to hurt him and to say that his concern filled her with a strange kind of hope that she couldn't fully explain, from the corner of her eye she noticed Justin fighting back a smug grin.

'Go away, Justin,' she hissed. 'I think you've done enough damage, and if there was any tiny spark of reconciliation possible then you've certainly put that out now.'

'So you won't talk to me at all? You can't give me five minutes?'

'You've had more than five minutes and you haven't convinced me yet. What's the point in another five? There's nothing you can say to me that will change my mind. The way I feel right now I could phone Grover Rousseau tomorrow morning and tell him to forget the inheritance deal entirely, and if anyone asked me why I would tell them it was your fault.

So I think you'd better go before you lose whatever little gift your aunt has promised you for trying to scam me in the first place.'

'Isla, you misunderstand—'

'Stop it! Please, just stop it! I don't want to hear any more of your bullshit. I just want to eat my dinner and go to bed ready for my flight tomorrow so I can get back to England and forget you ever existed. That's it. So please go. If what you've said is true, and you did care for me at all, then please do me this one kindness to prove it. Leave me alone and don't ever call me again.'

Justin's mouth opened and then closed again. If he was going to argue, Isla never got to hear what that argument was. She didn't give him the chance. She turned on her heel and headed through the doorway of Residence Alpenrose, slamming it hard behind her.

Isla made her way straight to the dining room and Dahlia rushed to the doorway to meet her.

'I was so worried,' she said. 'Did you get lost?'

Isla shook her head with a rueful smile. 'Not exactly.'

'Oh. Want to talk about it, honey?' She inclined her head at a relatively quiet dining room.

'A whole two waitresses?' Isla said, trying, but failing, to raise a playful smile. 'That's absolutely staggering. What's the special occasion?'

'For once nobody called in sick,' Dahlia replied, a smile of her own hovering about her lips. 'Seriously, Isla, you look shaken to the core. Want to tell me what's happened?'

'Do I?' Isla asked. She'd been convinced that she'd been keeping a lid on her emotions but it appeared she was wrong about that. Or perhaps Dahlia was more perceptive than most. 'Honestly, I'm fine.'

'OK. So convince me you're fine – talk to me.'

Isla glanced around the dining room. 'I'm sure you're too busy to listen to me witter on.'

'I wouldn't have asked if I didn't mean it. I won't pry if you don't want me to but I'm all yours if you need a friendly ear.'

'You might regret that offer.'

'I might, but I doubt it. Try me.'

Even as Isla was formulating a reply, Dahlia was herding her to a tiny office behind the bar. 'Sit down, honey,' she smiled. 'You can trust that anything you want to tell me won't go any further.'

Isla forced a smile in return. She didn't really care about that – what did it matter who knew what about her business? She was going home tomorrow and after a few days nobody in St Martin would even remember her name. Well, almost nobody.

'I think I might have just upset Seb,' she said.

'He's gone out. Said he needed some air – poor guy's been cooped up in his suite working all day.'

'I know, I saw him on the steps just now,' Isla replied. The mystery of where he'd been all day had been solved. She wished she'd just knocked and seen him instead of being silly about it. Perhaps then she wouldn't have been fighting Justin off and pissing off Seb into the bargain.

'Whatever happened between you two on the steps is what's upset you so?'

'Oh, God, no. It's something he happened to get in the middle of… it's nothing – silly really.'

'But you can tell me. Maybe I won't think it's silly.'

Isla sighed. 'Let's just say I think I've been taken for a mug and I ought to have known better.'

'Is this something to do with the meetings you've been having?'

Isla nodded as Dahlia took a seat across from her and folded her hands in her lap. 'My dad lives here in St Martin,' Isla said. 'I hadn't seen him since I was five, and one day I get a letter out of the blue from a solicitor's office to say I've inherited some property from my grandma.'

Dahlia's forehead wrinkled. And then her eyes widened as she processed the information and obviously came to a surprising conclusion. 'Wait… You're Ian McCoy's girl?'

'Yes.'

'Of course!' Dahlia smiled. 'I never made the connection even when I saw the name!'

'You know him then?'

'Honey, in a town this small we're all connected somehow. Though to be honest I didn't know he had a daughter other than Natalie.'

'And I don't suppose I'm someone he would have talked much about outside his family.' Isla broke into a wry smile. 'I don't suppose the fact that we're different skin colours would have helped you connect the dots either.'

Dahlia chuckled. 'I suppose not.' She held Isla in an appraising gaze. 'Well I never,' she added. 'Who'd have thought it? So he was with your mother before Celine?'

'Yes. We hadn't seen or heard from him for years – at least I hadn't. Apparently Mum had, but she kept it to herself for reasons she's not telling me.'

'So you came here to find him?'

'I came here because of the will, but I didn't expect much to come of it. Imagine my surprise when I found out I was inheriting a chalet here.'

'Sarah's holiday place?'

'Yes. You know it?'

'I've been up there once or twice with her. Beautiful house.'

'It is,' Isla agreed.

Dahlia paused, studying Isla carefully again before she finally spoke. 'So you're renting it out? To holidaymakers?'

'Renting it out?' Isla frowned. 'It's not even mine yet!'

'Only... well, I had a couple in here last week. They were passing through but loved the area so much they wanted long-term accommodation to come back and spend the summer here. I told them about a rental site and we looked at Serendipity Sound together.'

'What?'

'It's up on the site.'

'Should it have been taken down? Perhaps it was still listed from before Grandma Sarah died.'

'Sarah would never let that place to strangers – she loved it too much. It's been listed recently. I just figured Ian or Celine had listed it as I assumed they'd inherited it along with Sarah's house back home. I had no idea it wasn't theirs yet, and I hadn't bumped into them to ask.'

'You wouldn't know, of course you wouldn't,' Isla said, her mind racing. What the hell did any of this mean? 'Are you quite sure it was Serendipity Sound you saw listed? I mean, I don't even own it yet – none of us does – so I don't know how anyone can advertise it on a holiday let site.'

'I'd know it, and, besides, the name was in the information. I thought it was kind of odd at the time, but it's not really any of my business.'

'It's empty right now,' Isla said thoughtfully. 'I went up there yesterday and...'

The Christmas decorations. Suddenly it all made sense. Justin had the keys, so this was his doing? Was this why they were all so desperate to persuade her to take the inheritance? Because if nobody got theirs then what happened to the houses? What happened to the rental opportunities? She'd never thought to ask but it was safe to assume that they'd have to turn in keys and access to the properties.

Had the McCoys banked on her not wanting much to do with her place even if she was the official owner? Had they assumed that she'd rarely visit and the house would stand empty? That they could make a little money from it even if they couldn't own it? And by the McCoys, which members of that family was she talking about here? Not her dad, surely, not after all he'd said. Justin wasn't exactly a McCoy, but as Celine's nephew he was close enough. And he had keys. Hadn't he made clear all along his intention to look after the place for her when she was in England? Did that mean making a healthy profit from it on the side and never having to share it with her? Who'd know if he did? Was that the reason he'd tried so hard to make an effort with her? If he'd tricked her into a relationship then she'd be sure to alert him every time she planned to visit St Martin so he could make sure the house was empty for her visit. It was beginning to feel like she'd been scammed.

'Can you show me the website?' Isla asked. Dahlia nodded shortly and opened up a laptop standing idly on a nearby desk and typed in the address.

'There you go.' Dahlia sat back as they surveyed the page together.

'Bloody hell.' Isla sucked in a breath as she read the rental prices. 'I never even thought about renting it out. I mean, I suppose I might have done but... God, I'm an idiot.'

'I can't believe your dad would do this; he's so well respected around here.'

Isla shook her head. 'I don't think it's him... at least, I don't want it to be him. We've just found each other after twenty-four years, and he seems like he genuinely wants to make up for lost time but...' She shook her head again, more forcefully this time. 'He wouldn't – it doesn't make any sense.'

'Then who would?'

'I don't know. Maybe my cousin?'

'The guy who came here to see you earlier in the week?'

Isla turned to her. 'Of course – you didn't know him. I thought you knew the family.'

'I know Ian, Celine and the kids. Not him, though. I guess he doesn't live in town.'

Isla nodded thoughtfully. She'd never even thought to ask exactly where Justin lived – it never really seemed like an issue.

'How do you feel about the family members of mine that you do know?'

'They seem like decent folks, for the most part – pretty well liked around the village. Benet wasn't always easy growing up, but I guess they have it under control.'

'What was wrong with Benet?'

'Nothing in particular. You just get the impression that they've always been a little disappointed by him. I think he might pull his weight a little more than he does, and I don't think he makes the best choices when it comes to the types of people he associates with.'

Isla chewed on a nail and stared into space, weighing up the information Dahlia was giving her. It made her realise just how little she knew of this branch of her family and just how much of an outsider she really was.

'What are you going to do?' Dahlia asked.

Isla shrugged, her gaze returning to the photo of Serendipity Sound on the screen. 'I don't know. I'm not even sure this is a crime. I mean, I don't even know which of us owns the place at the moment because nothing has been sorted.'

'But you need to put a stop to it, surely? This is your place in all but name and, as far as I can tell, it's stealing.'

'Do you think I should email the website? Tell them to take it down?'

Dahlia nodded. 'It's a start while you get to the bottom of the mystery. And speak to your lawyer too – see what he has to say on the matter. Maybe you want to do that before you contact the site so you can show him the page and he can see for himself what's going on.'

'Good idea.' Isla looked up with a tight smile. 'Thank you. I wish I'd told you about this much earlier instead of trying to deal with it all myself – I'd have saved a lot of trouble.'

'Hey, you didn't even know me. I wouldn't have expected you to share all your private business with me as soon as you arrived but I'm glad we got a chance to uncover this now before you got ripped off big time.'

Isla looked up at the clock on the wall. 'I suppose it's far too late to contact Grover now and tomorrow I'm meant to be flying home so it might have to wait until I'm back in England. I could ask Dad but I don't want to let on that I know until I get Grover's take on things, and if I give any inkling that I know about it I expect whoever is responsible will take the listing down pretty sharpish so my proof will be gone too.'

'Why don't you eat now and think it over? You must be starving.'

'I must admit dinner is long overdue.'

'So you're feeling better?' Dahlia asked with a warm smile. Isla had to return it. Dahlia was a lovely woman, the sort of woman who'd make a gorgeous gran. She had no recollection of Grandma Sarah at all, but from what she'd heard the woman had been difficult, to say the least. How lucky Dahlia's family were, how blessed to have her. How come the good people always went to other families? What had she done to deserve the dysfunctional bunch she'd been landed with?

'Did Seb say he was coming back to dinner?' Isla asked, suddenly remembering that she had another problem to deal with. She hated the thought that she'd offended him and hated even more the idea that she might fly out tomorrow without having the chance to see him again.

'I think so. Did you two have a fight or something?'

'Not exactly. I think I might have offended him though. I don't know... I just wanted to explain before I went home.'

Dahlia's warm smile had now spread into a grin that was a little too smug for Isla's liking.

'What?'

'I think he really likes you.'

'I like him too.'

'No, really *likes* you.'

'Well that's just silly. We hardly know each other.'

'Isn't that how all love affairs begin?'

'A love affair! I hardly think so!'

'So you don't think he's handsome?'

'He's... well, he's cute, I suppose. In a handsome if slightly weird mad professor way. Like if someone zapped your history teacher with sex appeal. But he's absolutely not my type at all.'

'What exactly *is* your type? Because if a handsome, sweet man like that was interested in me I'd give him a shot. What do you have to lose?'

Isla gave a disapproving frown and Dahlia chuckled. 'OK, I get it. I'll zip it up. In answer to your question, he's coming back for dinner at eight so you could catch him then. Maybe you could share a table after all – it's not long to wait if you want to change your reservation.'

'I suppose I've pretty much missed my reservation anyway,' Isla said, glancing up at the clock. There was only ten minutes to go until

Seb was due back to eat. Would he welcome the intrusion, though? She supposed there was only one way to find out.

Isla rolled her eyes as she spotted that Dahlia had placed a single rose in a vase on the table right at the back of the restaurant. Where she'd even found a rose in the French Alps in the middle of the winter was anyone's guess. And there seemed to be candles everywhere; where there used to be a sprinkling of subtle tealights, there was now a riot of golden flames in heavy silver sticks, candelabras, glass jars and crystal dishes on every surface of the dining room. It was like Liberace had flown in and dumped his surplus. Isla couldn't help a sneaking suspicion that the display meant Dahlia was still clinging to the idea that she could throw Isla and Seb together like a fairy godmother on happy pills. Did she not see that they weren't suited one iota? Then again, Dahlia had been so wonderful, so supportive, how could Isla be cross? She only wanted to see two people she'd taken a shine to happy, and what was wrong with that? Besides, Isla had plenty more on her mind than Dahlia's attempts at match-making. The more she thought about it, the more she had to conclude that Justin was responsible for the house rental scam – and if not wholly, then he had to be involved somehow. At the very least, he had to have known about it, otherwise why would he have gone back to the house to clean it up the day they'd been there?

She'd barely had time to dwell on any of this when she looked up to see Dahlia ushering Seb over to the table. He looked faintly surprised to see her sitting waiting for him and threw a questioning glance at Dahlia, followed by a swift once-over of the room, which revealed that he was as confused by the candles as everyone else. But she simply shook her head and bade him to take a seat.

'Isla said she wanted to talk to you and you're almost always eating alone so I thought it would be a good idea to let you sit together for dinner tonight. It's Isla's last night in St Martin, so you should take the opportunity to get to know each other a little better.'

Isla was about to remind Dahlia that they'd already done that but then thought better of it; she'd already insulted Seb once that evening, and it might sound like a complaint.

'Oh,' Seb replied, looking confused but taking a seat across from Isla just the same. 'I suppose it's alright then.'

Now it was Isla's turn to be faintly offended. *I suppose it's alright then*? Was it that much of a hardship to sit with her for an hour? Or had she *really* upset him that much outside on the steps?

'Shall I get you some drinks?' Dahlia asked, seemingly oblivious to the strange atmosphere now settling over the table.

'That would be lovely,' Isla said, forcing a cheery smile. 'Thanks, Dahlia.'

After a quick confirmation of their order, Dahlia bustled off while Isla shot Seb an awkward smile.

'I'm sorry,' she said as he reached for the menu, moving a pongy scarlet candle out of the way. 'I did try to tell her this wasn't a good idea.'

'It's fine,' he said stiffly. 'Just unexpected.'

'If you'd rather eat alone I completely understand, I—'

'Of course not,' he cut in, looking up from the menu. 'I wouldn't hear of you moving. Forgive me, I'm just tired.'

'I suppose you must be, working all day. I just thought... well, I wanted to apologise. For the way I spoke to you outside on the steps earlier. It was a complicated situation and I didn't want to drag you into it. You understand, don't you? It came out all wrong and I didn't mean to be rude; I just panicked.'

'It looked like an unpleasant situation from where I was standing but I apologise that I waded in without being asked to.'

'God, you have nothing to apologise for! I mean, it's sweet that you wanted to help. But I just didn't want things to escalate.'

'And I suppose they would have with my help?'

'No. Maybe. Yes. I don't know.'

'He's your cousin?'

'Sort of. I suppose it just goes to show that what they say about not being able to choose your family is true.'

'What do they say?'

'You know, that thing about you can choose your friends but not your family? Essentially if you get landed with crap family there's not a lot you can do about it.'

'Oh. Right.' Seb's head went back into the menu. Isla fought back a frown.

'You're still angry with me.'

'Of course not,' he said, looking up. 'I'm just hungry.'

'Don't lie.'

'I'm not. It's just... what you said about families...' He shook his head. 'It's nothing.'

They were silenced for a moment as one of the waitresses on duty with Dahlia brought their drinks over. Isla threw a glance towards the bar and could see Dahlia herself watching them with interest, even as she tried to make it look as if she wasn't. Isla didn't know whether to laugh or hurl the little vase from the table at her, rose and all.

'So, your business in St Martin has been concluded satisfactorily?' Seb asked as the waitress left them again.

'Sort of.' Isla took a sip of her beer. It was cold and malty and very good. 'OK, not really. I thought it was, but then...'

'Was that what you were arguing about? On the steps outside with your cousin?'

Isla tried not to smile, but despite the subject of their conversation she was pleased to see that she was drawing Seb out of himself again. She liked chatty, open Seb, not the wounded puppy version of him who refused to talk.

'Not exactly. I suppose it was connected. It looks as though I'll be leaving tomorrow with things still in a bit of a mess. It means I'll very likely have to come back. Although I was planning to come back anyway, just not quite as soon as I might have to.'

'Could I be of assistance? I'm planning to stay on for a while.'

Isla glanced up from her own menu with a silent question.

'I know I said I was flying back for Christmas,' he said with a faint sigh. 'The truth is there's no reason to, so I've changed my mind.'

'No reason?'

'People are busy, you know…'

'Your family are too busy to spend Christmas with you?'

'It's not that simple. I, um… well, I have some more work to do on my current project and as I have to come back in the new year it seemed silly to go home in the first place. So I decided to stay on for Christmas and continue working straight after until I've finished. I had mentioned to Dahlia a couple of days ago I might so she was holding my suite for me.'

'Won't your family be upset you're not home?'

'I'm sure they'll get by just fine,' he said, and Isla got the feeling there was a lot he was holding back. More than a feeling, she knew the truth of it like she knew her own name.

'There's something you don't want to deal with at home? Something that feels worse at Christmas for some reason?'

'It's not that—'

'You can tell me; I'll understand. After all, look at the mess my family is in. I guarantee yours can't be any worse than mine.'

He shook his head. 'It's just bad memories, you know. Something that happened a long time ago.'

Isla narrowed her eyes. 'Something to do with that girl you won't tell me about? The one who broke your heart?'

He paused, opened his mouth to reply, but then Dahlia's voice cut across them and they both turned to see her standing at the table. 'Ready to order yet?' she asked, moving the candle that Isla had shifted back onto the table between them.

'Um… yes,' Seb replied, visibly flustered by the interruption, the old uncertain, slightly flaky version of him back again. 'At least I think I am. Isla?'

'Oh, I'll have the steak,' Isla said, almost shoving the menu at Dahlia.

'Steak, yes… sounds good – I'll have that too,' Seb agreed, though Isla was sure that if anyone had asked him thirty seconds later he wouldn't have been able to remember what he'd ordered. She'd been half amused and half annoyed at Dahlia's attempt to throw them together tonight but now she was irritated beyond measure at her interruption, just when she felt certain that Seb was about to say something massive and she desperately wanted to hear what it was. Somehow, something told her that the moment had been and gone and she might never hear it now.

Dahlia nodded amiably and glided away again, looking pleased with herself.

'Do you get the impression she's up to no good?' Seb asked as he watched Dahlia disappear into the door that led through to the kitchens.

Isla stared at him. But then she started to laugh as she picked up the candle again and placed it onto an empty table nearby. 'Oh, thank God it's not just me! She's impossible, isn't she?'

'But she means well.'

'Of course, and she's absolutely lovely. But barking up a very wrong tree.'

'Quite,' Seb said, and then his smile faded. 'Quite the wrong tree.'

If not exactly relaxed, dinner had been fascinating and Isla had barely drawn breath in the end. There was no more mention of Seb's secret – if indeed there was any secret at all – and Isla had the sense he didn't want to mention it again. So the conversation had been deftly turned onto her. At first she hadn't wanted to talk about Justin and his advances, but a few beers had seen that resolve crumble. So she told him about that, about Serendipity Sound and her theories on why it was being listed on a holiday letting site when it shouldn't have been, and she asked for his thoughts. She didn't even know why, but perhaps it was a diversionary tactic, a way of avoiding the real conversation they should have been having, the one that he'd started but that Dahlia had interrupted. They couldn't go back to it – the moment had truly come and gone and it looked like it was gone for good. Isla couldn't even consciously admit to what was hanging in the air between them but it was there all the same. As for his thoughts on her puzzle, he had as many theories as she had, but as she herself said, they couldn't be sure about any of them. There was only one way to get to the bottom of it, and that was to talk to the people involved. Which, as Isla explained again – as she had to Dahlia – meant showing her hand and giving them a chance to get rid of the evidence before she could act on it. So for the time being, it looked like they were all going to be kept guessing.

'Perhaps I could give you my phone number,' Seb said awkwardly as they finished their desserts. 'Just in case you might like to let me know how your dilemma pans out. I'd like to know how you're getting on and if you're alright. If that would be OK, of course. I mean, I wouldn't want to overstep any boundaries and I completely understand if you don't want to give it to me...'

He dragged in a deep breath and Isla relaxed into a warm smile.

'I'd like that,' she said. ' So what will you do here over Christmas? Surely it won't be all work?'

'I'll be keeping Dahlia company for Christmas lunch.'

'I'd like to see her with her party hat on eating Christmas dinner,' Isla said. 'I'll give you my phone number and you can send me a photo of that.'

'Perhaps we could even FaceTime?'

'Even better. And, you know, I'm interested in your research. So if you ever wanted to let me know what you're working on...'

'Really?' His face lit up as though she'd just announced he'd got six numbers on the lottery. 'You'd want to know?'

'Of course I would. I'm not a complete Luddite you know.'

'Right,' he grinned. 'I'd love that!'

They were silent as he held her gaze and she felt her world tilt into the depths of his eyes.

'What?' she asked, flustered, blushing as she tore her gaze away. When she looked back she could see he was blushing too.

'I'm sorry... zoned out there for a moment,' he said with a self-conscious laugh. 'Long day.'

'Me too,' she said. 'Long and weird day.'

'Just so you know,' he added as she dropped her napkin onto an empty plate, 'I had a brilliant day out at the lake. I've been there so many times by myself, it was amazing to share it with someone.'

'It was amazing having someone show it to me,' Isla replied. 'I'd never have seen it in quite the same way otherwise. Thank you.'

And then came another charged silence. Was this it? Goodbye? The idea pulled at Isla, and she felt a strange and sudden lump in her throat.

'I'd better get back to my room and finish packing,' she said, realising that if she didn't leave soon she might just cry.

'Oh…' he said, standing as she did. 'I suppose this is the last I'll see of you.'

'My dad's coming to pick me up for the airport. I think he wants to start out early to make up for the snow on the roads so, yeah… probably. But it's been lovely getting to know you.'

'You too,' he said, looking so earnest and so desperate that Isla wondered if some huge revelation was coming, something that might just make leaving him ten times worse. But he simply forced a smile and nodded. 'Goodnight then, Isla. Have a safe journey home.'

There was a pause. Then Isla gave a tight smile in return and made her way out of the dining room. Was that truly the last time she'd ever see Sebastian? She had a feeling it might be, but it wasn't a feeling she was happy to dwell on right now.

Chapter Fourteen

At least it had stopped snowing when Isla looked out of her bedroom window the following morning. The sky was still heavy, the mountain tops obscured by blankets of white, but the air was dry and promising. It looked as if she'd make that flight home after all, and though part of her felt a stab of regret at the prospect of leaving St Martin, a place which had gradually and unexpectedly crept into her heart, there was relief too. Home would mean distance, and distance meant time to collect her thoughts and figure out exactly where she was in her life. There was plenty to think about too, from her new relationship with her dad to which members of the family she could trust – even how she now viewed her mother.

And then there was Seb. She'd gone to sleep with his voice in her head and his face behind her eyelids, the things they'd talked about playing over in her mind, and she didn't quite know how she felt about any of it. They'd parted as friends, but she couldn't decide if that was enough. While she'd shared so much of her life with him there was one part of her she couldn't share, not with anyone. It was the real cost of witnessing her dad's betrayal and the life her mum had lived since that day, and it was the fear of getting too close to a man, certain that one day the same would happen to her if she did. It was like she'd programmed herself to gravitate towards relationships that would only ever end in disaster, like a self-fulfilling prophecy that proved her point that she would never find anyone who would make her truly happy and if she ever did she would lose them. But how could she admit this to anyone when she couldn't even admit it to herself? She'd convinced herself Seb wasn't her type, but perhaps that was the point? Her type had always been wrong, no good chancers like Justin, but perhaps that was just a defence mechanism dictating her choices. If she had a bad man then she had the perfect excuse for it not to last and she'd be spared the heartache of a good man abandoning her. Perhaps what she really needed was a man like Seb and the belief that she might not lose him.

Seb was holding back too – she understood it. She could feel he wanted to say more and there were moments when he almost did, but not quite. They'd agreed to stay in touch when she got home but surely things would change once she did? Ordinary life would start again and time would dull the stirring of emotions that had the potential to become so much more. She'd convinced herself she didn't fancy him but there had been a strange pull as she'd watched him across the table and it had to mean something, even if she didn't fully understand it herself.

He wasn't at breakfast that morning, though Dahlia went to great pains to let Isla know that he'd told her he'd be eating it late. Did Isla want to come back and eat when he did, she'd asked. Isla politely declined and the conversation had quickly moved on to what she was going to do about Serendipity Sound. Isla had made a quick phone call to Grover Rousseau's office after breakfast and he'd been shocked to hear her accusations, but he'd confirmed that the house had no right being listed on the website. He'd told her he would make enquiries of his own and Isla was so relieved to know that she wouldn't have to face dealing with it alone.

Once, she might have felt vindicated by the need to confront her dad about it – even quite enjoyed the idea. But now she wanted to believe, more than anything, that her instincts about her father were right. She wanted to believe that he was essentially a good man who'd made bad choices.

Isla was sharing a last coffee with Dahlia in the bar when Ian arrived. The snow had been falling steadily outside but they'd been having such a good time chatting that neither woman had noticed it. Now, as her father strode towards their table, Isla saw the troubled look on his face and guessed that he didn't come with good news. Her gaze flicked to the windows – the snowfall looked heavy out there. Had he come to tell her he wasn't able to drive her out to the airport after all?

She glanced at the clock meaningfully, hoping she was wrong. 'I wasn't expecting you quite this early.'

'Have you seen the forecast?'

'No, but…'

'It's bad. High winds, snow, blizzard conditions, danger of avalanche on the mountain passes. It's not going to be safe to drive to the airport and I doubt your flight will be taking off anyway.'

'But I checked and it's not cancelled—' Isla began.

'Not yet,' he cut in. 'But I guarantee it will be. There's no way anything will be taking off in this, even if we could get there. Best to sit it out and re-book.'

'But what about the cost? I can get the bus if you don't feel safe driving; I can't afford to re-book—'

'I wouldn't expect you to pay, but I do want you to be safe and if that means booking another flight then I'll pay for it.'

'But—'

'He's probably right,' Dahlia said.

Isla looked from one to the other. 'It's Christmas Eve. I'm supposed to be home for Mum.'

'Your mum wouldn't want you running the gauntlet of dangerous weather any more than I do,' Ian said. 'If you need me to, I'll call her and explain.'

Isla's mouth fell open. 'You'd do that?'

'If I had to, of course. I can't say it's an attractive prospect but your safety has to be my number one priority.' He gave a small smile. 'I'm not about to get you back and then lose you again in the same week.'

Isla shook her head. It said a lot that her father was willing to put years of conflict and pain behind him to speak to his ex-wife on her behalf. There was even a little spark of hope that perhaps one day they might all be able to stand in the same room and speak civilly to each other. All in good time, but the idea was a wonderful one.

'I need to go home. Besides…' she looked at Dahlia, 'my room's not available after today.'

'Not a problem,' Ian cut in before Dahlia had time to reply. 'I'll talk to Celine about you staying with us for a day or so while we get you sorted.'

'But…'

'I don't want you to argue. Just this once let me be your father; my decision is final.'

'You don't think any transport will be running to the airport?' Isla turned to Dahlia, filled with a sudden panic at the thought of sleeping under the same roof as the family she barely knew and barely trusted. How was she supposed to cope? Not to mention her suspicions, increasingly well-founded, that one or more of them was trying to rip her off. She'd hoped for time to mull things over at home, do a little digging before making her move. She wasn't even sure if any of her suspicions were grounded in fact, but while that doubt hung in the air the last thing she wanted to do was share Christmas dinner with them.

'Probably not,' Dahlia admitted. 'Sorry, honey. I can see about getting you a room elsewhere, if you need me to.'

Isla looked at Ian and shook her head. How could she say yes in front of him when he meant so well?

'I suppose I have Serendipity Sound if I could have the keys from Justin?' she said, the idea occurring to her all at once. If she were there she'd know if anyone arrived to take possession over Christmas and it would be a legitimate reason to get it all out into the open.

'I'd rather you weren't out there on your own in blizzard conditions,' Ian said. 'I'd hate to think of you being cut off and the power going – you'd freeze to death.'

'Lovely thought,' Isla said, and she saw him glance at her with a small smile.

'Just saying.'

'So no to Serendipity Sound?'

'I'd rather have you at our place while the storm is bad.'

Isla held in a sigh.

'You're packed and ready, right?' Ian asked.

'Yes.'

'Always Glory's daughter,' he smiled. 'I knew you'd be organised way in advance.'

'Of course,' Isla said, and she couldn't help a small smile despite the tension of the situation. It was nice – they seemed to be at a place where it didn't feel quite so sharp around the edges when they talked about her mum. In a funny way, they'd both suffered at her hand and, as much as Isla still adored her, even she could see the damage Glory had caused over the years. But there was no point in laying blame; it was the way it was.

'You have a few hours until I need your room,' Dahlia said. 'And the new guests might not even make it here if the weather is too bad, so you might find it's free after all. Why don't you wait to see before you hand me the keys? Might make life easier for everyone.'

Isla gave Dahlia a grateful smile. She might have acted like an eccentric fairy godmother at times but she had a sharper insight than anyone gave her credit for and now she appeared to understand Isla's predicament perfectly.

'Fantastic, thank you, Dahlia,' Ian said. 'I'll go home and speak to Celine just in case. And Isla, you phone me as soon as you know. But remember that the invitation for Christmas dinner will be open regardless. Can't very well have you here in St Martin and not see you on Christmas Day, can we?'

'I'd like that,' Isla said. But it was a good job he couldn't see how her stomach churned at the prospect.

'Please tell me you have something,' Isla said in a low voice as they watched Ian leave. 'A broom cupboard, a coal bunker, a grain silo… I'll take anything as long as I don't have to go and stay with my dad.'

'I guess it would be awkward,' Dahlia said. 'I'd love to help but if my guests arrive I'll have nothing. I'd let you stay in my own quarters but there's only one bed and—'

'I'd take the floor!' Isla said, but then she checked herself as she saw from Dahlia's expression how difficult that would be. Dahlia wouldn't allow Isla to sleep on the floor – it wasn't in her nature, and there was no way Isla would take her bed.

'I could stay at Serendipity Sound, couldn't I?'

'I guess you can do whatever you want but I don't think anyone would be happy about the idea. You've never seen a doorway get buried by snow before?'

'Well, no, but...'

'Let me tell you, it can make life difficult. Ian's right, if the power goes and you're snowed in there you could well find yourself in real trouble. At least here there's enough of us to work together if we had an emergency – safety in numbers.'

Isla let out a sigh. 'I suppose I can deal with my dad's place if I have to. I've done the hard work, and at least Dad is on my side even if no one else is.'

'You don't know that for certain yet.'

'There's that too. I suppose I'm overreacting.'

She was about to speak again when Dahlia's attention wandered. Following her gaze she saw Seb walk into the bar. He looked sheepish and set to turn around and walk out again when Dahlia called him.

'Morning! Or should I say afternoon because we're nearly there!'

He blushed, fiddling with a moss-green bow tie, his gaze flicking to Isla and then back to Dahlia again. 'I had some results I needed to get sent off before Christmas and the internet connection has been terrible so it's taken me all morning.'

'You didn't come down for breakfast,' Dahlia said reproachfully.

'Sorry about that. Work has to come first you know.'

'I'll get you something now – you must be famished,' she replied, pushing herself up from the table.

'Oh, I wouldn't hear of it—' Seb began, but Dahlia waved her hands in the air.

'Sit down. I wouldn't see you starve.'

'But it's almost lunchtime.'

Dahlia crossed her arms and frowned. 'Then you'll just have to eat both.'

'Perhaps some toast then…' With a sheepish smile he made his way over to Isla's table as Dahlia went in the opposite direction to the kitchens.

He turned to Isla. 'I thought you'd already be on your way to the airport.'

'So did I,' Isla said. 'You just missed my dad, actually, telling me that he can't take me today because of the weather.'

Seb looked across at the windows, seemingly surprised to see that it was snowing.

'I could take you to the airport if there's a problem… I have my hire car still.'

Isla looked to the windows herself. If anything, the storm seemed to be picking up pace, flurries now racing in circles, heaping in corners and window frames, and Isla was almost as surprised as he was to see the speed with which it had progressed. Before it had looked like snow – now it looked like something to be scared of. Tempting as it was to try to make her flight, there was no way she was dragging Seb out in this. Her dad was right; it was dangerous. She wasn't scared so much for herself but if anything happened to Seb she'd never get over it.

'It's OK, I'm going to try to find somewhere to stay overnight and see about getting home on a later flight.'

'But tomorrow is Christmas Day. There won't *be* any flights.'

'I suppose not.'

'But won't your mum be upset?'

'Ballistic. But she'll understand – eventually. When she gets over the disappointment and finishes telling me she told me so. So in about twenty years.'

'So, you're stuck here for Christmas?'

'Looks that way. Maybe there'll be room for another at Dahlia's Christmas lunch?'

'She does seem to like picking up waifs and strays,' he replied with a half-smile. 'What about your dad? Won't he invite you there?'

'He already has. Sort of. The trouble is…'

'You don't know if you want to go,' Seb finished for her. 'Of course, given the circumstances I can hardly blame you.'

'That sounds ungrateful, doesn't it?'

'Why?'

'Well, I have family here offering me a room and dinner and you're going to be working all through the holiday season…'

'I'm sure I'll take a couple of hours off somewhere.'

'But you won't be with your family, you'll be with… well, with Dahlia. Who's nice and everything, but she's not your family – she's a lady whose hotel you use sometimes – she's…'

'A virtual stranger,' he finished for her. 'But you know what they say about strangers?'

'What?'

'They're just friends you haven't met yet.'

Isla smiled. Then another conversation came back to her, something similar about strangers. Hadn't Dahlia reminded her that love affairs started in just the same way?

Her thoughts were interrupted by Dahlia herself returning with a plate of toast and a coffee. She set it down on the table. Seb sent an uncertain glance at Isla and she nodded. 'Sit here, I don't mind at all.'

'I'm sorry, honey…' Dahlia turned to Isla now as Seb took a seat. 'But the guests who are due to arrive and take your room have called ahead to say that they're making slow progress, but they are still coming. They said they've got so far now it's easier to carry on than turn back. So I'm afraid I don't have that room for you tonight.'

'But you could phone round, see if anyone else has a room?' Isla asked hopefully.

'I already did that and nobody has a spare.'

Isla frowned. Dahlia had called around all the hotels in the village that fast? It seemed rude to question her on it. She'd have to get online and check for herself, although if the internet connection was as bad as Seb had mentioned then that might mean simply walking the streets to find out, not a particularly enticing prospect in the current weather.

'It looks as though it's going to be Dad's then,' Isla said.

'I'm sorry,' Dahlia repeated. She gave an awkward smile and then left them to tend to a customer who'd just arrived at the bar.

'My suite is huge,' Seb said suddenly. 'There's a bed and a sofa.'

'But—'

'It's no problem. I can take the sofa for one night. Once you've camped out on a glacier you can sleep anywhere, you know. You can have my bed.'

'I couldn't—'

'Yes, you could. I know it's not ideal but I'm guessing the alternative is staying over where you're not entirely sure you're welcome. At least with me you know you're welcome…' He blushed, dipping his gaze to spread marmalade on his toast with far more concentration than the task merited. 'And I'd be the perfect gentleman – no funny business.'

Isla was reminded of when Justin had made the very same promise, and she was suddenly seized by the notion that if there was to be any 'funny business' she'd much rather it was with Seb than with him. She shook the idea away and turned her thoughts back to his proposal. Would Dahlia mind? She didn't suppose so. It certainly beat the alternative.

'I'd pay for the room for that one night.'

'No need,' he said, looking up from his toast. 'I've already cleared it with the university and they're happy to put the expenses through, so there's nothing to worry about on that score.'

'And I wouldn't be in your way? Stop you from working?'

'Not in the slightest. I can easily work around you.'

She might live to regret her decision, but Isla smiled and nodded. 'Thanks then – that would be brilliant.'

Seb grinned. 'I'll clear it with Dahlia but I'm sure she won't mind one bit.'

After a short conversation with Dahlia, Seb disappeared to tidy his equipment away so that Isla had space for her stuff and Isla ordered herself another coffee. There wasn't anywhere she needed to be and going out was going to be tricky for the next few hours anyway.

Dahlia had just placed the cup in front of her with a strangely knowing smile and gone off to answer the phone in reception when Isla's own phone rang. She groaned inwardly as she saw the name displayed on the screen. This guy just didn't take no for an answer.

'Justin.'

'Are you OK? Ian told me about your flight.'

'I'm fine. Is that all you wanted?'

'No… I wanted to say—'

'Don't. I don't want to hear an apology, or a proclamation of love, or how I do things to you that you can't control. I don't want any of that; I just want you to leave me alone.'

There was a brief silence at the other end. Across the room a group of young men broke into a tipsy rendition of 'Jingle Bells'. She hoped that they weren't going to get louder as the day went on – Dahlia's other guests were mostly stuck indoors like she was and that was a recipe for some serious boredom drinking.

'I'm sorry for the way things turned out,' Justin said finally. 'I never meant it to end up this way.'

Isla bit back the reply she really wanted to give. She'd bet a fair amount of money that much about it was true. Something had started between them and scuppered his well-laid plans, whatever they might have been. But it was up to Grover now to get to the bottom of it and Isla had to be content to let him if she wasn't going to make things worse. At least she wasn't staying at Ian's house now, running the risk of bumping into Justin if he visited.

'Is that all?' she asked.

'Merry Christmas?'

'Thank you,' she said stiffly. 'And to you too.'

Ending the call before he could say anything else, she stowed the phone in her pocket. Times had been stressful enough and the last thing she wanted to think about was Justin and his silky lies.

But her bad mood dissipated as soon as Seb came back down to the bar. She smiled broadly. He looked so damn pleased with himself she couldn't help it.

'All clear upstairs,' he said. 'Underpants removed from the light fittings and coffee-stained research papers kicked under the bed.'

Isla laughed. 'I'm thrilled to know you made such an effort for me.'

'So, whenever you're ready we'll move your cases in and leave your old room free for Dahlia to get ready for the next guests.'

Isla nodded and was about to suggest that he get a coffee and join her before they did that when her phone rang again. Pulling it from her pocket, she half expected to have to tell Justin to piss off again when she saw it was a number she didn't recognise.

'Miss McCoy – it's Grover Rousseau here. Have I caught you at a good time to talk?'

'It's as good as any. Have you got news for me already?' she asked, taken aback that he was still working at this time on Christmas Eve.

'Firstly, I know who registered your grandmother's house on the rental site. And now that I have the information I've taken the liberty of contacting the site to ask them to remove it. I hope that's alright with you.'

'Of course. I don't suppose I officially own it anyway yet so I couldn't complain if I wanted to.'

'I don't know how it slipped through the necessary checks to be honest, but I suspect the site administration might be a little on the sloppy side. The fact remains that without relevant paperwork it shouldn't have been on there. Of course, should you choose to reinstate the listing once the property passes to you then I would imagine that would be perfectly acceptable. Although, given what's happened here, perhaps you might want to choose a letting agent with more stringent checks – it doesn't bode well for the rest of their systems if they fail to fulfil the most basic ones.'

'I'll bear it in mind,' Isla replied, but she wasn't really thinking about letting agents and websites. She wanted to know who was behind it, and her heart was thumping as she waited. When she found out, what then? Was she supposed to confront them? Did she need to do something about it? Involve the police? Make some sort of formal complaint? Despite the betrayal, that wasn't a road she really wanted to go down. It would make life difficult for her and even worse for her dad if it turned out to be someone close to him. Was it worth all that hassle? Perhaps it would be easier for Grover to issue a quiet warning to the perpetrator and leave it at that? They'd get away with it, of course, and that stuck in her throat, but was the alternative any better? She'd just begun to mend her relationship with her dad and something like this might set them right back again, especially if he was forced to take sides. And there was no telling which side he might take.

'Who was it?' she asked, shutting her eyes.

Grover hesitated. 'You really want to know?'

'No, but I probably ought to. If it's my dad—'

'Gracious, no!' Grover exclaimed. 'Not Ian! He'd never...' He smoothed his tone again. 'Ian and I go back a long way and I'm sure he'd never...'

'Who then?'

Another pause. 'Your brother,' Grover said quietly.

'Benet?' Isla blinked. She'd considered it, of course, but her natural instinct had been to suspect Justin. Unless they were in it together? Justin had already admitted that Celine had offered him money to help win Isla over. Would he have seen another opportunity to screw a little more out of the situation? It made some sense now – his guilt over their failed relationship seemed all too intense to be just about that. If he'd been trying to make a much bigger wedge of money from her too then that would explain why he was so torn up about it. So, did that mean Benet and Justin *were* in cahoots? Or was she seeing patterns and connections that weren't there?

'What would you like to do?' Grover asked.

'I don't know. Nothing yet, I suppose. Should I tell my dad?'

'That's entirely up to you. Would it do irreparable damage to the relationship if you did?'

'That's what I was wondering. So I just leave it?'

'You could speak to Benet yourself and tell him you know. That might be enough to resolve the matter. You'd have to decide if you'd feel vindicated by such a small amount of action.'

'Do I have a legal case to prosecute?'

'I've never come across a situation like this before. Would you like me to look into it?'

Isla was silent for a moment. 'No,' she said finally. 'He'll know that we know when the rental agents contact him to tell him they've taken the house from their listings and I would hope that's enough to deter him from trying anything untoward again. Perhaps I'll talk to him, but not yet. I need to think about what to say first.'

'That sounds like a wise course of action to me. Please don't hesitate to call me any time if you need more advice or help. I'll be on standby, awaiting your next instruction.'

'Thank you, Grover – I appreciate that. And I really appreciate your help already with this. If I wanted to, would I be able to find out if anyone else has been involved?'

'You think Benet may have had an accomplice?'

'I don't know.'

'Natalie…' Grover began, but then stopped himself.

'You can say it,' Isla prompted. 'Whatever you need to say, please do.'

'It's just that I know the family of old and your grandmother spoke of Natalie many times. From what I know I don't imagine for a moment she'd be caught up in anything like this.'

'Well, at least that's one sibling not out to get me then,' Isla said with a faint smile. 'This brother and sister business is all new to me and I never imagined it would get this complicated.'

'For what it's worth, I'm sorry this happened.'

'It's not your fault. It's probably the last thing anyone would expect. If anything, it all seems like a lot of hassle for not very much payback.'

'That all depends on how long you stayed away from St Martin and how little interest you took in the house,' Grover said. 'It might have been very profitable indeed if you were never here and he could get away with keeping it covered up.'

'My dad would have been checking on it regularly, I'm sure.'

'Perhaps Benet never considered that.'

'He's not very bright then.'

'Hmm,' Grover replied, and made an odd sound in his throat that sounded like he was trying to swallow an undiplomatic reply.

But then it occurred to Isla again just how much interest Justin had shown in the situation. Hadn't he said he was happy to check on the house for her? He had the keys and Ian trusted him. He could have kept her dad away on the pretence of doing it for him. And if that were true, did that mean Celine knew? She'd already offered him money for getting Isla on side. Would she go that much further too?

'OK,' she said, holding in a sigh. Her brain was in knots over this thing and she was tired of trying to work it out. It was Christmas, she was stuck far from home and she just wanted this whole horrible business to go away. 'Thanks again for letting me know and for dealing with it. For now, I'm not going to do anything but let me know if there are developments that I ought to be acting on.'

'I will. I just need to warn you that I won't be available tomorrow.'

'I should think not!' Isla said, and she couldn't help a little laugh. 'I'd feel very sorry for you if you were!'

'Quite,' he replied, and she could hear the smile in his voice. 'Compliments of the season to you.'

'And to you,' she replied.

Ending the call she tapped the phone silently against her chin as she gazed the length of the restaurant. Seb sat next to her, a silent question in his expression, one she wasn't capable of answering until she understood it fully herself. Why was her life never simple? Swiping to unlock the screen, she brought up Justin's number. But then she paused, finger hovering over the call button for a moment before locking it again. What was the point? If he was involved he'd only deny it, and if she was honest she just didn't have the energy to get into a debate with him again about anything, least of all this.

The most galling thing was the lies. When she thought about it now, she almost felt she would have handed them the opportunity to rent out the house so that it was all above board if only they'd put it to her. She'd never asked for Serendipity Sound and she hadn't really cared about it all that much. It would have made sense for them to do it between them and share the profits, and she would have been happy with that arrangement.

'Is everything alright?' Seb asked, his voice low and respectful of the pain in her eyes. 'Something's happened?'

Isla shook herself. 'I don't want to ruin the day with all that crap and I have the rest of my life to think about it. Why don't we go and get my stuff moved into your room and try to remember that Christmas is coming?'

*

Once she'd dumped her belongings in Seb's room, Isla called her mum to explain she wasn't going to make it home for Christmas. The reaction was typical Glory – emotional fireworks, tears, recriminations and cold threats. But in the end she'd had to concede that Ian had been right to want to keep his daughter safe and decided that, although she'd never stop hating him, perhaps that one act would save him from the fiery damnation she'd wished on him so many times in the past. Still, this was going to be a Christmas that would live long in the memory of Glory McCoy – and for all the wrong reasons. She'd take great pleasure in trotting the story out year after year, embellishing it and turning it into legend. The story of how her ungrateful daughter had forsaken her at the most precious time of any Christian year to take off halfway across the world to find a dad who hadn't cared about her for all those Christmases before. It was already a classic.

She also phoned Dodie, who was expecting her in Bournemouth to take part in a charity sea swim on Christmas Day, to apologise for the fact she wasn't going to make that either. It was something they'd been doing for a couple of years now, a crazy tradition that Dodie seemed to love, and Isla hadn't the heart to tell her friend how much she wished they could do something just a little less radical for their fundraising efforts. Who wanted to splash around in the sea in zero temperatures when they could be tucked up in bed with Christmas champagne before wrapping up in a fluffy robe and ambling downstairs to open presents? But Dodie had a way of making even the most horrible things seem like a good idea and Isla always ended up getting roped in.

A small part of her relished the idea of spending Christmas holed up a hotel sharing a room with a virtual stranger. Although, this was Seb, and perhaps he wasn't such a stranger any more. She was finding it harder to fight the growing, confused feelings she had about him and as much as she craved his company, it scared her too. She was on the cusp, about to fall into something big, and she didn't know if she was ready. She didn't know if she'd ever be ready.

As she ended the call to her friend, she looked across to where Seb was hunched over his laptop, muttering to himself.

'You're a workaholic,' she said.

'I haven't got much else to do,' he replied, looking up. Isla raised her eyebrows. 'OK,' he laughed. 'Perhaps I have today.'

'I'll tell you one thing, we'll go stir-crazy in here all day.'

'Dahlia says there's a carol concert and service at the little church in the square tonight.'

'I doubt it,' Isla replied. 'Won't it get called off?'

'Too important to get called off…' Seb dipped his head back to a spreadsheet on his laptop.

'Even in a deadly blizzard?'

'So she says. They never call it off, not for anything. And everyone just battles through the snow to get there.'

'That's crazy.'

'I know.'

Isla flopped onto his bed. 'I'm bored already. Maybe we should try and get there.'

'You really want to?' he asked, looking up again.

'You said you weren't going to do any more work today,' she added, aware that she sounded vaguely like an unreasonable toddler but unable to help it. There he was, sitting at his desk with his silly bow tie and his floppy hair and freckles, and all she wanted to do was pull him up from his chair and rip his silly bow tie off, followed by his shirt and then his trousers. It was a ridiculous notion and along with all the other emotions that were spinning around in her head, she was about ready to explode and she didn't know what to do about any of it.

She went to the window and wrapped her arms around herself. He'd promised no funny business and she believed him because he was good. She ought to be thankful he wasn't just another Justin.

'I'm sorry; I did,' he said, closing the lid on his laptop. 'It's hard to break the habit of a lifetime.' She turned away from the window to face him. 'So, what do you want to do?' he asked.

Isla chewed on her lip and those wicked images invaded her thoughts again. 'There's nothing we can do,' she said with a shrug, feeling even more like a fractious toddler than ever. 'We're stuck. And I never thought I'd complain about having to lounge around all day.'

'How do you feel about Christmas films?' he asked.

'They're OK I suppose. Depends on what film it is. Why do you ask?'

'Because,' he said with a smile, 'I happen to know that Dahlia has a cupboard full of DVDs in her office and I'm sure she'd let us borrow some if we asked.'

As they sat together on the sofa in Seb's suite, Isla would have put a sizeable sum on the fact that Dodie was watching this exact same film right now.

'*It's a Wonderful Life* is my best friend's favourite movie,' she said. 'She's nuts about James Stewart and she watches this one every Christmas.'

'Really? I know it's supposed to be a Christmas classic and it's always on TV but I've never seen it before.'

'I have. About a *million* times.'

'Oh…' He sat up and turned to her. 'You want to watch something else? You should have said instead of letting me put it on—'

'It's fine,' Isla smiled. 'I don't mind watching it again. In fact, I quite like it. Just don't tell her I said that.'

'I'll be sure not to if our paths ever cross.'

Out of habit, she tucked her legs beneath her. The action spread her body so she took up more room on the sofa and she was suddenly aware of how much closer to him she now was; the heat of his arm resting against hers, his scent in the air she breathed. She sensed him tense up. Instinctively she pulled her legs down again and moved away.

'Sorry,' she mumbled.

'What for?'

'Taking up so much space.'

'It's fine…' he said, flipping up from the sofa and crossing the room to grab a high-backed chair. He set it beside the sofa and sat down.

'What are you doing?' she asked.

'Giving you the sofa so you can put your legs up.'

'Oh. Thanks.'

Sucking in a sigh, Isla got comfortable again. She didn't know whether his gesture was endearing or annoying. Just as she was about to tell him she didn't want him to vacate the sofa on her account her phone bleeped a message.

Did you get your room sorted? Celine says you're welcome to stay here if not.

Isla tapped out a reply. *Dahlia sorted me out. Thank you but no need to worry.*

How about Christmas lunch? As you're here would you like to join us?

She glanced up at Seb, who gave her an uncertain smile as he paused the film. 'Everything OK?' he asked.

She nodded. 'Just my dad, checking everything is OK.'

'And is it?'

'I think so. He wants to know if I'm eating with them tomorrow.'

'Perhaps you should. I mean, he's your dad after all. Won't he be offended if you don't?'

'Maybe. I don't know if I'm strong enough…' Isla shivered, overcome by a sudden wave of emotion that she hadn't even seen coming. 'I mean… it's a bloody mess, isn't it? My family is a shit-tip of a mess and I just don't know if I can cope with it any more. Honestly… I think I'd rather stay here.'

'He's your dad, though.' Seb was silent for a moment. 'I could come with you?' he said. 'Moral support if you're feeling nervous around your brother. Actually, ignore me. That's a stupid idea – your dad doesn't even know me and why would he allow that?'

'He'd probably allow it, but I wouldn't wish it on my worst enemy. I appreciate that you were willing to put yourself through that on my account, though.'

'So what are you going to do?'

Isla typed a brief reply and then locked her phone. She looked up at Seb. 'I've told him I'll sleep on it.'

'Probably wise.'

'Now, please come and sit on the sofa because you're making me feel guilty.'

With a sheepish grin he perched himself next to her. 'I just thought you might need some more space.'

'How fat do you think I am?'

'You're not at all fat, I think you're…'

Isla didn't get to hear the rest of his reply. They both jumped as the lights flickered twice and then they were plunged into darkness.

Chapter Fifteen

There were footsteps – Seb running across the room. Isla could see his lean silhouette in the dim light from the dusky skies beyond the window.

'Where are you going?' she asked as he headed for the door.

'Just checking on Dahlia. You'll be alright here for a minute?'

'Sod that, I'm coming too!'

Out in the windowless corridor it was total blackness. Isla heard other doors opening too and guests coming out mumbling about the loss of power. Once or twice she bumped into someone with an apology on her lips. She felt a hand grab hers and knew by the scent close by that it was Seb. There was a jolt of desire, a spark so charged he must have felt it as well. The darkness and the uncertainty of their predicament brought a sense of urgency, but it was strangely thrilling too, almost sexy. His hand closed in, a gentle, reassuring squeeze and her free hand itched to pull the rest of him closer. She balled it into a fist and fought the urge. Hadn't he just said Dahlia would need them? This was not the time for crazy fantasies.

'Stairs,' he said, and pulled her to follow him.

'Won't it come back on in a minute or two?' Isla asked uncertainly as they felt their way along to the stairwell door and opened it. He'd flicked his phone torch on but she was still impressed by his confidence. He wasn't fazed at all.

'Last time I was here we lost power. Dahlia has a backup generator but it's in a really tricky location; the steps are lethal, especially when they're covered in snow like they will be today. I'd rather she didn't go down there.'

'So you're going down there so you can break your neck instead?'

'Exactly.'

Isla didn't reply. As she wasn't about to let go of his hand, it looked as though she was going down there too. Together they emerged from the bottom doors of the stairs and out into the main reception corridor. Flashing his torch around the space, Seb quickly revealed that Dahlia wasn't there. Beyond the main desk Isla could see the bar was full of customers. The remains of Dahlia's candles from the previous evening were still burning, dotted around the restaurant with a warm, reassuring glow. It looked so pretty and festive it was tempting to believe that they didn't need their electricity at all. Seb led her to the key rack behind the reception desk.

'The key's gone... she must already be on her way down,' he said, his voice unmistakably tense.

Without waiting for a reply, he tugged at Isla again and took her through a side door that emerged into the freezing cold of the world outside. Snow slapped in her face and took her breath away, more ferocious than any snow she'd ever been in. It had looked beautiful and magical from the safety and warmth of Seb's room, but outside it was wild, unpredictable and totally terrifying. He grasped her hand tighter and they crossed a narrow lane to a kind of bunker, a dark, squat doorway buried in snowdrifts. The door was already open.

'Dahlia!' Seb cried into the darkness. He crossed the threshold, and Isla followed him, the smell of damp assaulting her. He shone his phone down a set of steep stone steps. The top few were inches deep in snow that had drifted beneath the door, and the ones falling away looked slick with icy moss and lichen. 'Dahlia! Are you down there?'

'Here!' called a cheery voice. 'I'm having a bit of trouble with the switch though. Arms aren't as strong as they used to be.'

Seb cursed under his breath. Isla had imagined that he simply didn't swear and she was taken by surprise. 'I knew she'd do this. I told her to call me if the power went out. Stay here – it's too dangerous to go down.'

'But you're going down?' Isla clamped her hands on her hips as he gently pushed her away. 'Why is it more dangerous for me than you?'

'I won't be long. I don't want you to fall.'

'I didn't ask what you wanted – and I won't fall.'

'Isla…' He moved closer, held her in a pleading gaze, and once again there was a moment when she found herself drowning in the pools of his eyes, where the candlelight from the windows of the hotel beyond played tricks with the colours swirling there. But she jutted out her chin and shook herself from the spell. 'You're not backing down, are you?' he asked, the half-smile about his lips belying the half-exasperated tone of his voice.

'No. So the quicker we agree I'm going down, then the quicker we'll get to Dahlia.'

After a heartbeat's pause, he simply nodded and for a second she almost thought that he'd move in and kiss her, like some action hero in a movie just at the moment of ultimate peril. But instead he gave her that exasperated smile again and turned for the steps once more.

'Does this happen a lot?' Isla asked as she followed him gingerly down, the bravado she'd shown for his benefit now dissipating in the reality of the damp and dull cellar. Instinctively she reached for his hand again, but he was too far in front and to grab it from here might have sent them both tumbling down the steps. She had to satisfy herself with reaching for the clammy walls, rough and unpredictable under her palms, to steady her path.

'Imagine how hard it is to get power up here in the first place, and then imagine the force of the blizzards battering the equipment. That's what the generator is for.'

As they hit the bottom step, the tiny, low-ceilinged space was lit by a larger torch to reveal Dahlia wrestling with a huge rusting lever.

'Why didn't you fetch me?' Seb asked, rushing over.

'Oh, don't be silly. You're not here all the time so I need to be self-sufficient.'

'Not at the expense of a broken limb… Remember what happened last time?'

'That was last time. I'm not stupid enough to let it happen again.'

'What happened last time?' Isla asked.

'Fell down the steps,' Seb grunted as he threw his weight into the lever and pushed hard. 'Broken ankle.' The lever inched up and, with a loud clunk, slotted into place. The room flooded with yellow light and there was a muffled cheer from the hotel above.

'Guess that's done it.' He grinned, wiping his hands down his trousers. He turned to Dahlia. 'I know I'm not here all the time, but I'm here now so you should have asked me to come down.'

Dahlia looked sheepishly from him to Isla and back again. 'I figured you would be busy.'

'It doesn't matter how busy you think I am, next time fetch me.'

'Yes… OK,' Dahlia said, pouting like a chastised child. Seb offered his arm.

'What about Isla?' Dahlia asked pointedly. 'Shouldn't she have your arm?'

'I don't think we'll get up those steps three abreast,' Isla said, throwing a surreptitious grin at Seb. 'If I break an ankle the worst that will happen is I have to take some time off uni. You have a hotel to run, and who's going to cook my divine pancakes if you can't?'

Seb led Dahlia, complaining, up the stairs and back out into the snow as Isla followed. It was funny hearing her complain because she was always so agreeable. Anyone would think they'd seriously scuppered some cunning plan by coming down to the basement to save her.

The snow was still heavy, but it had calmed enough to venture out, and it seemed half the guests of Residence Alpenrose were trekking through the snow alongside Seb and Isla as they made their way to the little church in the main square. The power was back on in the village so Dahlia had been able to divert the hotel back onto the main grid from her backup generator, and now their way was lit by streetlamps and fairy lights in the windows of homes. They walked side by side, Isla wishing he'd take her hand like he did before, but he didn't. He did talk, however. A lot.

'I'm interested to see what the service is like,' he said. 'I've never been to a Christmas church service before. I suppose it'll be in French and mine isn't brilliant but I should be able to follow it. Do you need me to translate as we go along?'

If Isla hadn't known better she'd have said it was nervous chatter, though he certainly had no reason to be nervous. At least she didn't think so.

As they got closer to the church they were joined by more groups of people from around the village – some guests of other hotels and some village residents, some greeting with a friendly hello and some with *bonsoir* or *salut*. Everyone was smiling and although Isla had never been particularly sentimental about the holiday season, it was difficult not to get caught up in the warmth of the crowds that swept away the cold of the night. Old, young, parents, children, couples and friends – everyone wore the same expression of joyous expectation.

The church was small, made of old rendered stone with a grey bell tower. The exterior was lit from the ground, throwing a warm glow across the square which teemed with crowds so large Isla wondered how on earth such a tiny village could house them all.

'It's lovely,' Isla said. She'd passed it during the day when it had looked pretty but unassuming, but now the light and the atmosphere in the square had turned it into something altogether more enchanting. Some people in the crowds carried lanterns and others gave out warm, spicy drinks. There were no snazzy coloured fairy lights, no blow-up Santas, no jangly music playing over loud speakers, just simple and elegant touches that harked back to a peaceful, more simple time. A time where the real meaning of Christmas was still fresh in the minds and hearts of men. Isla didn't ordinarily mind the bling that went with the holiday season at home, but this was something so refreshing that she already loved it.

As they approached the church entrance, swept along with the crowds, Isla was given what looked like a hymn sheet.

'*Joyeux Noel!*'

'*Merci*,' she replied.

Seb laughed. 'Speaking the lingo.' Isla nudged him in the ribs.

'I'll have you know I'm not completely useless.'

'Just a little bit.'

She tried to frown but it turned into a grin. 'I admit that I'll struggle with anything more than telling someone my name, or asking where the train station is.'

If the outside of the church had looked pretty but unassuming, the inside was as different as could be. Ornately carved wooden panels adorned the seating, sculpted figures of cherubs and saints were everywhere painted in rich hues, frescoes stretched across high-vaulted ceilings and row upon row of candles lined the walls.

'Wow!' Isla stood and stared, almost causing a line of people behind her to topple like dominoes. 'Sorry,' she mumbled as she blushed, but it seemed the spirit of Christmas was working its magic on everyone and the nearest man merely waved away the apology with a smile. She turned back to Seb, who was scanning the room for a vacant seat. 'This place is incredible!'

'It's beautiful, isn't it?'

'Gorgeous! Have you been here before?'

'Dahlia told me about it last time I was here so I came to have a look around. It was a lot quieter then.'

'I'm sure it was,' Isla said with a smile as he indicated a space for them to sit on the end of a row. 'I wish I knew more about religious iconography now so I could understand some of these pictures.'

'You don't need to understand them to appreciate them. It's a bit like glaciology in that way; you can still see it's beautiful even if you don't understand what makes it tick.' Seb gave her a strange sideways look as he said this.

'Well, I wish I did,' she replied, uncertain what to make of his expression.

'I'll tell you one thing I do know,' he said with a soppy grin that looked like him again. He pointed to the gold-embellished altar. 'See those fine fellas in those paintings there? Saints. Saint Martin, Saint Joseph, and the best one, obviously, Saint Sebastian.'

'Saint Sebastian?' Isla smiled and peered to get a closer look. 'He's better looking than you, though,' she said. 'More muscles.'

'Yes, but that's how they painted everyone in those days. It was like Photoshop for the sixteenth century. In real life they were flabby and useless like the rest of us.'

'You're not flabby,' Isla giggled. 'I've never seen such a bendy beanpole of a man.'

'You think I'm a beanpole?' Seb looked vaguely offended.

'No,' Isla laughed. 'I don't really. I think you're just right.'

The voice of the priest suddenly filled the space. Isla looked up in surprise, not realising they'd been almost ready to start as she and Seb chatted. He seemed to have that effect on her – that whenever he was talking the rest of the world somehow faded away. How funny that she hadn't noticed it before. After one last brief smile from him, she faced the front. She had absolutely no idea what the priest was saying and even less about what the order of service was, but it didn't matter. She was sure she was going to love every minute no matter what.

'Isla!'

She spun round at the sound of her name being called. The service was over and the congregation was spilling out into the square, lanterns aloft again, the chattering and laughter of a crowd in high spirits, ready to start the festive season in earnest. She looked to see Ian trudging through the snow towards her with Celine, Benet and Natalie following.

'I didn't know you were coming tonight,' he said, throwing a glance at Seb before turning back to her. 'You could have come along with us.'

'I didn't know myself I was coming until an hour before I did,' she said. She looked behind him, half expecting to see Justin bringing up the rear and was relieved that she couldn't see him anywhere. 'I just… *we* just decided it might be a nice idea.'

Ian looked at Seb again, clearly under the impression he was missing something. But he merely gave him a stiff smile and turned back to Isla.

'And did you enjoy the service?' he asked.

'It was lovely,' Isla said. 'I didn't understand a word, of course, but I enjoyed the sentiment. And Seb translated a little for me.'

'Did he now?' Ian replied, looking at Seb again, and if she hadn't known better Isla would have said it was the look of suspicion that all fathers gave to new potential suitors for their daughters. But then, Ian wasn't like all fathers, Isla wasn't like all daughters and Seb wasn't a suitor.

'Will you come back to our house for drinks now?' Celine asked. She looked at Seb now, weighing him up in a subtler way than Ian but still seeming to weigh him up just the same. 'Your friend is welcome too.'

'Sebastian.' Seb nodded. 'Pleased to meet you.'

Isla was almost dazed as everyone greeted him briefly, as if events were somehow always two steps ahead of her. She barely knew herself how she felt about Seb and now he was meeting her family as if all this was normal. As for him joining them for drinks, she didn't know what to make of that either and the idea of them all sitting together seemed overwhelming. And would Justin be there? Seb and Justin in the same room. Now there was a prospect, Isla thought wryly. Even less appealing was the idea of spending time with Benet, who now stood nonchalantly, hands dug in his pockets and barely concerned with proceedings at all. At least that was the impression he was trying to give. Natalie stepped forward to link arms with Celine and smiled.

'It would be good to get to know my new sister,' she said. 'I know things are still strange, but perhaps in time they will be easy, as with all sisters.'

Isla stalled. 'I don't know, I… well, I'm quite tired, you know. And it's dark and cold, and I'm worried that the snow will get heavy again. I would really rather get back to the hotel if you don't mind.' She looked up at Seb, who smiled, happy, it seemed, to acquiesce to whatever plan for the evening she had in mind.

'I understand,' Celine said. 'Perhaps we will see you tomorrow then? For lunch?'

'Well, I was going to have lunch with Seb… as he's here alone…' she said, noting the thinly disguised look of disappointment on Ian's face. Isla guessed he was hurt that she didn't want to spend Christmas lunch with him. After all, they'd missed the last twenty-four Christmases and it hadn't been completely his fault. But the situation was just too prickly at the moment, and as she thought about Seb standing silently beside her, she realised she really did want to spend it with him, not just as a necessity, but as an event she had a feeling she might enjoy.

'Oh, I don't mind,' Seb put in. 'I can sit with Dahlia and keep her company if you want to go to dinner with your family.'

'We would like that, wouldn't we?' Celine said, glancing at her family members in turn. It was clear also that they wanted her but the invitation for dinner didn't extend to Seb. What Isla had said was true; she didn't want to leave him alone and she wasn't enamoured with the idea of lunch with the McCoys. She didn't feel like she could refuse now, though.

'OK,' Isla said. 'Thank you, lunch would be nice.'

'Fantastic!' Celine smiled. 'One more place is no problem!'

Isla took a moment to assess the situation. Celine seemed pretty genuine despite what Justin had told her. Perhaps her intentions hadn't been completely bad when she'd employed Justin to charm Isla. Perhaps she had only panicked about losing their inheritance and had seen a way to solve that problem – perhaps she hadn't seen anything wrong in it. Likewise, now that she looked at Natalie, Isla was inclined to trust Grover's judgement on her integrity. In an instant she'd made a decision to put Ian and Benet to the test.

'I'm glad I've caught you actually,' she said to Ian. 'I wanted to ask you something. What do you think about me renting Grandma Sarah's house out when I'm not here?' Isla tried to sound casual, her gaze flicking from him to Benet, watching closely to gauge her brother's reaction. 'Would I be allowed to do that?'

'I suppose so,' Ian replied. 'It's going to be your house after all. Want me to ask Grover about it?'

'So you think it's a good idea?'

'If it means maintaining a link to St Martin for you, then I think it's a brilliant idea. It would solve your problem of affording the upkeep of the house and it would mean you'd have it there to use whenever you wanted. Be a nice income too, I expect, a house that size. Life-changing perhaps, and I'd rather see you do that than sell it, if I'm honest. I'd be happy to keep an eye on things from this end and make sure your customers behaved while they were there.'

Ian looked genuinely pleased, which was more than could be said for Benet. There was no way her dad had any inkling that Grandma Sarah's house was already down to make a nice income for someone – just not her. The idea was one that made her happy and by airing the proposal now it meant that Benet had also been given a warning shot across his bows. If he didn't already know she was on to him (and she didn't think he did at the moment) he would realise that his scam would have to be wrapped up anyway.

What she'd wanted more than anything, though, was to know that it hadn't been her dad. Benet shifted, his gaze dropping to his feet. It was evidence enough to convince her that Grover was right.

'Let me know what you decide about that and I'll do whatever I can to help.'

'Thanks, I'd appreciate that.'

Ian smiled and this time it was warm and genuine. Celine looked relieved and wrapped her arms around Natalie as Benet continued to look at his shadow across the snow.

'And the house would always be there for you when you visit,' Celine said.

'You want me to visit again then?' Isla asked. 'I'd have thought you'd have had your fill this time around.'

'More than anything,' Ian said. 'And maybe it wouldn't be so bad if I came to England to see you?'

'I'm sure it wouldn't be terrible,' Isla smiled. 'I could probably spare half an hour sometime for you as long as I can keep you off Mum's radar.'

'Half an hour is all I need,' he said. 'I know I've been a terrible father, but…' He waved a hand to silence her argument. 'There's no way of getting around that. But now you're back in my life I want to keep it that way. I can't make up for all the years I was missing but I can make whatever we have left count. If that's what you want.'

'I do. I'd like that very much.'

He reached to give her a tentative kiss on the cheek. But then she pulled him into a hug, completely taken by surprise when sudden tears burned her eyes and fell quickly onto his coat.

'Sorry,' she said, pulling away and rubbing furiously at her eyes. 'I don't know why I'm being so stupid about it.'

'You're not,' he said, catching a tear with his thumb. 'You've never been stupid about anything in your entire life. I'm the one who's been stupid.'

'Well, it looks as if you're stuck with me now then. So there's your reward.'

'It's a happy day,' Celine said. 'Perhaps from now we can be good friends.'

'I'd like that,' Isla said, her eyes blurring again. She rubbed a hand across them. Perhaps, in time, even Benet would accept her into the family, but for now she was happy to make progress with Celine and Natalie at least.

Benet stepped forward and said something to his mother in French and she nodded shortly before turning to Isla. 'We must leave you now – we have a function to attend.'

'Of course,' Isla said.

Celine stepped forward and kissed her on both cheeks, and Isla was content to let her this time. 'Goodnight, Isla.'

'Goodnight.' Isla glanced at Ian.

He nodded at her and Seb in turn. 'Goodnight. Merry Christmas. In fact, I wish you many merry Christmases. All the Christmases we've ever missed.'

Isla had no way of speaking through the lump in her throat. She nodded and smiled as her eyes burned. Ian paused as he looked at her, almost said something else, but then he turned and walked away, rubbing his own eyes as he went.

*

'Are you alright?' Seb asked as they made their way back through the drifts. Snow was still falling but now it was pretty and Christmassy. Isla realised, somewhere in the periphery of her thoughts, that she probably could have gone home today after all. So why had she let her dad and everyone else persuade her so easily not to? Was it, perhaps, because she wanted to stay? Perhaps she wasn't ready to let go of St Martin and its residents just yet? There was no doubting that this Christmas would be like no other – it would be infinitely more peaceful for a start. No nagging from her more overbearing female relatives, no strict timetable to be here at this time, there at that, dinner to be finished in time for the afternoon movie. No rain outside, no rolling of eyes as the neighbours got drunker and louder, no knocking on the wall at 11 p.m. when the party really kicked in, no constantly trying to please her mum and failing at every hurdle. Here it was just her and whomever she chose to let in. If not for Seb, perhaps she would even have been happy enough to spend it completely alone.

Her thoughts were interrupted by an arm round her shoulder and she realised that, in his own adorably awkward way, Seb was trying to comfort her, mistaking her silent musing for distress. It didn't matter where the gesture had come from – she liked it.

'It must have been difficult for you back there,' he said, 'knowing what you know about your family now.'

'I'm OK,' she said. 'In fact, I feel quite calm about it for the first time. I trust Grover to sort things and it looks as though Benet has got the message that, even if I don't know about his scheme, he won't be able to rent a house I'm already renting out.'

'Are you going to tell your dad?'

'Not yet. Not until I'm sure it's the right thing to do. It may never be the right thing to do and then I suppose I'll never tell him.'

'That's very noble of you.'

'I suppose it must be. Not like me at all.'

'Oh, I don't know... I think you could be very noble. You must be to take all that's happened to you here and still have the capacity to forgive.'

They lapsed into silence and the snow creaked beneath their steps. Seb moved his arm and let it dangle to his side again, and Isla wondered how he would react if she reached for his hand. What about if she kissed him? He had once liked her, she knew it instinctively, but did he still? Or did he just see her as a friend in need? Perhaps that was exactly what she was – she certainly came with enough baggage.

The warm orbs of streetlamps that lit the way suddenly went out, plunging the town into darkness. Along the rows of wooden houses, the only lights were candles in the windows. Isla halted and she sensed Seb do the same beside her. A moment later he produced a hefty torch and switched it on.

'Took a spare from the store cupboard at the hotel before we left,' he said in answer to her silent question.

'Lucky,' Isla replied, and they began to walk again. Less than five seconds later they both stopped again at the same time and turned to look at each other, the realisation hitting them both at the same instant.

'Dahlia!' Seb exclaimed, and he grabbed her hand as they broke into a run.

Chapter Sixteen

They were laughing, breathless and soaking wet as they arrived back at Residence Alpenrose. Just as they reached the entrance, the lights went on in the town. But they made their way back to the basement again and found Dahlia coming up the steps.

'Looks like I didn't need it after all,' she said. 'Which was just as well as I was having a devil of a time with that lever.'

'Why on earth don't you ask for help?' Seb chided.

'Disturb my guests? I couldn't do that.'

Seb clicked his tongue as they exchanged glances.

'Perhaps we need brandy now,' Isla said, kicking chunks of compacted snow from her boots before walking into the main reception of the hotel. Dahlia went back to tend the bar. 'Like you get from those dogs who rescue people.'

'St Bernards?'

'Those, yes. Do they even exist?'

'I'm sure they do,' Seb grinned.

'But do they actually rescue people with barrels of brandy around their neck?'

'That I couldn't tell you – I've certainly never seen it happen. We'll have to quiz Dahlia on it.'

'I'm sorry I won't be around much tomorrow,' she said. 'I had wondered if we might do Christmas lunch together but... You understand, don't you?'

'Absolutely. We hardly know each other and he's your dad. Of course you must go to lunch there.'

'I wasn't going to, but then he looked so disappointed that I thought...'

'Please, don't feel you need to explain. We'll get a drink in the evening if you manage to get back.'

'I will,' Isla said. 'That sounds good.'

As they passed the door to the bar Dahlia was serving drinks to a middle-aged couple and laughing uncontrollably as she did.

'Looks like she's been having a few herself,' Isla said.

'God, and she went down to the generator like that. I hadn't even noticed she was half-cut,' Seb said, and Isla turned to see he'd gone pale.

'She manages all the time you're not here,' Isla replied gently. 'Which is quite a lot of the year.'

'I know, but...'

'It's sweet. That you worry about her. You worry about everyone. Your parents did a good job.'

He seemed to wince at this, but it was fleeting and Isla couldn't be sure she'd seen it at all. Then he smiled. 'We could get a drink... a nightcap. If you're not too tired that is. I know you said to your dad...'

'I don't know. The bar seems sort of busy.' It wasn't that the bustle of the bar was a problem on any other day, but Isla had to admit to being emotionally exhausted. It was hard to believe that only that morning she'd been due to fly back to England, ready to see her mum and get back to normality. Now she was here in St Martin and her life seemed to be moving at a pace she could barely keep up with.

'We could take something back to our room then.'

Our room. It sounded funny when he said it like that, as if they were a proper couple.

'Just one.' She smiled. 'And maybe we could finish watching that DVD too, if the power holds out.'

It had been weird, getting ready for sleep with another person in the room. They'd finished their DVD together, sharing a bottle of house red, and Seb had gently chided Isla for not saying earlier she wanted to go to bed when she'd begun to nod off beside him. There was a moment when she pretended to insist that he take his bed back and let her sleep on the sofa, but they both knew that he would never do that.

And so now she lay in the darkness, listening to him breathe. They'd turned out the lights over two hours ago, but despite her tiredness earlier on, she was wide awake. The bed was soft and comfortable but it felt somehow vast and too empty. Outside there was only profound silence. It was Christmas Eve. What would she be doing at home? Zonked, that was for sure, not lying awake listening to a man she barely knew breathing softly.

Unable to stand it any longer, she dropped out of bed and padded to the window. The weather had deteriorated again. There were little snowy mounds everywhere that probably contained cars, and flakes as big as her fist blowing down in dense bursts, high winds gusting the eddies in all directions. There were no stars in the sky, only a heavy, featureless blanket of dark cloud.

'What are you doing?'

Seb's voice came from the sofa.

'Sorry, I didn't mean to wake you.' Isla let the curtain drop back into place.

'I wasn't asleep.'

'Me neither.'

'I guessed that,' he said, sitting up. 'Is there something the matter?'

'No, I was just restless, that's all.'

'What for?'

'I don't know…' She shrugged. 'It's Christmas Eve. Looking out for Santa.'

He let out a chuckle. 'Fair enough.'

'As a kid I could never sleep on Christmas Eve. I always thought my dad might come back… you know, to see me because it was a special day. When other kids looked for Santa I looked out for him, walking up the drive of our house. But he never did.'

'That's tough,' he said quietly, a sudden tenderness in his tone that might have made her cry, even if the thought of all those years without her dad didn't. She tried not to dwell on it.

'I suppose so, though I haven't thought of it in a long time now.'

'You have him now, though. So I suppose this one Christmas your wish came true.'

'I suppose it has. Funny, it doesn't feel quite like I thought it would.'

'How did you imagine it?'

'Easier than this. Less scary. Like we'd slip into the father–daughter vibe as if we'd never been parted. And it would be just me and him, not complicated by half-brothers and sisters and stepmothers. I suppose that's just life, isn't it? I was being silly.'

'You were a child – you can be forgiven.'

'And what about now? I'm not a child now.'

'No. But that child is always in there, isn't she? Just as it is in all of us. The things that occupied your childish thoughts never really leave you.'

Isla went back to the bed and perched on the edge. She looked across to see his silhouette in the dim light from the window and had the sudden urge to go and fold herself into his arms and snuggle on the sofa with him. But that was just her uncertain, new-found vulnerability talking.

'I bet your parents are lovely,' she said. 'They must be if they made you. Do you have brothers, sisters? You never did tell me.'

'There's just me,' he said. 'Do you want a warm drink?'

'What?'

'Something to help you sleep?'

'I think you need it more than me?'

'It's nothing out of the ordinary; I'm often awake during the night.'

'Thinking about rocks and ice?'

'Something like that. So, do you?'

'We can't wake Dahlia – it's not fair.'

'We wouldn't have to. I'm sure she wouldn't mind if we helped ourselves and asked her to put it on the tab tomorrow.'

'As long as you're sure she'll be OK with it.'

'I can't imagine her being mad.'

'I can't imagine her being mad about anything. She's the loveliest woman on earth.'

Seb chuckled. 'True.' The next minute the room was flooded with light as he switched the lamp on. He was before her, sitting up on the sofa wearing a T-shirt and boxers, and it was strange to see him without a tie and sweater, like she wasn't looking at the same Sebastian at all. 'How do you feel about cocoa?' he asked.

'Cocoa's good.'

'Brilliant,' he said, crossing the room and pulling a sweatshirt over his head. 'Cocoa it is.'

'I'll come with you.'

'You'll get cold down in the kitchen and then you'll never get to sleep.'

'You'll get cold too.'

'Probably, but that doesn't matter.'

'It matters if I get cold but not you. How does that work?'

'I don't know. Don't analyse it, just indulge me.'

'Nope.'

'Are you always this difficult?'

'Yep. Just ask my dad.'

He grinned. 'I wouldn't dare. Let's go then, but don't say I didn't warn you.'

They'd snuck like naughty children down to the kitchen, using the mood lighting in the units to save drawing attention to themselves. Neither of them knew how to make cocoa, but they'd made a good fist of it and eventually they had a mug of pan-warmed milk each with clumps of bitter chocolate floating in it.

Isla giggled. 'It tastes horrible.'

'Sorry. I thought it would be easier to make than that. I mean, you read it in books all the time and see it in films and it looks easy.'

'Not your fault. I've never made it before either. Pathetic, eh? Both of us pushing thirty and neither of us has ever made a cup of cocoa.'

'I blame Starbucks – it's too easy to walk down the road and buy one.'

'Not here it isn't. Imagine living here with no Starbucks.'

'Could you?' Seb asked, leaning across the kitchen counter. 'Imagine yourself living here?'

Isla set her mug down and rested on her elbows across from him. 'If you'd asked me yesterday I'd have said no. Today… maybe it wouldn't be so bad. Do you come here a lot?'

'I'll have to for the next two years. Months at a time. It'd be nice to know you were here when I come back. A friend…'

Before she knew it, she was moving closer, holding his gaze. 'A friend…' she murmured, closer still. 'Is that all?'

'I…' He closed his eyes, and Isla closed hers, lips grazing lips…

They leapt apart as the kitchen door swung open and Dahlia stood before them, baseball bat held above her head, dressing gown flapping around her ankles.

'What the *hell*?' she cried, looking from one to the other. 'I thought I was being robbed!'

'Dahlia, I'm so sorry!' Seb had turned a shade of red so deep he looked in serious danger of spontaneously combusting. 'We couldn't sleep, we didn't want to wake you, we—'

'Didn't want to wake me?' Dahlia clutched at her chest and sat at the table. 'You damn near gave me a heart attack!'

'We're sorry,' Isla said. 'We'll go back to bed, out of your way. We didn't mean to cause trouble.'

'Take your drinks,' Dahlia said, peering into Isla's mug with a grimace. 'Whatever the hell they are.'

'Right,' Seb nodded, rushing back to claim the mug he'd abandoned as he headed for the door.

Isla stood and waited for him, mortified by the idea that Dahlia was angry with them, but as she dared to glance her way, she saw that though their host was frowning, arms folded tight, she didn't look angry. If anything, her eyes showed the glint of someone mildly amused by the situation. Isla didn't know whether to smile in recognition or scuttle away in shame. In the end, they both left looking shamefaced.

'She didn't look happy,' Seb said.

'Maybe,' Isla replied, but she couldn't imagine their sweet, cheery landlady staying mad with anyone for long, even if they had woken her in the middle of the night trying to make cocoa in her kitchen. 'She actually didn't look all that mad when we left her – probably just wondered what the hell was going on.' She peered into her mug. 'What on earth were we thinking? All that effort and embarrassment for this?'

Seb looked into his own mug as he opened the door into their room and frowned. But as he looked up at Isla again, there was a split second of silence, and then they both burst into laughter.

Being caught red-handed in Dahlia's kitchen was their own fault, but Isla couldn't help but wonder what might have happened had Dahlia not chosen that exact moment to come in. It felt as if that perfect, never-to-be-repeated moment, where the stars were aligned and everything would happen as it should would never come again. The possibility now hung in the air between them, unsaid and unrealised. They drank their terrible cocoa, making pointless small talk, skirting round the questions that had both of them so charged up.

Turning off the lights with a brief goodnight, Isla lay awake in Seb's bed, listening for the tell-tale slowing of his breath that signalled sleep. She must have fallen asleep waiting, because the next thing she knew daylight was edging into their room from behind the curtains. Christmas Day had arrived, and it was time to go and meet the family.

*

Breakfast was strangely quiet at Residence Alpenrose. The tiny dining room was only half full, and most of the guests there were nursing hangovers. At home, Glory would have been racing around the kitchen by 7 a.m. barking out orders while her sisters got under her feet.

Isla sidled into the dining room feeling sheepish and wishing that she could break into Dahlia's kitchen again and get her own meal now, instead of having to face her. Seb shuffled behind her looking similarly sheepish. To her relief, Dahlia came straight over to their table with a bright smile.

'Did you two have a good night?' she asked. 'Before I'd chased you from my kitchen, that is.'

'Dahlia—' Seb began, but she stopped him.

'I know what you're going to say. Last night I was taken by surprise – I didn't expect to find anyone in my kitchen. But it's fine, there's no need to apologise.'

'We didn't want to wake you,' Isla said. 'That's why we went to get our own drinks. And we would have told you about it in the morning so you could add them to the bill.'

'I know you would, honey,' Dahlia said. She folded one hand over the other and smiled. 'So you stayed up pretty late. Both of you. Together. You didn't get any sleep at all?'

Isla resisted the urge to frown. 'We couldn't sleep.'

'That's nice,' Dahlia said. 'Staying up together.'

'We didn't stay up together, it just happened that neither of us could sleep and we were awake at the same time.'

'Of course.' Dahlia's knowing expression was infuriating. 'So, I guess you're pretty hungry this morning.'

'I could eat a horse,' Seb said, and Dahlia looked delighted.

'Pancakes,' she said, tapping the side of her nose. 'Lots of pancakes. How does that sound? You need to keep your strength up.'

'Wonderful,' Seb smiled. 'If it's no bother.'

'No bother at all. Christmas morning is just like any other for me. Be back soon.'

'Well,' Isla said as they watched Dahlia go to the kitchen, 'at least she's still talking to us.'

'I couldn't imagine her holding a grudge against anyone for long,' Seb replied. 'Come on, we'd better get a seat before she comes back – I don't want to give her another excuse to tell us off.'

'God no!' Isla agreed fervently, prompting huge grins from them both.

An hour later Isla was back in the suite getting ready for lunch with her father. The snow had calmed and the landscape outside was greeting-card pretty, prompting Seb to announce he was going for a walk. Isla suspected it was his chivalrous way of making himself scarce so she could get ready in peace. The room seemed quiet and too empty without him. As she passed his open laptop she ran a finger along it with a small smile. Everything you needed to know about Sebastian was probably contained in there. She supposed that was the thing about coming from a stable, affluent background: you had time to obsess and pursue your passions without the worries that ordinary people had. It was no wonder he was so well-educated, so knowledgeable and accomplished. Like Dahlia said, you could tell he had breeding. Too much for a scrub like her. She'd been desperate to kiss him and they'd come so close last night, but in the cold light of day it had been a foolish impulse. Even if she admitted her feelings and they got together, even if they had the most wonderful few hours together, she'd have to fly home tomorrow and he wouldn't want to wait for a girl like her.

And even if he did, it wouldn't last. Their backgrounds and lives were worlds apart and she couldn't imagine how she could ever fit into his. There would be expectations, disappointments – not least on the part of his parents when he took her home. She was probably everything they wouldn't want in a girl; perhaps he'd even be embarrassed.

He was too good for her and he'd only leave her in the end. Better to steer clear in the first place, because she was beginning to feel like this could be something more than she could ever have hoped for, and to lose it would destroy her completely. Better not to let it grow in the first place. Better to pull up the drawbridge of her ice castle and lock him out. Lonely, but safe.

She spun with a start as the door of the suite opened.

'Are you decent?' Seb called.

'Don't worry, you can come in.'

He peered round the door. His cheeks were flushed with cold, his nose red, hair dishevelled and curled from the damp. He gave a wide grin as he came in and shut the door behind him again.

'You look lovely,' he said.

'It's the best I can do – I didn't exactly bring formal wear with me. Where have you been?'

'Up to the church. You should hear the bells ringing this morning – so pretty. It really felt like Christmas.'

'What do you normally do on Christmas morning?' Isla asked. 'I don't suppose it's always like this.'

'It's never like this,' he said.

'I suppose not. I'm bricking it over this lunch, but I suppose it's worse for you being stuck here. At least I have someone to eat lunch with.'

'Oh, I've got Dahlia,' he said cheerfully. 'And it's just another day, after all.'

'Only it's not.'

'Do you make a big deal of it at home?' Seb sat on the edge of the bed and yanked off his boots.

'Mum does. She goes all out – table full of food, more guests than we have room for, Queen's speech – the lot.'

'Sounds good.'

Isla laughed. 'It's a nightmare. I didn't think I'd miss it, but a little bit of me does this morning.'

'You're bound to – family is important no matter where you are.'

'I suppose they are. I suppose you'll be busy making phone calls back home later.'

'I'm glad you're giving your dad this chance today,' he said. 'That has to take priority.'

'I feel terrible about leaving you.'

'Don't. I'll be happy to look forward to that drink later, if you can make it.'

Isla smiled. 'You bet I will.'

She was nursing her first glass of wine of the day. A majestic tree stood in the corner of the sitting room, decorated tastefully in gold and red, the scent of fresh pine still there beneath the stronger smells of cooking meat and vegetables. Celine and Natalie were in the kitchen, and she could hear them conversing in rapid French as they worked. Benet kept his eyes firmly on the screen of his phone while Ian tried his best to start a conversation that wouldn't quickly descend into profuse apologies for all their missed Christmases.

'Your house is lovely,' Isla said. It was, and she'd felt the pull of longing as she walked over the threshold. It felt warm, lived-in, occupied by a normal functioning family. It was traditionally styled in rustic woods and stone, delicate pink rendering over the fireplace making a striking feature of it. She could smell cinnamon on the air.

'Thank you,' he said.

'I feel I should be helping in the kitchen.'

'Celine would hate that,' he smiled. 'She likes to do it herself. You're our guest after all.'

Benet looked up and said something to Ian in French and Ian frowned.

'We're eating it again,' he replied in English, 'because Isla is here and the rules are different in Britain.'

'What's that?' Isla asked.

'Christmas dinner,' Ian said. 'Nothing to worry about.'

'You've eaten already?'

Ian sighed. 'We had it last night. After the church service. It's how we do it here. But Celine was more than happy to prepare another one from the leftovers. In fact, it was her idea because she knows that you'd normally eat it today and it's not unheard of for us to do it – we've done it when Grandma Sarah visited. Besides, I can always make room for more turkey, no matter how many times we eat it. Benet is pulling his face because he chooses to forget that eating the leftovers from our Christmas Eve feast on Christmas Day is as much of a tradition here in St Martin as cooking a turkey on Christmas Day is in Britain.'

'Oh,' Isla said. So much for keeping under the radar. It looked as though sulky Benet was happy to seize on any excuse to hate her. It was possible that he already knew she was on to him, but perhaps he didn't even need that much.

'So, did you have any more thoughts on what you were going to do with your house once you get it?' he asked.

'Sarah's house?'

'Yours now,' Ian smiled. 'I think we can safely say that now, can't we? At least I hope we're on the road to reconciliation now… We still have to provide something official for Grover, of course, but as far as you and I are concerned we're good, right?'

Isla acknowledged his statement with a short nod. 'Some,' she said carefully, looking to see that Benet had stopped tapping on his phone.

'That's good. By the way, who was that man you were with last night? I had thought… well, you'd mentioned Justin and…'

'Justin and I are friends,' Isla said. 'Just like Seb and I are friends.'

'Right. So there's no boyfriend? Back at home?'

'No.'

'I'm not prying; I'm just interested. In your life, what you've been doing.'

'Not getting boyfriends, that's for sure.'

'Because I want you to know I'm proud of you. I'm proud of the woman you've become despite the hand you were dealt. And I'm not pretending that I didn't have a huge part to play in that, which makes me even prouder and wretched with guilt all at the same time.'

'You don't have to keep apologising.'

'But I do. I can never stop apologising because the damage I caused will never stop affecting your life – it's written into everything you are. I can do my best to make it up to you—'

'And you're already doing that,' Isla cut in with a smile that bordered on desperation. She didn't want to keep coming back to this conversation. 'We're here now and I know you're trying. That's all I need from you.'

'Come!' Celine shouted from the kitchen. Isla looked at her dad, relieved by the timely interruption.

'Looks like lunch is ready,' he said, nudging Benet with his foot to get off his phone and walk to the kitchen to eat. Benet had been bent over his phone, staring intently at it the whole time Isla and her father had been talking but Isla didn't think for a minute he was quite as absorbed as he pretended. More likely he was listening for clues as to what Isla knew or didn't know about Serendipity Sound, about where her relationship with Ian was going and what that might mean for him and his future financial security.

Isla followed Ian to a bright, warm kitchen with huge windows looking out over the snowy slopes at the feet of the nearby mountains. The snow glistened as the sun peeked out from behind a thick bank of clouds, like a glitter-strewn Christmas-card scene. She took her place at a table bedecked with gorgeous claret and gold cloth and matching napkins, crystal glasses and sparkling silverware. At its heart was a centrepiece of evergreens and winter fruit sprayed with gold flecks.

Cold meats, potato and bean salads, vegetables and crudités and bowls of lush green leaves and sauces filled the huge dining table that dominated the room. There was a half-carved turkey at one end and a slab of thick-cut ham at the other. It wasn't Christmas dinner as she knew it, but clearly Celine was proud of her efforts.

'This looks wonderful,' Isla said. And it did. Ordinarily she would have been happy to dig in, but all morning, despite her efforts, something hadn't been right with her. She should have been salivating at the sight of so much food, but her mind somehow wasn't on it at all.

'Thank you,' Celine said. 'Please… eat.'

Isla was seated next to Ian, Natalie at her other side. Benet sat across from her, throwing her baleful looks while Celine fussed about the kitchen. Whatever her stepmother's motives had been for making her pact with Justin, Isla didn't want to believe that she was a bad person. Maybe she was neither good nor bad, but somewhere in between like the rest of the world, someone who sometimes just made bad decisions. Where money was concerned, that was easier to do than anybody liked to admit.

Isla tried to show enthusiasm; digging a spoon into the potato salad she ladled a mound onto her plate. Then she went for the green beans soaked in a vinaigrette dressing and a slice of cold turkey. Everyone else followed her lead and began to help themselves amidst the usual dinner-time chatter; comments on how beautiful it looked, what the ingredients were in certain dishes, what was in season and what was harder to come by, and so on.

It was lovely, but for Isla it was all starting to feel like hard work. As much as she wanted to win favour and fit in with her new family, her mind kept slipping away to somewhere across the village and she had to keep dragging it back.

'I suppose this Christmas is very different for you,' Celine said, handing a basket of bread to Isla.

'It is. But it's a nice change if I'm honest. My mum would kill me if she could hear me say that though.'

'I'm glad it's not too miserable for you. I think perhaps you may begin to like it here in St Martin?'

'It's nice. Very pretty. Nice people.'

'You looked so happy when we saw you outside the church last night,' Natalie agreed. 'As if you had always belonged here.'

'It's a very welcoming place.'

Celine nodded. 'Perhaps one day you will understand why we made this place our home.'

'I think I already do,' Isla said. 'But I believe that sometimes home is as much about people as places. I mean if you have the people you love around you then you can make anywhere home. You make *them* your home.'

'Just so.' Natalie nodded eagerly. 'Who was that man at the church last night?'

'Sebastian?' Isla said, a sudden rush of heat at the mention of his name.

'You have met him here? In St Martin?'

'Yes.'

'You seemed good friends.'

'He's... well, he's nice.'

'Handsome.'

'I suppose he is. If you like that sort of thing.'

Ian looked from one to the other, trying, and perhaps failing, to keep up with the subtext of the conversation. Benet frowned at his sister but Celine shot her daughter a knowing smile. At least one member of the McCoy family had caught up.

Natalie seemed to know what was in Isla's heart before Isla did herself. A few seconds' delay and then the truth of her words hit her too. When had she felt happiest, most content in St Martin? Where did her thoughts keep leading her? Something had felt wrong about today and it wasn't the awkward family conversation or the change of routine. Something was missing, and it wasn't her mum, even though she missed her, because her mum would be there when Isla got home – her mum would always be there.

When Sebastian wasn't there everything felt a little colder, a little greyer. They had nothing in common, no shared background or common interests, and yet she felt they somehow fitted together perfectly. If she didn't tell him would she wave goodbye the following day never to see him again? He had to feel the same, didn't he? Surely it had to be worth a shot?

'He is staying at the Residence Alpenrose?' Celine asked, interrupting Isla's feverish thoughts.

'Yes. He's there now.'

'With family? Friends perhaps?'

'With nobody. Completely alone,' Isla said slowly.

'Perhaps you would like to call him? He is welcome to join us,' Celine replied, looking to Ian for approval, who nodded. Whether he quite knew what he was agreeing to was another matter entirely.

Isla hesitated. She still didn't know exactly what her feelings meant and if he shared them. Phoning him now to invite him might put pressure on him to attend when he didn't really want to.

'I think he may already be eating. At the hotel. I mean, I'm pretty sure Dahlia has it covered. But thank you.'

Celine didn't push it, but Isla thought she saw a shared, knowing look pass between her and Natalie.

'This all looks amazing,' Isla said, turning back to the table in a bid to change the subject. She was fast running out of things to say that didn't make her think of Seb. All she could think about was that he was sitting in their hotel while she was here and with every second they were apart he seemed to move further out of her reach. But she couldn't go to him now, because doing that would jeopardise the fragile relationship she was building here. Like it or not, she was going to have to get through this lunch. But then it seemed Lady Luck threw her a favour.

'*Alors!*' Natalie shot upright in her seat, shooting a sudden glance at the kitchen clock. 'Pierre is waiting!'

'Pierre?' Celine raised her eyebrows and Natalie gave a sheepish grin.

'I promised to meet him.'

'Today? When we have our visitor?'

'But I did not know we would have a visitor when I arranged it,' Natalie replied helplessly. She turned to Ian with a beseeching look. 'Papa?'

'I don't mind,' Isla cut in. 'I presume Pierre is someone pretty special?'

'He is,' Natalie beamed. 'Very special.'

'Then I would be the last person to complain about you going to him.'

'But—' Ian began, but Isla shook her head.

'Honestly, it's fine.' She turned to Natalie. 'It's been lovely getting to know you and I'll see you again before I leave, for sure.'

Natalie glanced at her father, who gave a nod of resignation. 'I suppose if Isla is OK with it then I can't really complain. Though don't think I'm happy.'

'*Merci*, Papa!' Natalie flew round the table and kissed Ian and Celine in turn. Then she crossed to Isla and gave her a peck on the cheek too. 'Until next time, *ma soeur*.'

'Sister,' Ian translated in reply to Isla's bemused smile. Then he turned an indulgent eye to his younger daughter, dashing from the room. If he was trying to look stern he was fooling no one.

'May I be excused too?' Benet asked.

'No. You may stay at the table.' Ian's smile faded. 'You know my feelings on this—'

'It's OK,' Isla said. 'To be honest...'

Talk of boyfriends had brought Seb to mind again, and Isla felt that hole at her core, that unfinished business, the opportunity slipping away from her with every second she was away from him. If Natalie had gone to meet Pierre and Benet was itching to disappear too, perhaps this was a good point to wrap things up anyway. Prematurely, maybe, but they'd made enough progress today to allow for it, hadn't they? To Isla it was worth taking a chance.

'I realise this is going to sound incredibly rude,' she said slowly, taking a breath. 'But I really need to go too.'

Ian's head flicked up. 'Have we done something wrong?'

'God no! Of course not! It's not you at all, it's just—'

'Are you ill? Do you need me to take you back to your hotel? Call a doctor?'

'Honestly I'm fine. I just need an hour to sort something and I thought perhaps…'

Celine smiled. 'Natalie has gone to meet Pierre and perhaps there is someone you wish to meet?'

Isla said lamely, 'Well… there's something I need to do. I'm sorry I can't say more than that…'

Ian's brow creased slightly. Isla supposed it was one thing to tell his son he had to stay put, but perhaps another entirely to do the same to the daughter he was only just getting to know. 'So important that you have to drop everything and go now?'

'You've got every right to be annoyed at me, but yes.' If they'd known each other better perhaps Ian would have been angrier. Perhaps if they had known each other better she could have explained it. But she couldn't, because she barely understood it herself. All she knew was that she needed to find Seb now, while she had the courage to tell him how she felt. Another hour and it may well fail her again.

'I'm really, really sorry, but please don't take it personally, it's just…'

'Well…' Ian looked helplessly in turn at the remaining family gathered round the table. 'I suppose if it means that much to you then you must go.'

Isla gave a tight smile. 'Thank you. And I am really sorry for all this.'

'Will you come back?' Celine asked.

Would she? Isla didn't know how this was going to play out.

'Go to see your friend,' Celine said. 'Perhaps you would like to bring him with you when you return – he is more than welcome.'

Isla nodded. Letting her napkin fall to the table, she dashed from the room.

Chapter Seventeen

Soaking wet, flushed and freezing from her run through the drifts outside, Isla stopped and frowned at the doorway to the dining room of Residence Alpenrose. Dahlia was crossing the floor of the restaurant with a tray of drinks, the low strains of Christmas tunes played in a jazz style being piped in through the sound system, the room festooned with tinsel and streamers and the smell of roasting meat and vegetables on the air. Almost every table was occupied by guests, but there was no sign of Seb. When he'd told her he'd be eating Christmas lunch with Dahlia she'd assumed they'd be sitting down together. Which she felt silly about now because Dahlia was running a hotel, one which was open all over Christmas; of course she wasn't going to have time for a cosy candlelit meal with Seb.

Dahlia broke into a broad smile when she saw Isla. Depositing her drink order in front of a waiting family, she made her way over.

'Everything OK, honey? I thought you were eating with Ian and Celine today? Has something happened?'

'No, I… I was looking for Seb. I thought he said he was having lunch with you.'

'I asked him if he was coming down today, and he had too much work to do. I tried to persuade him to take an hour off, but he was insistent.'

'Oh. So, he's in his suite?'

'Yes.'

'Working? On Christmas Day? He told me he wouldn't do that.'

'Afraid so. It's not right and I said as much.'

'It isn't.' Isla paused. 'Dahlia, I don't suppose you can do me a couple of turkey dinners to go?'

Dahlia gave her a knowing smile. 'Take a seat at the bar, honey. I'll be right with you.'

With both hands full, Isla had to kick at the door of the suite. She was sweating now in the huge coat that was brilliant for walking in alpine winters, but not so suited to labouring in a heated hotel under a huge tray containing two turkey meals with all the trimmings, a bottle of wine and two glasses. The sweat pouting off her was not very romantic, but she tried not to think about it as she waited for Seb to answer.

'Who is it?' he asked, his voice muffled from within the room.

'Father Christmas!' Isla shouted.

A few seconds later Seb's face appeared. 'Isla! I thought…'

'I know you did.' As he rushed to take the tray from her, confusion written over his features, she shrugged her coat off with a sigh of relief.

'What are you doing here? Did something happen with your dad? Is it all off?'

Isla shook her head. 'It was all fine. Better than fine – we got on really well.'

'Then why are you here?'

'I could ask why you told me you'd be eating with Dahlia, and now I find you working – on Christmas Day… Why did you lie to me?'

'I didn't lie… OK maybe it was a white one. But you wouldn't have gone to dinner with your family if I'd told you what I was planning to do and I knew it was important. I didn't want you burdened with worrying about what I was going to be doing today and miss out on visiting your family.'

He shrugged and turned to the tray of food he'd just placed on a small table.

'I hope you're hungry,' Isla said, fighting a blush.

'Two plates?' He raised an eyebrow. 'I thought you'd just eaten.'

'I did. Sort of. I mean I picked. I can totally eat another dinner. Come on,' she insisted. 'Sit down. And merry Christmas!'

'It looks wonderful. It's very kind of you.'

'Don't worry, I've charged it to your room…'

He looked up with a small smile. Not his usual goofy grin, but something sad and lost, and Isla was suddenly thrown into unfamiliar territory. She'd come to tell him how she felt about him but she realised that all wasn't well here. How could she bare her soul when something was so clearly amiss?

'Seb,' she said gently. 'Let's eat. I'll tell you my troubles, if you'll tell me yours.'

'I'm fine.'

'I disagree.'

He paused and then let out a sigh. 'You can't fix mine. Nobody can. There's no point in worrying about something that can't be fixed. We can talk about it all you want, but nothing will change.'

'How do you know if you don't share?'

'Trust me, I know.'

'What if I'd said that to everyone who has helped me deal with the reunion with my dad? What if I'd shut everyone out? You would have insisted I accept the help and you'd have been right. I'm returning the favour now, so please just let me.'

'That turkey looks good,' he said, making his way over to the table.

'Doesn't it?' Isla replied, realising that she would need a new tactic if she was going to get him to open up. And it was nice, strangely, being the person to hand out support for once, instead of being supported. She'd spent the last week being supported by just about everyone she came into contact with and she was beginning to feel like a burden on the entire population of St Martin.

'I wasn't going to eat, not really that hungry.'

'Really?' Isla raised her eyebrows.

'I was too busy to stop.'

'Am I interrupting you?'

'Yes… But I don't mind. I thought I was going to be spending the day alone so it made sense to use the time for work. But I don't mind that you're here.'

Isla poured two glasses of wine and handed him one as they both pulled chairs over to the makeshift dining table. 'Aren't you a bit sad you couldn't get back home for Christmas?'

'Does that mean you are?'

'I miss my mum, of course. This is the first Christmas I've spent away from her so it's bound to be weird. But this is turning out OK.'

'It's going well with your dad?'

'It's going OK.'

'That's brilliant.'

'So what do you normally do on Christmas Day? Your parents don't mind you being here now, away from them? Did you call them this morning?'

'They're…' With a sigh he placed his cutlery carefully on his plate. 'Isla… I haven't been completely honest with you.'

'Go on…' she replied, her breath catching in her throat.

'There's just me.'

'I don't follow.'

He gave a vague shrug. 'There's no one to go home for.'

'You don't get along with your family?'

'I don't have any family.'

Isla's glass stopped halfway to her mouth. She stared at him. '*None?*'

'Not a single person.'

'But I thought…'

'That I would have a lovely set of middle-class parents who paid for piano tuition and private schools and took me skiing in Verbier in the winter? I suppose that's the impression most people have when they first meet me, and I don't deny that it's been an advantageous one when it comes to landing research jobs. For some reason, academic institutions seem to like that version of my past. They don't want to give research posts to people who might come with emotional baggage. Nobody thinks anything different about where I came from and so I choose to let the reality be whatever makes them happy.'

'So where *do* you come from?' Isla asked, reeling from his sudden revelation, her own issues melting into the background.

'I grew up in a children's home in Croydon.'

'Where are your parents?'

'No idea. Drug addicts, apparently. They're probably dead, and if they're not they certainly haven't made any effort to find me so they might as well be.'

Isla clapped a hand over her mouth. 'Oh, God, Seb! I'm so sorry!'

He gave a wan smile. 'There's no need for you to be sorry.'

'But I said all those things – about my family – and you never said a word! I complained and complained and all this time you listened and wondered what it must be like to have family to complain about! You must have thought I was so pathetic!'

'Of course not. That's your reality, and this is mine. I completely understand how affected you are by yours. In many ways one could say I'm luckier than you not to have anyone – at least there's nobody to worry about but myself. And I was happier than I could say to see you make peace with your dad.'

'Because you wished you could do the same?'

'Perhaps. I've never known anything different, though.'

Isla took a gulp of her wine. This was huge. How did he keep this bottled up all the time? 'But you must have friends? A foster family? There must be someone in your life – you can't be completely alone in the world.'

'Somehow I never seemed to get settled in a foster home – there was always a reason why it didn't work out. I wasn't bitter, I just got used to the idea that I'd have to forge my own path in life and I couldn't rely on anyone to help me. It made me strong. Then I learned that if I really wanted to pursue my dreams of a career in academia then I'd have to reinvent myself as someone academia could relate to. So when I went to university I didn't tell anyone about my past. I painted a picture of someone from a perfectly normal, average family. I pretended to go home in the summer. People would offer to come visit me and I'd have to lie to keep them from the truth. I couldn't bear the looks of pity if my university friends found out. I worked hard on my course, managed to get some lucky breaks and eventually I got this job, which is the best thing that ever happened to me. I've been able to travel the world and indulge my passion and not worry about anything else.'

Isla leaned back and studied him. He looked every inch the university professor, the perfect example of the man he'd tried so desperately to become. Suddenly, she understood him in a way she never imagined would be possible, as if he'd shone a torch right through himself. Though why he'd chosen this moment to tell her was a mystery. Perhaps it was the idea that he might never see her again, perhaps he thought he had nothing to lose. Or was it that he trusted her with a secret he'd never trusted anyone with before? She didn't know whether to be flattered or terrified.

'I don't know what to say.'

'You don't have to say anything,' he replied. 'But now you know the real me, and I have to say it's quite a relief to finally share it with someone after all these years.'

'I would imagine it is. I don't know why you'd choose me, but thank you.'

It was his turn to study Isla and she felt the heat travel to her face even as he did. 'Really?' he asked softly. 'You really don't know why I'd choose you to share my secret with?'

'We're friends, right?'

'Yes,' he said. 'I hope so.'

'And we could be...' Isla faltered. The moment was here but how could she tell him this now, after what he'd just shared? He'd only just begun to open up and surely he needed time to finish the story. And yet, as she felt the moment slipping through her fingers, she knew that if she let it go she might never find another.

'I wish I had a Christmas present for you,' Seb said. Isla looked up from her plate and smiled.

'This is a Christmas present. You, being here with me.'

His expression brightened. 'Really?'

'Of course. Besides, I don't have a present for you, so we're equal.'

'This is good,' he said, waving his fork at his plate. 'I don't usually bother with Christmas dinner. Could never see the point.' He spoke without maudlin or melancholy, but that alone made Isla's heart suddenly lurch for him. She could picture the years going by, every one with him in some lonely place as Christmas came and went. It certainly put the injustices she saw in her own life into perspective. She'd had her share of disappointment and betrayal, but at least she'd had a mother who loved her and a place to call home.

'Has it always been horrible?' she asked gently.

'What?'

'Christmas Day?'

'Oh no,' he smiled. 'I'm used to it. Sometimes I even get invited to the odd lunch. But you feel it, you know, the fact that you're an outsider even when people try to include you. The best ones were in the care home, actually, with the other kids. The place was a battleground most days but they were the closest to family I've ever had.'

'Do you keep in touch with any of them?'

'I tried, at first. It's not so easy these days; we're all so busy with our own lives. I often think of them, though.'

'Did you have a girlfriend?'

'No,' he said, blushing a little. 'That was difficult too, particularly if it was a girl in the home. The people in charge didn't like that sort of thing.'

'But you had a girlfriend after? A serious one, I mean. You said something… back at Lake Blanc. It sounded as if…'

'It didn't end well,' he said. 'She went to work in South America and I haven't seen her since.'

'Why didn't it end well? Because of the job?'

'Sort of. A bit because of the cheating too. But I suppose that was partly my fault.'

Isla frowned. 'Why would it be your fault?'

'I introduced her to my best friend. The first proper friend I'd made outside the home when I started at university. At least, I thought he was my friend. Turns out it didn't mean that much to him. He knew I was nuts about her. Perhaps that was the attraction.'

'What a bastard!'

'It's old news now. I don't think about it all that much.'

'But you find it difficult to trust anyone now?'

He gave a small smile. 'I try not to let it have that effect on me. I want to be optimistic and forgiving. It would be too easy to go through life being miserable and blaming it on every one of my past misfortunes but that would be a waste of the life that could follow. A life I'm sure would be infinitely better and more productive than one spent wallowing in self-pity.'

'You're right,' Isla said, her thoughts wandering back to her own experiences so far. It had been so easy to wallow and blame everything on everyone who had ever wronged her. But things were different now – she was moving on and it felt good.

'Have you been with anyone since?'

He shook his head slowly. 'I suppose the right person just hasn't come along.'

'I suppose it's quite hard meeting people wandering around glaciers,' she said, trying to lighten the mood. But in reality, she hardly felt like joking at all.

He smiled. 'It could be a large part of the problem.'

'You miss being with someone?'

'Yes. But I don't want to be with someone who doesn't mean anything to me. I'd rather be alone than do that.'

'Nobody should settle for second best.'

He sipped at his glass of wine in silence for a moment. 'So you wouldn't?'

'Absolutely not. Where's the sense in that? It's love – or nothing at all.'

Isla's gaze fell on the pair of Christmas crackers Dahlia had sneaked onto the tray with their food. Seb, following her gaze, picked one up.

'Where did these come from?'

'Dahlia of course. God knows where she got them from; I have no idea if Christmas crackers are even a thing in France.' She smiled. 'Want to pull it?'

He shrugged. 'Why not?'

He took hold of one end and Isla took the other, yanking hard until it came apart with a CRACK! She peered inside the long end she now held, convinced that he'd deliberately let her win, and retrieved the party hat stashed within.

'It suits you,' he said as she jammed it onto her head and then tipped the cracker upside down to shake out the elusive prize. A plastic ring tumbled out onto the table and Seb picked it up.

'Wow – this could be worth a fortune.'

'Millions,' Isla grinned. 'Looks like my cousin Pamela's engagement ring… only classier.'

He held it out across the table. 'Will you marry me, Isla?'

What had started as a flippant joke became something far stranger and more charged as she stared at him. His grin died too and he stared back, the ring awkwardly held in the space between them, his words heavy with meaning that neither of them had seen coming. Perhaps the day was already too strange and full of meaning for this to be a joke they could laugh off. And for one crazy moment she considered saying yes. It didn't matter that he wasn't serious, or that they barely knew each other, the response simply bounced around her head, taunting her, threatening to come out. She forced out a laugh in its place, one that sounded vaguely hysterical.

'Don't be silly.'

He shook himself, blushing. 'I gave it a shot. I might have known you'd refuse me. Way out of my league...'

'Not that,' Isla said quickly. She gazed at him – the floppy hair, the freckles, the nose that crinkled when he smiled. He'd been there all along – her perfect match, and she'd never seen it because she couldn't see past the ridiculous template she'd set for herself for love. Those men had only ever caused her pain and heartache, and here was a man who was cute and funny, intelligent and kind and good-looking. If he wasn't perfect boyfriend material she didn't know what was. 'Not that at all...'

She reached across and took his hand. 'I can't marry you because I don't know you. Yet. But maybe we could do something about that.'

In one synchronised movement they were both on their feet, kissing across the table. Isla plunged her hands into his hair and pulled him in, a prisoner in her embrace that she never wanted to release, moving with him as if this was a dance delicately choreographed and rehearsed a thousand times before. Now the moment was real and Isla couldn't care less about Christmas lunch or missing families or the fact that she'd only known him for a week. She was burning in a fever of need, the smell of him and the taste of his mouth on hers driving all other thoughts from her head.

He broke off suddenly. 'I don't want pity. Please... that wasn't what I wanted.'

'Pity?'

'I'm alone and I'm OK with that.'

'You don't have to be.'

'That's not why I told you about my parents. I just thought… you'd understand. More than anyone.'

'And I do,' Isla said, moving in again. 'I understand and it doesn't change a thing.'

'But…'

'You like me?'

'Oh, Isla, you know I do…' He screwed his eyes tight, letting out a sigh of barely contained desire. 'You know I adore you.'

'I couldn't be sure.'

'How can you say that? I'd fall down and worship the ground under your feet – you must be able to see that.'

'I don't think we need to go quite that far,' she said with a faint smile.

'You like me?' he asked uncertainly.

'Would I be doing this if I didn't?' was her lazy reply as she reached for his bow tie and pulled it loose.

'What are you doing?'

'Undressing you. It's a bit forward, I know, but I figure it's Christmas, and since neither of us has any presents to open, we'll just have to unwrap each other…'

Chapter Eighteen

Doing her best to shake away the fog of her sleepy brain, Isla pulled a sweatshirt on and hurried to the window to check the weather. Crisp snow covered the ground – a new fall must have come down while she'd slept in Seb's arms – but it was calm and clear now, the sky pastel pink over the mountains as dusk cloaked the village of St Martin, giving the snow a glittering, icy hue. It should have been beautiful, but the sight only made Isla sad. It meant there was no excuse to stay now. Just when she most desperately wanted to.

It had been the strangest and most incredible Christmas Day. None of her mum's prawn cocktail starter, no figgy pudding and brandy sauce that nobody had room for, no falling asleep in front of a film, or charades. No aunts screeching with laughter and no pretending to love presents she'd later hide in a drawer. None of the things that were supposed to mean Christmas, and yet everything that Christmas meant was asleep in the bed where she'd left him. Christmas was about love, and she'd found that in spades.

Crossing the room, she checked her phone. Missed calls and text messages from her mum, but that wasn't surprising. She was probably still fuming about Isla's no-show, even though she knew perfectly well it was out of Isla's hands. She would return the calls, but right now she wanted to hold onto the feeling of intense happiness and contentment that had stolen over her.

'What are you doing?'

Isla turned to see Seb was awake and looking at her. Naked, his limbs draped across the bed as he stretched, he looked like him, but not like him. Like an insanely sexy version of him. A naughty twin who didn't wear a bow tie and study glaciers, but who swore and drank and did dirty things with girls.

'I was checking the weather,' she smiled. 'And then I thought I'd look to see how many angry texts my mum could manage in an hour.'

'And how many is that?'

'Surprisingly only two. She's thawing out in her old age.'

He sat up. 'Did we actually just do that?'

'I'm afraid we did.'

'What now?'

'We could do it again...'

His grin was brief and bright, but then he was serious again, the old, thoughtful, uncertain Seb back.

'I mean for us. You have to go home tomorrow?'

'Yes. I'd quite happily check back in and stay for another month, but I don't suppose that's a realistic prospect.' She crossed to the window and peered out again as the sky above the Alps turned from pink to lilac. Seb appeared at her side and together they stood at the window watching new, stuttering snow flurries gently drift to the ground. Her hand found his and slid around it.

'Maybe it will snow like crazy again tonight and then I'll *have* to stay,' she said.

'I wish it would snow forever.'

She turned to him. 'I may have to go home, but I have no intention of leaving you. Why would you say that after today?'

'I suppose it's just the way I'm conditioned to think.'

'I might have asked the same of you.'

'Why on earth would you think I wouldn't want to see you again?'

'I sort of have a track record.'

'Isla, I…'

She smiled up at him and pushed a finger to his lips. 'Don't worry – I know. I feel the same way.' Reaching up, she looped her arms around his neck to pull him in. Pulse racing, desire coursing through her, their lips smudged across one another's; she knew instantly that this was good and right. All her doubts, all her pretending, all her denial, all was washed away in the heat of this moment.

He pulled her closer and his hand gently traced the line of her arm, across her shoulder, his fingers finding the nape of her neck and gently stroking. She groaned, desire exploding deep inside her.

'Don't go,' he whispered, his lips close to her ear as he breathed her in. 'I can't lose you, not now.'

'You know I have to.'

'What if I never see you again?'

'You will.'

'How can you be sure?'

'We'll make it happen. One way or another.'

He pulled away and shook his head. 'I should have said something sooner; you'll be leaving in the morning and it's my fault we have such little time.'

'I think we could both take some blame for that. And besides, I'm leaving in the morning, but the morning is hours away.'

*

'I think your wish came true.'

Isla stood at the window of their room and gazed out onto a fresh fall of snow. It looked as if it had been snowing all night and it didn't show any signs of stopping. They'd slept for a few hours but something had woken her early. It was Boxing Day morning and already Christmas Day seemed like a strange and distant dream. Except it wasn't a dream, and Seb came to stand beside her, folding her into his arms as they took in the scene together, just to remind her of how real it had all been.

'If I'd known it would be that easy I'd have tried wishing for things a lot sooner.'

'So what should I do? I've already cancelled one flight and I can't keep putting off my trip home.'

'But you haven't rebooked it yet?'

'Dad said to wait and see what the weather was doing. He didn't think it would be an issue to get something last minute.'

'Looks like it was good advice. I guess you could phone the airport and find out if anything's taking off their end but, honestly, I'd wait a while.'

She swivelled to get a better look at his face. 'Is that because you don't want me to go?'

'Could be,' he grinned. 'Would another day be so bad?'

'I suppose I've already missed Christmas Day and I doubt I could enrage my mother any more by missing Boxing Day. I think she's already at maximum capacity.'

'There you go then – decided.'

'Oh no you don't…' Isla giggled. 'You make it sound too easy.'

'Isn't it? One more day? I've only just found you and I have to let you go already? Please, one more day isn't going to hurt anyone, is it? I'll help you book tomorrow's flight, but give me today. And the weather's on my side too, so how can you argue?'

Isla let out a sigh. She wanted to stay, God only knew how much. But the longer she stayed with Seb, the further away real life seemed and the less she wanted to go back to it. If she stayed too long she might never go back. She had Serendipity Sound and Seb there for the next couple of months; St Martin was looking like a very appealing prospect right now.

'I'd better phone my mum and let her know. She is *not* going to be happy.'

'You're joking, right? This is a joke…'

'No, Mum.' Isla shot a frown at Seb as he watched her make the call. He pulled a sympathetic face before returning his attention to the batch of emails he'd promised he'd reply to as quickly as he could while she was busy on the phone.

'You said you'd be home for Christmas and here you're telling me you're not even coming home on Boxing Day?'

'I can't do anything about the weather.'

'You wouldn't have been stuck in snow if you hadn't gone in the first place! I knew this would happen—'

'Mum, it's one Christmas out of a whole life of Christmases.'

'For you maybe. How do I know you won't want to go there every Christmas now that you have your fancy house?'

Isla chewed on her lip. She *had* thought about spending more time in St Martin and she couldn't deny that in the end Christmas here had been amazing.

'If I did, you could come with me.'

'Unbelievable! Why on earth would I want to do that? Christmas is here, with family!'

'But I have family here now too. And it's so beautiful, Mum... if you could only see it I know you'd love it—'

'Me? Set foot in the same town where your father lives with another woman? Are you crazy?'

'Maybe a little.' Isla shot a furtive glance at Seb as he tapped on the keyboard of his laptop. His forehead was creased in a vague frown and his tongue poked from the corner of his mouth. She couldn't help but smile. If her mum thought things had changed for Isla while she'd been in St Martin, she couldn't even begin to imagine how much. 'There's something else and I might as well tell you because it means I'll be coming here again in the next couple of months. I've met someone.'

There was silence. Seb looked up from his work with an expression of mild surprise.

'Mum?' Isla said. 'Did you hear what I said?'

'A local?'

'No; not a local.'

'Thank the lord.'

'Mum!'

'I only mean that if it was a local I wouldn't be happy.'

'Why? What difference does it make?'

'Well, you'd be moving there.'

'Mum... you need to stop doing this. I can't stay with you forever and you need to get used to that.'

'Yes, but *he* lives there...'

'You mean Dad?'

'You know who I mean.'

'He does, but that shouldn't matter. I'm not a kid who needs your protection any more. If I choose to build a relationship with my dad then that's my choice, and if it all goes wrong then that's my problem. If I marry a Frenchman and come to live here – not that I'm going to – that's my choice too and I live with the consequences. You'll always be important and no matter what happens I'll always love you, but I can't keep living in your shadow.'

'Isla, what the hell—'

'I'm sorry, Mum – I know you don't want to hear this but I need to say it. I need to make my own mistakes because while I'm making yours the world is shrinking around me and pretty soon the only life I'll have is the one you have.'

Isla drew a breath. There was a faint sniff at the other end of the line.

'I didn't mean to hurt you, Mum.'

Silence.

'You're angry?' Isla glanced across at Seb. He stood and took her into his arms as she waited for her mum to say something.

'No…' the strangled reply finally came. 'I just… I had no idea you felt that way. I thought you were happy living with me.'

'I am! God, Mum, I've been so happy living with you! But things change – it's inevitable and right that they do – and I'm not saying I'm not still happy, but I want to see what else life has to offer. You understand, don't you? Can you see why I want to know more about Dad, why I want to see more of this beautiful town I'm in, why I want to be with a man who makes me happy.'

'You've only just met him.'

'It doesn't matter that I've only just met him; I *know* him.' She looked up and smiled at Seb, who beamed in return. She did know him already, and she knew he was right, and she knew that if she was very lucky he might just be her future – the only future she needed.

'So you're not coming home? Is that what you're saying?'

'God, no…' Isla swallowed the squeak of frustration building in her throat. 'I'm not saying that at all. I'll be home as soon as the weather allows and we'll talk more. OK?'

'I'll definitely see you? Tomorrow?'

'Hopefully.'

'There you go again. Are you coming home tomorrow or not?'

'I'll try. I'll do my best, and I can't promise any more than that.'

'OK,' Glory said stiffly. 'See you tomorrow then.'

'Bye, Mum. Love you.'

The line went dead.

'Well, that went well,' Isla said, turning her face to Seb's again. He wrapped her tighter in his arms and kissed her lightly.

'I'm honoured that I got a mention so soon in our relationship. I could have understood if you wouldn't want to tell her about me, I mean it's—'

'Shut up.' Isla smiled, placing a finger on his lips. 'Why would I want to keep my hunky glaciologist a secret?'

'Well, I think you've hit it on the head right there actually,' he said, laughing. 'The glaciologist bit is usually the bit that puts people off.'

'It doesn't put me off. In fact, it rather turns me on…'

'Oh…' Seb blushed as she pulled him into a passionate kiss. 'Does this mean we're about to…'

'Oh yes,' Isla said. 'It most certainly does.'

*

Are you still in St Martin?

Isla tapped out a reply in the affirmative as Seb returned from the bathroom, rubbing a towel over his wet hair.

'Dad wants to know if I'm still here,' she said. 'I suppose he must have guessed that the weather would scupper things.'

How about dinner with us this evening? Celine and Natalie would love it. Bring your man too. We might as well meet him properly.

Isla frowned. 'He wants us to go to dinner at their house.'

'I don't mind if you need to go; there's plenty of work to keep me busy here.'

'Not *me*. *Us*.'

'Oh. You told him?'

'He sort of guessed.' Isla gave a sheepish smile. 'I wasn't doing a brilliant job of keeping a lid on my feelings to be honest.'

Seb blushed. It really was the most adorable thing and Isla wondered if she'd ever get sick of seeing it.

'I guess we should go then,' he said. 'The last person in the world I need to be offending is your dad.'

'My dad's a pussycat. The person you really need to worry about is my mum, but I wouldn't dream of subjecting you to that meeting just yet. So, I'll tell him yes?'

Seb nodded. 'I'm probably going to regret it, but go ahead and tell him yes.'

'You must love me then,' Isla grinned, and he blushed again.

*

They'd trudged through the snow hand in hand, and though St Martin had always looked beautiful to Isla, today it was not only beautiful, but it felt like home. They'd barely talked, each content with the feel of a gloved hand in theirs and to know that they were together, but at the door of the McCoy family home, Isla paused and looked up at Seb with a silent question.

'Knock,' he said, smiling. 'I'll be OK.'

'It's just… you know, the family thing. Does it make you sad? I would hate to think that you were sitting there thinking about your own situation while we were all laughing and joking.'

'Will there be a lot of laughing and joking? I thought it was hard work seeing them?'

'It was,' she replied with a small smile. 'I suppose it doesn't seem so bad now. In fact, I quite liked it yesterday. Apart from the bit where I couldn't stop thinking about you, that is.'

Seb's cheeks flared briefly and she reached up to kiss him.

He shook his head as they parted. 'I can't believe how lucky I am.'

She smiled. 'I can't believe how lucky *I* am.'

'No, it's me…'

Isla pressed a finger to his lips. 'Shush, silly. Now, are we going to argue all day about who's the lucky one or are we going to knock on this door?'

'Do you want the honest answer to that?'

'You worry too much – he's going to love you.'

Almost as soon as she'd rapped her knuckles on the door it opened to reveal a smiling Celine.

'Welcome, welcome…' she said as she ushered them in with kisses for both. 'Please… everyone is waiting to see you.'

They followed her into the kitchen where a table full of people rose to greet them. Benet was there, his usual grudging self; a smile on his face that Isla was convinced was solely the product of threats from Ian. Natalie greeted her warmly; next to her was a man Isla had never seen before.

'This is Pierre,' she announced, and Pierre stepped forward to greet Isla.

'I have heard much about you,' he said. His English was rougher than Natalie's but he spoke it clearly. He stood perhaps three or four inches shorter than her, slight but with an undeniable boyish charm and quick, intelligent features. Isla smiled.

'I hope it was good.'

'Very.'

'Some of you have already met him, but this is Sebastian.' Isla grabbed Seb's hand to indicate just what their relationship was in case anyone was in any doubt. 'Admittedly we've only met this week in St Martin, but...'

She blushed, almost as hotly as Seb himself, but he squeezed her hand gently and gave her a quick smile.

Ian stepped forward. He kissed Isla briefly on the cheek. They'd come a long way in a week. Then he turned his attention to Seb, who stuck out his hand.

'It's a pleasure to meet you properly, sir,' he said, and he was so breathless Isla wondered whether she'd have to administer CPR at some point. She wanted to tell him to calm down and chill out, but she supposed he would have to work that out for himself. Besides, it was sweet that he already cared so much for her that he was desperate to make a good impression. She could see by the look on Ian's face that he was almost as desperate to make a good impression on Seb for the same reasons.

With the introductions and greetings over, they took seats at the table. Celine poured champagne while Ian informed them that dinner would be ready shortly.

'I hope we've no vegetarians,' he said, glancing at Seb, who shook his head. 'I hadn't really considered it when I planned the menu and the shops are closed today so I couldn't get anything else.'

'I'm sure whatever it is will be lovely,' Isla said. There was a rich, meaty smell on the air, warm with spices and perhaps the tang of red wine. Whatever it was it smelt good and Isla's stomach groaned in agreement.

Celine placed a delicate fluted glass in front of Ian and angled her head at Isla. 'Perhaps you would like to share our interesting development now?'

'Aye, perhaps so.' Ian turned to Isla. 'I've had a phone call this morning. Care to take a guess at who it might have been?'

Isla froze, glass halfway to her lips. Had Grover called him to tell him about Serendipity Sound? Were they really going to have this discussion now? 'I've no idea,' she said carefully.

'Your mother.'

Isla's mouth fell open. If she'd been dreading his reply, nothing could have prepared her for the shock of hearing this. It might have been easier if it had been Grover Rousseau telling him about Benet's misdemeanours. 'Mum? When did this happen?'

Ian nodded. 'This morning. In fact, about twenty minutes ago.'

Isla ran the events of the morning through her mind. When had she spoken to Glory? Perhaps a couple of hours ago? So this had been since then.

'But she doesn't even have your number, she…'

'Hates me?' Ian said with a wry smile. 'Wouldn't spit on me if I was on fire? I know. As for where she got the number, she must have called the shop phone – we have that on divert to the house when we're closed; it would be easy enough to find for anyone who had the will. The reason why? Well, that's an interesting one…'

Isla glanced at Seb, then at Celine, Benet and Natalie in turn. Then she turned back to Ian. 'Why?' she asked, though she wasn't sure she wanted the answer.

'I'm sure you can guess it was mostly about you. We had a wee chat about what had been going on here, and about your inheritance. She wanted to know if you were happy. I said I believed so, and she said she thought so too. And she wanted to give us her blessing.'

Isla's eyes widened. 'What?'

'I know. She told me I had her blessing to make peace with you if it was what you wanted and she believed it was.' He smiled. 'Don't think it didn't come without a warning that she would be straight on the first plane to smash something over my head if I ever hurt you again. She told me in no uncertain terms that I'd never have *her* forgiveness or acceptance, but she was OK with us, going forward.' He leaned back in his seat. 'What do you make of that?'

'I think it's a bloody Christmas miracle,' Isla said quietly, and Ian burst into laughter.

'Couldn't have put it better myself.'

'What do you think it means?' Isla asked. 'What's she up to?'

For a moment Ian looked taken aback, then he relaxed. 'I'd like to think it means progress, at long last.'

Lunch consisted of escargots for starters, served in the traditional way and rich with garlic butter. Isla tried not to wrinkle her nose as the dish arrived on the table and Ian smiled as he watched her. 'Don't feel you have to try them if you really don't want to.'

Isla shook her head. 'I'll try them,' she decided, looking to Seb, who was already happily tucking in. If he was eating them they couldn't be that bad. So she bit gingerly into a corner and was surprised that where she'd expected some slimy, bitter mouthful, she could barely taste anything but sweet, melting garlic. The texture was a little on the springy side but it wasn't too bad once you put the idea that it was a snail out of your mind.

The main course was a different matter – duck in cranberries. Not a dollop of supermarket sauce from a jar like Isla would have with turkey at home, but a rich, fragrant jus with a hint of peppercorns giving it a kick. It was as she was joyfully shovelling this delight into her mouth that there was a knock at the front door. Celine glanced up at the clock.

'Justin is here,' she said. She looked at Isla. 'I hope you don't mind, but he wanted to say goodbye before you flew home so I told him you would be here today.'

Isla stopped chewing and suddenly the divine duck didn't seem quite so tasty. She swallowed hard and shot Seb a look of vague alarm. He reached under the table and gave her hand a reassuring squeeze, so Isla forced a smile for Celine and nodded.

'Of course.'

Stupidly, it hadn't even occurred to her that if she was going to be spending a lot more time in St Martin she was going to run into Justin again sooner or later, and probably more often than she'd like.

A moment later, Celine returned to the dining room with Justin in tow. He stalled for a moment as his gaze settled on Seb sitting next to Isla, before regaining his composure and greeting everyone airily. If he'd been rattled by Seb's presence he was doing a good job of hiding it. Isla wondered if Justin had come here for one last attempt to seduce her. She imagined that one look at the glow between her and Seb would send out a clear message that even Justin couldn't fail to understand. At least she hoped so.

'You will stay and eat with us?' Celine asked.

Justin glanced at Isla and Seb again and shook his head. 'I see you have started already and I do not want to impose. Perhaps another time?'

'We have more,' Celine insisted. 'I can easily find you a chair for the dinner table.'

'I think...' Isla began, interjecting before he could be persuaded to stay, 'that perhaps Justin has places to be.' She gave him a tight smile. 'I do appreciate you dropping by to say goodbye to me, though.'

'You will fly home soon?' he asked.

'Tomorrow,' Isla said.

'You will come back?'

'I expect so; I've got Serendipity Sound for starters.'

He nodded, and now his uneasy glance went to Benet, some silent signal passing between them. It would have been missed by anyone else, but Isla knew exactly what it meant. Their scheme was over. Then he made a move towards Isla, as if he might kiss her or embrace her, but stopped short, giving a stiff nod instead. '*Bon. Au revoir, Isla. À bientôt.*'

A minute later Justin was gone. Seb turned to her as Celine fetched another bottle of champagne, Benet on hand to help her uncork it, and Ian was engaged in a conversation with Natalie and Pierre.

'You OK?' he asked in a low voice.

'I think so. I wish I knew what was going through his head right now, but I suppose time will tell.'

'You think he'll make another move on you?'

'Not that. I just don't think he likes to lose.'

'Perhaps if he played more fairly he wouldn't.'

They were interrupted by the return of Celine and the fresh bottle. After filling everyone's glass, Ian raised his.

'A toast,' he said, looking at Isla. 'To new beginnings.'

Isla smiled, and then glanced at Seb as she raised her glass and then everyone else followed.

'New beginnings indeed.'

And then a thought occurred to her. She couldn't come straight out and challenge Benet about Serendipity Sound, but she could now put it in a way that he'd understand.

'I've decided,' she added, 'that I'm going to keep Serendipity Sound.' She looked directly at Benet. 'And I'm going to use it as often as I can. After all, there's a reason that Grandma Sarah left it to me, and I think this is it. She hated the thought of complete strangers staying there, and I intend to respect her wishes to that end too. So no renting out, no one but friends and family staying there – not ever. And, *Dad…*' She smiled. She'd called him Dad and it was easy and natural for the first time. 'I'd be honoured if you'd take the keys and keep them safe for me. I trust you.'

'You don't need to worry about a thing, sweetheart,' Ian beamed. 'I'll take good care of it while you're away.'

'I know you will, Dad.'

When Isla and Seb arrived back at Residence Alpenrose for what looked to be their last night together, Justin was waiting outside.

'I had a feeling this might happen,' Isla muttered.

He looked up at their approach and nodded shortly at Seb before speaking to Isla.

'You are together?' he asked.

'We are,' Seb replied for her.

'And this is what you want?' Justin looked at Isla, ignoring Seb's intervention.

'Of course it is,' Isla said. 'Do you think I don't know my own mind?'

'No, but...'

'You think I'm trying to make you jealous or something? Come on – grow up, Justin. I don't play those games. Seb and I are together and that's all you need to know.'

He was silent for a moment, glancing between the two of them before he spoke again.

'Can I speak to you in private for a moment?'

'Whatever you've got to say you can say in front of Seb.' Isla felt Seb's hand tighten around hers, silently thankful for his support. Her voice was calm and clear; her emotions were anything but.

'It is a delicate matter,' Justin said.

'Something to do with the covert letting of Serendipity Sound?'

Justin's reply faltered.

'Seb knows all about it,' Isla said. 'And my father will too if I ever feel the need.'

'You have not told him yet?' Justin let out a huge breath, his features instantly relaxing.

'No. I don't think you or Benet are hardened criminals, just two stupid men who made a stupid decision to embark on a stupid scheme. I'm annoyed – of course I am – but I don't want to see either of you get into trouble. You've spoken to Benet about the situation?'

'Of course.'

'Then I shouldn't have to tell my dad, should I?'

Justin nodded. 'You have my word.'

'And Benet?'

'I pledge for him too.'

'Then there's nothing else to say. I want you to give my dad your keys to Sarah's house; he's going to take care of it while I'm away. He's expecting to see you about it over the next few days.'

'OK.'

'Tell me one thing – honestly. Was there anyone else in the family involved?'

Justin shook his head. It was the answer Isla had been desperate to hear. For the most part, she was beginning to feel at home with the French branch of the McCoys – slowly, but they were getting there. She didn't know if she could deal with the news that their fledgling relationship was already a lie.

'Bye then,' she said, turning to go into the hotel, her hand still enveloped in Seb's, drawing strength from the contact.

'Goodbye, Isla,' Justin said. 'And *bonne chance.*'

Isla was shaking as they walked into the reception of Residence Alpenrose.

'I don't know how you stayed so calm then,' Seb said quietly as they got through the door.

'I don't know either,' Isla replied, her voice now cracking.

A flicker of panic crossed Seb's face and he pulled her into his arms. 'Hey… I thought you were keeping it together out there… Don't break on me now…'

'I wasn't. God knows I was a wreck inside. I talk the talk pretty well, huh?' she said, laughing through her tears.

'Well I was convinced. Remind me never to get on your bad side, because I'd be terrified, even if it was an act.'

Isla buried her face into his shoulder and took a deep breath to calm herself. 'I'll be OK, I'm just—'

'OH MY LORD!'

They both spun to see Dahlia staring at them with a look of glee on her face. 'You two...?'

Seb gave a sheepish nod in reply as they broke apart, Isla hastily drying her eyes.

'Oh, I just KNEW it!' Dahlia squeaked, clapping her hands. 'I just knew you were perfect for each other! I'm so happy! Come into the bar for a nightcap – tell me all about it! It's on the house!'

Seb turned to Isla, happiness tempered by a look of concern. 'How are you feeling? Up to it?'

She squeezed his hand and gave him a watery smile. 'I think it might be just what the doctor ordered.'

Chapter Nineteen

Dawn was rising, grey and pale beyond the curtains of their room. During the early hours Seb had gone to the window to check the progress of the snow and found it had finally petered to halt. He'd returned to her arms, a new sadness in his eyes, and she'd done her best to hold him and kiss it away. But they both knew the sting of abandonment, how it felt to be lost – how it felt to be alone.

They made love, but where it had been fire and energy the times before, now it was intimate and gentle, consolation for what they were about to lose.

Now, as morning arrived, she felt him stir and looked up from where her head lay on his chest to see him smile down at her.

'How long have you been awake?' he asked.

'Not long. I keep thinking about how I ought to go and check on my flight, but I can't bring myself to do it.'

He kissed the top of her head. 'I don't want you to do it either. Are you sure you can't just stay here with me?'

'In this bed?'

'I would have settled for St Martin, but this bed will do nicely, if you're offering.'

'I wish I could. You have no idea how much. But my mum is expecting me home and… well, you don't know her. If you did you'd be trying to get home too.' His smile faded and instantly she regretted her quip. 'God, I'm so insensitive,' she said.

'Don't be silly…' He wrapped his arms tight around her and pulled her close. 'You can't walk on eggshells for me and I wouldn't want you to. I've never known anything different from what I have and you know how they say what you don't have you don't miss.'

'But it must bother you a bit. To hear me complain about my parents when you don't have any.'

'Honestly, it doesn't. And you're not complaining – you're just talking through your feelings. I like when you do that with me because I like the idea that you trust me enough to do that.'

'I do. More than anyone I've ever met. That's weird, right? How a week can change so much.'

'I suppose it is. Will you think I'm mad if I tell you something?'

'Probably. But you could try me.'

'I think I love you.'

He was silent, and Isla could feel the thump of his heart against her cheek as she lay on his chest, and for a moment she was convinced that it was beating that much faster as he waited for her reply. He'd said what they'd both been too scared to say until now.

'I've thrown you, haven't I?' he asked. 'You don't have to reply. I'm sorry I said anything.'

'A little. But not because of what you've said. Because I think I feel it too, and I shouldn't. It's not sensible or logical or safe to fall in love with someone you've known for a week. My head is telling me to stop being an idiot, but my heart won't listen.'

'What are we going to do about it?'

'We could do *it* again. You know, just to check.'

He gave a low chuckle, her joke diffusing the situation instantly. 'I'll miss you like crazy.'

'I know. Me too.'

'Come back then. Come back to St Martin and stay with me while I finish this research project. You've got your grandma's house to live in.'

'That's three months – you know I can't do that; I've got my own studies at home.'

'Can you distance learn? Online tutorials? Lots of people do it.'

'My mum. I have to think about her too, remember. We've made progress, but I can't expect her to deal with too much at once.'

'I don't know how I'm going to concentrate on anything without you near. Now that I've found you I don't want to let you go, not ever. I don't want a day to go by when I don't see your face or hear your voice or feel your touch. It sounds ridiculous and melodramatic but it's how I feel. My chest hurts when I think about continents and oceans between us.'

'You could come back to England with me.'

'But this project… I'll lose the funding. The university would probably fire me and nobody would employ me again if they thought I was that unreliable. Isla….' He let out a long sigh. 'Then we're stuck. Three months without you will be the worst kind of hell.'

'Nobody said it had to be three months. I can't come back right away, and I can't promise anything at all – it depends on finances. But if I can find a way I'll come back to visit before your research stint is up. I told my dad I'd come back anyway so it makes sense; I'd be able to see you both.'

'But maybe you'd see a little more of me?'

Isla smiled. 'Greedy.'

Seb folded her into his arms and kissed the top of her head. 'I'll hold on to that hope. At least it's something to keep me going when I'm lonely.'

'It's lucky how things turned out, isn't it? I mean, if you hadn't come to this hotel, and if my flight hadn't been cancelled, and if Dahlia didn't have a booking for my room…'

'About that,' Seb said.

Isla pulled away to look up at him. 'What?'

'Don't be mad at her, but I think she might have been telling us a little white lie.'

'About what?'

'I haven't seen anyone go in or out of your old room. And the key is on the hook in reception.'

'The conniving little minx!' Isla squeaked. 'So she…'

'Yep. I think her plan was to throw us together all along. She obviously saw what we were both too stupid to see.'

'I don't know whether to go downstairs and thump her or kiss her.'

'Perhaps you should settle for a friendly hug before you leave.'

'Shall we tell her we know about her little plan?'

'What do you think?'

'Perhaps we will. One day. But right now, let's keep her guessing.'

'Now who's the little minx?'

'I've got plenty more where that came from.'

'I don't doubt it for one minute.'

She snuggled down, back into the sanctuary of his arms. For the first time in her life, Isla understood what it was to want time to stand still. She wanted to hold back the dawn forever, to stay warm and safe in this bed with a man she now realised was the most perfect man on earth, a man who would never hurt her or manipulate her or leave her. A man who was kind and gentle and true and would be there when she needed him no matter what. It had been the most extraordinary week and an even more extraordinary Christmas. She'd found a father, new friends, fallen in love with a village and a man. Life would never be the same, and she'd never been happier to know that.

Acknowledgements

The list of people who have offered help and encouragement on my writing journey so far must be truly endless, and it would take a novel in itself to mention them all. However, my thanks goes out to each and every one of you, whose involvement, whether small or large, has been invaluable and appreciated more than I can say.

There are a few people that I must mention. Obviously, my family, the people who put up with my whining and self-doubt on a daily basis. My colleagues at the Royal Stoke University Hospital, who have let me lead a double life for far longer than is acceptable and have given me so many ideas for future books! The lecturers at Staffordshire University English and Creative Writing Department, who saw a talent worth nurturing in me and continue to support me still, long after they finished getting paid for it. They are not only tutors but friends as well. I have to thank the team at Bookouture for their continued support, patience and amazing publishing flair, particularly Kim Nash, Peta Nightingale, Lauren Finger, Jessie Botterill and Lydia Vassar-Smith. Their belief, able assistance and encouragement means the world to me. I have to mention Jessie especially, whose little editing touches have made this book so much more than it was. If you laughed at the unwrapping scene (and by now you should know all about it) then you have her to thank!

My friend, Kath Hickton, always gets a mention, and rightly so for having put up with me since primary school. Louise Coquio also gets an honourable mention for getting me through university and suffering me ever since, likewise her lovely family. And thanks go to Storm Constantine for giving me my first break in publishing. I also have to thank Mel Sherratt and Holly Martin, fellow writers and amazing friends who have both been incredibly supportive over the years and have been my shoulders to cry on in the darker moments. Thanks to Tracy Bloom, Emma Davies, Jack Croxall, Dan Thompson, Renita D'Silva, Christie Barlow and Jaimie Admans: not only brilliant authors in their own right but hugely supportive of others. My Bookouture colleagues are also incredible, of course, unfailing and generous in their support of fellow authors – life would be a lot duller without you all. I have to thank all the brilliant and dedicated book bloggers (there are so many of you, but you know who you are!) and readers, and anyone else who has championed my work, reviewed it, shared it, or simply told me that they liked it. Every one of those actions is priceless and you are all very special people. Some of you I am even proud to call friends now.

Last but never least I have to thank my agent at LAW, Philippa Milnes-Smith, for her counsel and support.

A Letter from Tilly

I really hope you've enjoyed reading *A Cosy Candlelit Christmas* as much as I enjoyed writing it. I'm very proud and excited to share this story with my readers. You can sign up to my mailing list for news on what's coming next. I promise never to hassle you about anything but my books. The link is below:

www.bookouture.com/tilly-tennant

I hope you've fallen for the charms of St Martin-de-Belleville and love it as I do. If you liked *A Cosy Candlelit Christmas*, the best and most amazing thing you can do to show your appreciation is to tell your friends. Or tell the world with a few words in a review. It can be as short and sweet as you like, but it would make me so happy. In fact, hearing that someone loved my story is the main reason I write at all.

If you ever want to catch up with me on social media, you can find me on Twitter @TillyTenWriter or Facebook.

So thank you for reading my little book, and I hope to see you again soon!

Love Tilly x

Made in the USA
San Bernardino, CA
25 February 2019